DATE DUE

4-6-15			
			PRINTED IN U.S.A.

WATER

TALES OF ELEMENTAL SPIRITS

ROBIN McKINLEY
PETER DICKINSON

G. P. PUTNAM'S SONS ✦ NEW YORK

Designed by Gunta Alexander. Text set in Aurelia Book.
Library of Congress Cataloging-in-Publication Data
McKinley, Robin.
Water: tales of elemental spirits / Robin McKinley and Peter Dickinson.
p. cm.   Contents: Mermaid song / Peter Dickinson—The sea-king's son/Robin
McKinley—Sea serpent / Peter Dickinson—Water horse / Robin McKinley—
Kraken / Peter Dickinson—A pool in the desert / Robin McKinley.
1. Short stories, American. 2. Short stories, English. [1. Ocean—Fiction.
2. Mermen—Fiction. 3. Mermaids—Fiction. 4. Short stories.]
I. Dickinson, Peter, 1927-   II. Title.   PZ5.M2335 Wat 2002   [Fic]—dc21   2001041642
ISBN 0-399-23796-8
1 3 5 7 9 10 8 6 4 2
First Impression

TO ANNE WATERS

CONTENTS

MERMAID SONG ✦ 1

by Peter Dickinson

THE SEA-KING'S SON ✦ 30

by Robin McKinley

SEA SERPENT ✦ 78

by Peter Dickinson

WATER HORSE ✦ 119

by Robin McKinley

KRAKEN ✦ 170

by Peter Dickinson

A POOL IN THE DESERT ✦ 208

by Robin McKinley

MERMAID SONG

Her name was Pitiable Nasmith.

Her grandfather had chosen Pitiable so that she and others should know what she was, he said. All the People had names of that kind. He was Probity Hooke, and his wife was Mercy Hooke. Their daughter had been Obedience Hooke until she had married Simon Nasmith against their will and changed her second name to his. Because of that, the People had cut her off from themselves, and Probity and Mercy had heard no more of her until Simon had come to their door, bringing the newborn baby for them to care for, and told Probity of his daughter's death. He said he was going away and not coming back. Probity had taken the baby from him and closed the door in his face without a word.

He had chosen a first name for the baby because she had neither father nor mother. She was pitiable.

The Hookes lived in a white wooden house on the edge of the town. Their fields lay a little distance off, in two separate odd-shaped patches along the floor of the steep valley, where soil deep enough to cultivate had lodged on the underlying granite. The summers were short, but desperately hot, ending usually in a week of storms, followed by a mellow autumn and then a long, bitter winter, with blizzards and gales. For night after night, lying two miles inland in her cot at the top of the ladder, Pitiable would fall asleep to the sound of waves raging along the outer shore, and wake to the same sound. Between the gales there would be still, clear days with the sun no more than a handsbreadth above the horizon, and its light glittering off mile after mile of thigh-deep snow. Then spring, and thaw and mud and slush and the reek of all the winter's rubbish, rotting at last. Then searing summer again.

It was a hard land to scrape a living off, though there was a good harbour that attracted trade, so some of the People prospered as merchants. Fishermen, and others not of the People, came there too, though many of these later went south and west to kinder, sunnier, richer places. But the People stayed "in the land the Lord has given us," as they used to say. There they had been born, and their ancestors before them, all the way back to the two shiploads who had founded the town. The same names could be read over and over again in their graveyard, Bennetts and Hookes and Warrens and Lyalls and Goodriches, but no Nasmiths, not one.

For eight years Pitiable lived much like any other girl-child of the People. She was clothed and fed, and nursed if she was ill. She went to the People's school, where she was taught to read her Bible, and tales of the persecution of her forebears. The People had few other books, but those they read end-lessly, to themselves and to each other. They took pride in their education, narrow though it was, and their speech was grave and formal, as if taken from their books. Twice every

Sunday Pitiable would go with her grandparents to their church, to sit still for two hours while the Word was given forth.

As soon as she could walk, she was taught little tasks to do about the house. The People took no pride in possessions or comforts. What mattered to them in this world was cleanliness and decency, every pot scoured, every chair in its place, every garment neatly stitched and saved, and on Sundays the men's belts and boots gleaming with polish, and the women's lace caps and collars starched as white as first-fall snow and as crisp as the frost that binds it. They would dutifully help a neighbour who was in trouble, but they themselves would have to be in desperate need before they asked for aid.

Probity was a steady-working, stern old man whose face never changed, but Mercy was short and plump and kindly. If Probity was out of the house, she used to hum as she worked, usually the plodding, four-square hymn tunes that the People had brought with them across the ocean, but sometimes a strange, slow, wavering air that was hardly a tune at all, difficult to follow or learn, but once learnt, difficult to let go of. While Pitiable was still very small, she came to know it as if it had been part of her blood, but she was eight before she discovered what it meant.

The summer before that, Mercy had fallen ill. At first she would not admit it, though her face lost its roundness and became grey and sagging, and sometimes she would gasp and stand still while a shudder of pain ran through her and spent itself. Probity for a while did not notice, and for another while chose not to, but Pitiable found herself doing more and more of her grandmother's tasks while Mercy sat on one of the thin upright chairs and told her what she did not already know. By winter Mercy could not even sit and was forced to lie, and the neighbours had come to see why she no longer came to church, but Probity had sent them away, saying that he and the child could manage between them. Which they did, but Pitiable's days were very long for a child, from well before dawn until hours after dark, keeping the house clean and decent, and seeing to her grandfather's meals and clothes, and nursing her grandmother.

On a Sunday near Christmas (though the People did not keep Christmas, saying it was idolatrous) there was a storm out of the west, driving snow like a million tiny whips, fiery with cold. Still, Probity put on his leather coat and fetched out his staff and snowshoes, and told Pitiable to get ready so that he could drag her to church on the log sled.

"Let her stay," said Mercy. "I am dying, Probity. I may perhaps die while you are gone. May the Lord deal with me as He will, but I am afraid to die alone."

Probity stared at her with his face unchanging, then nodded and tied on his snowshoes and went out into the storm without a word. Mercy watched the door close.

"He had love in him once," she said. "But he buried it the day your mother left us and set the tombstone on it the day she died. Bear with him, Pitiable. Deal with him as best you may. It will not be easy."

"Are you really going to die?" said Pitiable.

"As we all are, when the Lord calls to us."

"To-day? Now?"

"Not to-day, I think. I am better to-day. The pain is almost gone, which is a bad sign. My body has no more messages to send me."

Pitiable knelt by Mercy's cot and put her head on the quilt and wept, while Mercy stroked her shoulders and told her she was glad to be going, because she trusted in God to forgive her the small harms she had done in her life. She told Pitiable to fetch a stool and sit by her and hold her hand.

"I have a story to tell you," she said. "My mother told it to me, and her mother to her, through seven generations since *The Trust in God* was lost. You remember the story of Charity Goodrich, our ancestress, yours and mine?"

Pitiable nodded. Every child among the People, even those who were not directly descended from her, knew about Charity Goodrich. It was almost the only story they knew, outside the ones in the Bible. They were told that the stories other children knew were superstitious nonsense, inventions of the devil, to distract believers from the narrow path to salvation. Two hundred years ago, three small ships had set out to cross the great ocean. They had been given new names before they left, *The Lord is Our Refuge, The Deliver Us from Bondage* and *The Trust in God.* Apart from their crews they carried the People, 287 men, women and children who had determined to leave the country where they were oppressed and imprisoned and burnt for their beliefs, and settle in new land where they could worship as they chose. After a dangerous voyage they were in sight of land when a storm separated them. Two ships came safe into the providential bay which was now the harbour of the town, but the third, *The Trust in God,* was driven against the cliffs to the north of it and lost with all hands. All hands but one, that is, for five days later a child was found wandering on the shore, unable to say how she had come there. Her name was Charity Goodrich.

"I am going to tell you how Charity was saved," said Mercy. "But first you must promise me two things. You must remember it so that you can tell it to your daughters when they are old enough to understand. And you must tell it to nobody else, ever. It is a secret. You will see why. Charity Goodrich was my great-grandmother's great-grandmother. There are other descendants of hers among the People, but I have never asked, never even hinted, and nor must you. Do you understand?"

"Yes, and I promise," said Pitiable.

"Good. Now this is the story Charity told. She remembered the storm, and the breaking of the mast, and the shouts of the sailors, and the People gathering on the deck, standing all together and singing to the Lord Who made the sea, while they clutched at ropes and spars and the ship heaved and wallowed and waves swept foaming around their legs. Some of them were washed away, still singing, and then the ship was laid on its side and the deck stood upright and they all went tumbling down into the roaring sea. Charity remembered her hand being torn from her father's grasp, and then a loose sail tangled round her and she remembered nothing more.

"Nothing more, that is, until she woke. A shuddering cold roused her and told her too that she was not dead, but alive. Her clothes were soaked, but she was lying on dry sand. She sat up and looked around. She saw a dim, pale light to one side of her. It was just enough for her to make out the black water that stirred at her feet, and the black rock all around her and over her. Somehow she had been washed up in a small cave whose entrance was beneath the water.

"Beside her was a small sea chest of the sort that the People had used to store their possessions for the voyage. With numbed fingers she opened it and found that it had been well packed, with all its contents wrapped tight in oilskins. There were dry clothes, far too large for her, but she stripped off, spreading out her own clothes to dry on the rocks, and wrapped herself in these others, layer on layer, and nursed her body back to warmth.

"Now she began to wonder what had happened to her and how she had come to this cave. She remembered the sinking of the ship, and herself being tumbled into the sea and tangled in the sail, and remembering that she saw that the sail was lying half out of the water, over against one wall of the cave. So she supposed that some current had washed her in here, and the sea chest too, and the tide had then gone out and left her in air. But why was it not dark? The light came from the other side of the cave, low down, and when she went to look she found that the water washed in along that wall, making as it were an inlet in the waterline, and partway up this was a pool where lay a coiling fish like a great eel, which shone with points of light all along its flanks. It stirred when it saw her and the light grew stronger, and now she saw that it was trapped in that place by a wall of small boulders, piled neatly against one another across the inlet.

"Then she grew afraid, for she could see that the wall had not come there by chance. She searched the cave, looking for a place to hide, but there was none. Only she found that the inlet was formed by a little stream of water, sweet to drink, that ran down the back of the cave. After that she prayed and sang, and then fell asleep, weeping for the mother and father she would never see again.

"When she woke she knew before she opened her eyes that she was not alone. She had heard the whisper of a voice.

"She sat up and looked at the water. Two heads had risen

from it. Four eyes were gazing at her. She could not see them well in the faint light, but her heart leaped and her throat hardened. Then one of the heads spoke, in a weak human voice, in a language she did not know, though she understood it to be a question.

" 'Who are you?' she whispered, and they laughed and came further out of the water, so that she could see that they were human-shaped, pale-skinned and dark-haired, wearing no clothes but for what seemed to be collars or ruffs around their necks. She stood and put her palms together and said the Lord's Prayer in her mind while she crept down to the water's edge. As she came, the creatures used their arms to heave themselves up through the shallows. Closer seen, she thought they were children of about her age, until she saw that instead of legs each had a long and shining tail, like that of a fish. This is what Charity Goodrich said she saw, Pitiable. Do you believe her?"

"If you believe her, I do too."

"Then you believe her. Now it came to her that these two were children of the sea-people, and the cave was a place they had found and made their own, as children like to do. They had caught the fish and prisoned it here to give light to the cave, for their own amusement, and in the same way they had found Charity and brought her here, and the chest, floating them in when the tide was high and dragging them onto dry land.

"They fetched the sail and by signs showed her that somehow a pocket of air had been caught in it with her, allowing her to breathe for a little beneath the water. All this and other things Charity learnt as the days passed. She could count those days by the coming and going of the tide.

"They had brought food for the shining fish, so she made signs that she wanted to eat and they swam off. She was afraid that they would bring her raw fish, but instead they came with human stores from the wrecked ship. Some were spoilt with salt, but some were in canisters that had kept the water out, wormy bread and dried apples and oatmeal which she mixed with fresh water from the stream at the back of the cave.

"She tried to talk with the sea-children. Their voices were weak, and they could not breathe for long out of the water. What she had thought to be ruffs around their necks were plumy growths with which they seemed to breathe the sea-water, as a fish does with its gills. Their language was strange. She told them her name, but they could not say it, nor she theirs. Instead they sang, not opening their mouths but humming with closed lips. You have often heard me humming the song of the sea-people."

"This one?" said Pitiable, and hummed the slow, wavering tune that she had heard so often. Mercy joined her, and they hummed it together, their voices twining like ripples in water. When they finished, Mercy smiled.

"That is how I used to sing it with my own mother," she said. "And then with yours. It needs two voices, or three. So Charity sang it with the sea-children in their cave, and they hummed the tunes she taught them, *The Old Hundredth* and *Mount Ephraim* and such, so that they should be able to praise their Creator beneath the waves. So as the days went by a kind of friendship grew, and then she saw that they began to be troubled by what they had done. At first, she supposed, she had seemed no more than a kind of toy, or amusement, for them, a thing with which they could do as they chose, like the shining fish. Now they were learning that this was not so.

"They made signs to her, which she did not understand, but supposed them to be trying to comfort her, so she signed to them that she wished to return to her own people, but they in their turn frowned and shook their heads, until she went to the place where the shining fish was trapped and started to take down the wall they had built. They stopped her, angrily, but she pointed to the fish as it sought to escape through the gap she had made, and then at herself, and at the walls that held her, and made swimming motions with her arms, though she could not swim. They looked at each other, more troubled than before, and argued for a while in their own language, the one trying to persuade the other, though she could see that both were afraid. In the end they left her.

"She sat a long while, waiting, until there was a stirring in the water that told her that some large creature was moving below the surface. She backed away as it broke into the air. It was a man, a huge, pale man of the sea-people. If he had had legs to walk upon, he would have stood as tall as two grown men. She could feel the man's anger as he gazed at her, but she said the Lord's Prayer in her mind and with her palms together walked down to the water's edge and stood before him, waiting to see what he would do.

"Still he stared, furious and cold. She thought to herself and closed her lips and started to hum the music the sea-children had taught her, until he put up his hand and stopped her. He spoke a few words of command and left.

"She waited. Twice he came back, bringing stuff from the wreck, spars and canvas and rope, which he then worked on, in and out of the water, making what seemed to be a kind of tent which he held clear of the water and then dragged back in, with air caught inside it, so that it floated high. He then buoyed it down with boulders to drag it under. He took it away and came back and worked on it some more, and then returned, having, she supposed, tried it out and been satisfied. Meanwhile she had gathered up her own clothes and wrapped them tightly in oilskin, and stripped off the ones she was wearing, down to the slip, and tied her bundle to her waist.

"When he was ready, the man, being unwilling himself to come ashore, signalled to her to break down the wall that held the shining fish, which she did, and it swam gladly away. So in utter darkness she walked down into the water, where the man lifted his tent over her and placed her hands upon a spar that he had lashed across it for her to hold and towed her away, with her head still in the air that he had caught within the canvas and her body trailing in the water. She felt the structure jar and scrape as he towed it through the opening and out into the sea. By the time they broke the surface, the air had leaked almost away, but he lifted the tent from her and she looked around and saw that it was night.

"The storm was over, and the sea was smooth, with stars above, and a glimmer of dawn out over the ocean. Charity lay along the sea-man's back with her arms around his shoulders as he swam south and set her down at last in the shallows of a beach. Oyster Beach we call it now.

"She waded ashore, but turned knee-deep in the water to thank him. He cut her short, putting the flat of his hand against his lips and making a fierce sideways gesture with his other hand—so—then pointed at her, still as angry-seeming as when she had first seen him. She put her palms crosswise over her mouth, sealing it shut, trying to say to him: Yes, I will keep silent. She had already known she must. She did not know if any of the People were left alive after the storm, but they were the only folk she knew, and who of them would believe her, and not think she was either mad or else talking profane wickedness? Then she bowed low before him, and when she looked up, he was gone.

"She took off the slip she had worn in the sea and left it at the water's edge, as though the tide had washed it there. Then she dressed herself in her own clothes, dank and mildewy though they were, and walked up the shore. Inland was all dense woods, so she walked along beside them, past Watch Point to Huxholme Bay, where three men met her, coming to look for clams at the low tide.

"So. That is the story of Charity Goodrich. Tomorrow you shall tell it to me, leaving nothing out, so that I can be sure you know it to tell it truly to your own daughters when they are old enough to understand."

Probity sat by Mercy's bed throughout the night she died, holding both her hands in his. They prayed together, and from time to time they spoke of other things, but in voices too soft for Pitiable, in her cot at the top of the ladder, to hear. In the end she slept, and when she came down before dawn to remake the fire, she found Probity still in his clothes, sitting by the fire with his head between his hands, and Mercy stretched out cold on her cot with her Bible on her chest. For two days Probity would not eat or dress or undress or go to bed. He let the Church Elders make the arrangements for the funeral, simply grunting assent to anything that was said to him, but for the ceremony itself he pulled himself together and shaved carefully and polished his belt and boots and dressed in his Sunday suit and stood erect and stern by the graveside with his hand upon Pitiable's shoulder, and then waited with her at the churchyard gate to receive the condolences of the People.

Mercy in her last hours must have spoken to him about their granddaughter, and told him to take comfort in her and give her comfort in return, and this he tried to do. He read the Bible with her in the evenings, and sometimes noticed if she seemed tired and told her to rest. And around Christmas, when all the children of the townspeople were given toys, he whittled a tiny horse and cart for her to set upon the mantelshelf. By day he worked as he always had to see that the two of them were warm and fed, fetching in the stacked logs for the stove, and bringing in more from the frozen woods to make next season's stack, and digging turnips and other roots from the mounds where they were stored, and fetching out grain from the bins and salted meat from the barrels, and mending the tools he would need for next summer's toil, while Pitiable cooked and stitched and cleaned as best she could, the way Mercy had shown her. She was young for such work, and he did not often scold her for her mistakes. So the neighbours, who at first had felt that in Christian duty they must keep an eye upon the pair, decided that all was well and left them alone.

Spring came with the usual mud and mess, followed by the urgent seed-time when the ground dried to a fine soft tilth and had not yet begun to parch. It was then that Probity, after brooding for a while, went to the Elders of the People and asked for their permission to bring his daughter's body up from the town cemetery and bury it beside Mercy's in the graveyard of the People. The Elders did not debate the question long. They were all of one grim mind. Obedience Hooke had cut herself off from the People by marrying the outwarder, Simon Nasmith. When the Lord came again in Glory, he would raise the bodies of His faithful People from their graveyard to eternal life, but Obedience Hooke had by her own act cast herself into damnation and would not be among them.

Probity sowed his crops as usual, but then, as June hardened into its steady, dreary heat, he seemed to lose heart. The leafy summer crops came quick and easy, and there was always a glut of them, but the slow-grown roots and pulses that would be harvested later, and then dried or salted or earthed into clamps, were another matter. He did not hoe them enough, and watered irregularly, so that the plants had no root-depth and half of them wilted or wasted. He neglected, too, to do the rounds of his fences, so that the sheep broke out and he had to search the hills for them, and lost three good ewes.

Pitiable was aware that the stores were barely half-filled, but said nothing. Probity was her grandfather, her only protector, and absolute master in his own house. He did what he chose, and the choice was right because it was his.

September brought a great crop of apples from the two old trees. Mercy had always bottled them into sealed jars, but that was a skill that had to be done just right, and Pitiable did not know how. Probity could well have asked a neighbour to teach her, but he was too proud, so he told her to let them fall and he would make cider of them. Most of the People made a little cider, keeping it for special days, but this year Probity made a lot, using casks he would not now need for storage as he had less to store. He shook himself out of his dull mood and took trouble so that the cider brewed strong and clear. He took to drinking a tankard of it with his supper, and became more cheerful in the evenings.

Winter came, with its iron frosts, and Probity started to drink cider with his dinner, to keep the cold out, he said. And then with his breakfast, to get the blood moving on the icy mornings. By the time the sunrise turned back along the horizon, he was seldom without a tankard near by, from the hour he rose until the hour at which he fell snorting, and still in his day clothes, onto his bed.

He began to beat Pitiable, using his belt, finding some fault and punishing her for it, though both of them knew that that was not the cause. He was hurt to the heart, and sick with his own hurt, and all he could think of was to hurt someone or something else, and doing so himself to hurt himself worse, dulling the pain with new pain. One night Pitiable watched as he took the horse and cart he had made her and broke them into splinters with his strong hands and dropped them into the fire.

Pitiable did not complain or ask anyone for help. She knew that anything that happened to her was a just punishment for her having been born. Her mother and father should never have wed. By doing so they had broken God's law. And then Obedience, Probity's lovely lost daughter, had died giving birth to Pitiable. So Pitiable was both the fruit of her parents' sin and the cause of her mother's death, and of Probity's dreadful hurt. Nothing that was done to her could be undeserved.

On Sunday mornings Probity did not drink. He shaved

and dressed with care and took Pitiable to church. They made an impressive pair, the big, gaunt man and the pale and silent child. Neighbours remarked how much they meant to each other, now Mercy was gone. Once a woman asked Pitiable why she wept in church, and Pitiable replied that it was because of her grandmother dying. The woman clucked and said that she was a good little girl—how could she have known that Pitiable had been weeping with the pain of having to sit still on the hard bench after last night's beating?

They came through the winter, barely, scraping out the old and mouldy stores from the year before. Probity butchered and salted one of his ewes, saying she was too old for bearing, which was not true. So they did not quite starve.

The mush of spring dried to the blaze of summer, and Probity pulled himself together and drank less and worked in his fields and brought home food and kept his belt around his waist, but he did almost nothing to provide for the coming winter. One noon in the late summer heat wave, Pitiable went out to tell him that his dinner was on the table and found him at the door of his store shed, staring into its emptiness, as if lost in a dream. He started when she spoke and swung on her, and snarled, "The Lord will provide." That evening he undid his belt and beat her for no reason at all.

From then on he was as harsh as he had been last winter, but at the same time strangely possessive. He seemed unable to bear to let her out of his sight. Having no harvest to gather, he took to wandering along the shore, in the manner of the truly poor and shiftless townspeople, looking for scraps of the sea's leavings, driftwood and such, which he might use or sell. Almost at once he was lucky, finding a cask of good sweet raisins, unspoilt, which he sold well in the town. After that he would go almost every day, taking Pitiable with him to help search and carry, but the quiet days of the heat wave brought little to land.

That dense stillness broke, as usual, with a week of storm. There was a proverb in the town, "The hotter burns the sun, the wilder blows the wind," and so it proved that year, with gales that brought down trees and chimneys and stripped roofs and scattered haystacks, while day and night huge rollers thundered against the shore. On the ninth night the storm blew itself out and was followed by a dawn of pearly calm.

Probity was up before sunrise and gulped his breakfast and pulled on his boots and told Pitiable to leave the dishes unwashed and the hearth unlaid.

"The Lord spoke to me in the night," he said. "We must be first down on the shore, for this is the day on which He will provide."

The town was barely stirring as they hurried towards the harbour, and left up Northgate to the beaches. On Home Beach there were men about, seeing to their boats, many of which, though drawn well up above the tide-lines, had been tossed about by the storm, overturned, piled together or washed inland. Probity hurried past, and on over Shag Point to Huxholme Bay, which was steep small shingle. Here they stopped to search. The waves had brought in a mass of new stuff, piles of wrack and driftwood, tangles of half-rotted cording, torn nets, broken casks and crates, as well as sea-things, shells and jellyfish and small squid and so on. Probity had a piece of chalk with which to mark anything he wanted to collect on his way back, but he was not looking for timber or firewood to-day and marked nothing.

Next came Watch Point, both sandy and rocky. Here Pitiable picked out of the sand an ancient leather boot with a spur, which Probity tested with his jack knife to see if it might be silver. It was not, but he put it in his sack and poked around with his staff in the sand, in case it might be part of some buried hoard exposed by the storm, but again it was not.

Beyond Oyster Bay lay the Scaurs, two miles of tilted rocky promontories with inlets between, like the teeth of a broken comb, and beyond them black unscalable cliffs. The Scaurs were the best hunting ground, but slow work, full of crannies and fissures where trove might lodge. If Pitiable had been less sore from last night's beating—lengthy and savage after Probity had been nine days cooped up by the storm—she might have enjoyed the search, the jumping and scrambling, and the bright sea-things that lurked in the countless pools. As it was, she searched numbly, dutifully, her mind filled with the dread of their homecoming, having found nothing. That failure would be made her fault, reason enough for another beating.

She searched the upper half of the beach and Probity the lower. They were about half way to the cliffs, and could already hear the screaming of the tens of thousands of gulls that nested there, when her way was blocked by the next jut of rock, a vertical wall too high for her to climb. She was hesitating to go shoreward or seaward to get past the barrier when she heard a new noise, a quick rush of water followed by a slithering, a mewling cry and a splash. After a short while the sounds were repeated in the same order. And again. And again.

They seemed to come from beyond the barrier to her right,

so she turned left, looking for a place where she could climb and peer over without whatever was making them becoming aware of her. She came to a pile of rocks she could scramble up. The top of the barrier was rough but level. Crouching, she crept towards the sea and discovered a large, deep pool, formed by the main rock splitting apart and then becoming blocked at the seaward end by an immense slab, trapping into the cleft any wave that might be thrown that far up the shore. The seal at the top end wasn't perfect, and enough water had drained away for the surface to be several feet down from the rim, leaving a pool about as wide as one of the fishing boats and twice as long, or more.

As Pitiable watched, the surface at the seaward end of the pool convulsed and something shot up in a burst of foam. She saw a dark head, a smooth, pale body, and a threshing silvery tail that drove the creature up the steep slope of the slab that held the pool in. A slim arm—not a leg or flipper but an arm like Pitiable's own—reached and clutched, uselessly, well short of the rim, and then the thing slithered back with its thin despairing wail and splashed into the water. From what Mercy had told her of Charity Goodrich's adventure, Pitiable understood at once what she had seen.

Amazed out of her numbness, she watched the creature try once more, and again, before she silently backed away and looked down the shore for her grandfather. He was standing near the water's edge but gazing landward, looking for her, she guessed. She waved to him to come and he hurried towards her. She held her finger to her lips and made urgent gestures for silence with her other hand. By now he must have heard the sounds and understood that something living was concerned, which must not be alarmed, so he made his way round and climbed cautiously up the same way that she had. She pointed and he crept forward to peer into the pool.

She lost count of the cries and splashes while he stared, but when at length he backed away and turned she saw that his eyes were glistening with a new, excited light. He climbed down, helped her to follow, chalked his mark onto the rock and led her up the beach.

"The Lord has indeed provided," he whispered. "Blessed be His name. Now you must stand guard while I fetch nets and men to bring this thing home. If anyone comes, you must tell them that the find is mine. See how excellent are His ways! This very week He brings the fair to town! Stay here. Do not go back up the rock. It must not see you."

He strode off, walking like a younger man, picking his way easily across the broken rocks. Pitiable sat on a sea-worn slab and waited. She felt none of Probity's excitement. She was now appalled at what she had done. Probity and his helpers would catch the sea-child and sell her—from what she had seen, Pitiable was almost sure it was a girl—sell her to the showmen at the fair. That in itself was dreadful. The People had no dealings with the fair that came each autumn. It was an occasion of frivolity and wickedness, they said. But now Probity was going to take the sea-child to them and haggle for a price. More than anything else, more than the ruined farm, more even than her own beatings, this made Pitiable see how much he had changed.

Obediently she sat and watched him go. When he came to Oyster Bay, he turned back, shading his eyes, so she stood and waved and he waved back and vanished into the dip, leaving her alone with the sea and the shore and the strange, sad cries from the pool. By now Pitiable was again too wrapped in her own misery to hear them as anything more than cries, as meaningless to her as the calling of the gulls. It struck her perhaps that Probity would perhaps not sell the sea-girl, but would join the fair, taking Pitiable with him, and show her himself. She would be dead by then, of course—in Charity Goodrich's story the sea-people could not live long out of water—but people would pay money to see even a dead sea-child.

The cries and splashes stopped for a while. Probably the sea-child was resting for a fresh attempt, and yes, when it came the swirl of the water was stronger and the slap of the body against the rock was louder, and the wail as the child fell back yet more despairing than before—so lost, so hopeless, that this time Pitiable heard it for what it was, and when it came again she felt it was calling to her, to her alone, in a language she alone knew, the language of a child trapped in a pit of despair by things too powerful for her to overcome.

Weeping, she realised that she could not bear it.

She dried her eyes and rose and climbed back up to the pool. This time as she watched the sea-child's desperate leapings she saw that there must be something wrong with the other arm, which dangled uselessly by the slim body as it shot from the water. Still, one arm should be enough, if Pitiable could lean far enough to reach it, so she made her way round to the sloping rock, knelt and craned over.

The sea-girl was on the point of leaping again. For a moment Pitiable gazed down at the wan, drawn face with its too-small mouth and its too-large dark eyes, but then the sea-girl twisted from her leap and plunged back below the surface, leaving nothing but the swirl of her going. Pitiable reached down, calling gently and kindly, telling the girl she wanted to help her, though they must hurry because her grandfather would soon be back. But the girl hid in the depths, invisible behind the sky-reflecting surface, and did not stir.

Pitiable stood up and looked along the Scaurs, but there was still no sign of Probity. He must have reached Home Beach by now, but perhaps the men there were too busy with their boats to listen to him. Well, she thought, though I cannot swim, if the girl will not come to me, I must go to her. At its shoreward end the pool narrowed almost to a slit, into which a few boulders had fallen and wedged, so she made her way round, sat down and took off all her clothes. Then she lowered herself into the slimy crack and, using the boulders for footholds, climbed down to the water.

Despite the hot summer it was chill from the storm, which had churned up the underdeeps and thrown them here ashore. The salt stung the weals where Probity's belt had cut, but she forced herself down and down, clutching a jag of rock beside her. With her chin level with the water she spoke.

"Please come. Please trust me. I want to help you. I will take you back to the sea."

Nothing happened. She was about to plead again, but then changed her mind and lowered herself a little further, drew a deep breath and ducked beneath the surface. Through closed lips she started to hum the music Mercy had taught her, and now she discovered why it needed to be hummed, not sung. It wasn't just that she couldn't open her mouth under water— the sea-people spoke with words, so they must be able to. It was because now her whole body acted as a sort of sounding-board from which the slow notes vibrated. She could feel them moving away from her through the water, and when she rose to draw breath and sank again, they were still there, the same wavering air that she had heard Mercy hum so often, but this time coming out of the depths where the sea-child lay hidden.

Pitiable joined the music, weaving her own notes through it as she had learned to do with Mercy those last days, until she needed to draw breath again, but before she sank back, the surface stirred and the sea-girl's head appeared, staring at her from only a few feet away, lips parted, desperate with fear.

Pitiable smiled at her and hummed again, in the air this time. The sea-girl answered and moved closer, slowly, but then came darting in and gave Pitiable a quick, brushing kiss and swirled away. Pitiable smiled and beckoned. Now the girl came more gently, and stayed, letting Pitiable take her good arm by the wrist and wind it around her own neck and then turn so that the girl's body lay along Pitiable's back and Pitiable could try to climb out the way she had come.

She gestured first, trying to explain that though they had to start inland, she would turn seaward as soon as they reached the top of the rock. The girl seemed to understand, and hummed the tune again, with a querying rise at the end.

"Yes," said Pitiable. "I will take you to the sea."

The great fish tail became desperately heavy as she dragged it from the water, but the girl understood the need and spoke and knocked with her closed knuckles against Pitiable's shoulder to stop her climbing while she deftly swung her tail sideways and up so that it lodged among the fallen boulders and Pitiable was now lifting only half her weight as she climbed on. Pitiable's small body was wiry from its household tasks, and since Mercy had fallen ill, she had had to learn how to lift and shift burdens beyond her apparent strength, so she strove and grunted up the cleft, with the girl helping as best as she could, until she could roll her out onto the surface and climb gasping beside her.

From then on she could crawl, with the sea-girl's arm round her neck and the chilly body pressed against her back and the tail slithering behind. The rock promontory that held the pool tilted steadily down towards the incoming tide. It had weathered into sharp ridges, painful to crawl on, but Pitiable barely noticed, because a tremendous thought had come to her and given her fresh strength. She herself belonged body and soul to Probity, to beat and use in whatever way he chose until he finally killed her. Until then she was utterly trapped in that pit, with no escape. But here, now, there was this one thing she could prevent him from doing. He would not have the sea-girl, to join her in the pit. Not now, not ever.

So she crawled on. Soon the sea-girl was gulping and panting from being too long in the air, but she lay still and trusting as the sea came slowly nearer. At last one flank of the promontory sloped down with the small waves washing in beside it, and Pitiable could crawl down until the sea-girl, judging her moment, was able to convulse herself sideways into the backwash and slither on through the foam to deeper water. In the haze of her huge effort Pitiable barely saw her go, but when her vision cleared and she looked out to sea, she saw the girl beckoning to her from beside the tip of the promontory.

Wearily she rose and staggered down. The sea-girl gripped the rock with her good hand and dragged herself half out of the water. Pitiable sat beside her with her feet dangling into the wave-wash. Her knees and shins, she noticed, were streaming with blood. The sea-girl saw them and made a grieving sound.

"It's all right," said Pitiable. "It is only scratches."

Face to face they looked at each other.

"You must go now," said Pitiable. "Before he comes back."

The sea-girl answered. She craned up. Pitiable bent so that they could kiss.

"I must dress myself before the men come," she said. "Good-bye."

She gestured to herself, and up the shore, and then to the sea-girl and the open sea. The sea-girl nodded and said something that must have been an answering good-bye. They kissed again, and the sea-girl twisted like a leaping salmon and shot off down the inlet, turned in the water, rose, waved and was gone.

As Pitiable dressed, she decided that now Probity would very likely kill her for what she had done, take her home and beat her to death, half meaning to, and half not. And then, perhaps, he would kill himself. That would be best all round, she thought.

And then she thought that despite that, she had done what Mercy would have wanted her to. It was why she had told her the story of Charity Goodrich, though neither of them could have known.

When she was dressed she shook her hair out and sat combing her fingers through it to help it dry in the sun, but still he did not come, so she tied it up under her shawl and waited where he had left her. Her mood of gladness and resignation ebbed, and she was wrapped in terror once again.

✦   ✦   ✦

The men came at last, four of them, carrying nets and ropes, a stretcher, and a glass-bottomed box of the sort that crab-catchers used to see below the surface of the water. From their dress Pitiable saw that the three helpers were townspeople, as they would have to be—Probity would not even have tried to persuade any of the People to come on such an enterprise. From the way they walked, it was obvious that even these men were doubtful. A tall, thin lad in particular kept half-laughing, as if he was convinced that he was about to be made a fool of. But Probity came with a buoyant, excited pace and reached her ahead of the others.

"Has anyone been near?" he whispered.

"No one, grandfather."

"And have you heard anything?"

"Only the gulls and the sea."

He stood and listened and frowned, but by now the helpers had come up, so he told them to wait with Pitiable and make no noise, and himself climbed up onto the ridge and crept out of sight. After a while he climbed down and fetched the glass-bottomed box, and this time he allowed the others to come up with him, but Pitiable stayed where she was. She heard his voice, gruff and stubborn, and the others answering him at first mockingly and then angrily, until he came down again and strode over to where she sat, with the others following.

Pitiable rose and waited. She could see how the others glanced at one another behind Probity's back, and before he spoke, she knew how she must answer.

"I tell you, the child saw it also," he shouted. And then to Pitiable, "Where has it gone? How did it get free?"

"What do you speak of, grandfather?"

"The sea-child! Tell them you saw the sea-child!"

"Sea-child, grandfather?"

He took a pace forward and clouted her with all his strength on the side of her head. She sprawled onto the shingle, screaming with the pain of it, but before she could rise, he rushed at her and struck her again. She did not know what happened next, but then somebody was helping her to her feet and Probity and the others were shouting furiously while she shook her head and retched in a roaring red haze. Then her vision cleared though her head still sang with pain, and she saw two of the men wrestling with Probity, holding his arms behind him.

"The wicked slut let her go!" he bellowed. "She was mine! Mine! You have no right! This is my grandchild! Mine!"

His face was terrible, dark red and purple, with the veins on his temples standing out like exposed tree roots. Then he seemed to realize what he had done and fell quiet. In silence and in shame he let them walk him back to the town, with the young man carrying Pitiable on his back.

Though there were magistrates in the town, there was so seldom any wrongdoing among the People that it was the custom to let them deal with their own. After some debate the men took Probity to the Minister and told him what they had seen, and he sent for three of the elders to decide what to do. They heard the men's story, gave them the money Probity had promised them, thanked them and sent them away. They then questioned Probity.

Probity did not know how to lie. He said what he had seen,

and insisted that Pitiable had seen the sea-child too. Pitiable, still dazed, unable to think of anything except how he would beat her when he had her home, stuck despairingly to her story. She said that she had been looking at the pool when Probity had climbed up beside her and looked too and become very excited and told her to wait down on the shore and let no one else near while he went for help.

At this Probity started to shout and his face went purple again and he tried to rush at Pitiable, but the elders restrained him, and then a spasm shook him and he had to clutch at a chair and sit down. Even so, but for his story about the sea-child, the elders might have sent Pitiable home with him. She was, after all, his granddaughter. But a man who says he has seen a creature with a human body and a shining fish tail cannot be of sound mind, so they decided that in case there should be worse scandal among the People than there already was, Pitiable had best be kept out of his way, at least until a doctor had examined him.

Pitiable spent the night at the Minister's house, not with his own children but sleeping in the attic with the two servants. First, though, the Minister's wife, for whom cleanliness was very close indeed to godliness, insisted that the child must be bathed. That was how the servants came to see the welts on Pitiable's back and sides. Her torn knees they put down to her fall on the beach when Probity had struck her. The elder servant, a kind, sensible woman, told the Minister. She told him too that if the child received much more such handling, she would die, and her blood would be not only on her grandfather's hands.

The elders did not like it, but were forced to agree. A home would have to be found for the child. As a servant, naturally—she was young, but Mercy Hooke had trained her well. So on the second day after the business on the Scaurs, a Miss Lyall, a very respectable spinster with money of her own, came to inspect Pitiable Nasmith. She asked for a private room and the Minister lent her his study.

Pitiable was brought in and Miss Lyall looked her up and down. Not until they door closed and they were alone did she smile. She was short and fat with bulgy eyes and two large hairy moles on the side of her chin, but her smile was pleasant. She put her head to one side and pursed her lips and, almost too quietly to hear, started to hum. Pitiable's mouth fell open. With an effort she closed it and joined the music. At once Miss Lyall nodded and cut her short.

"I thought it must be so," she said softly. "As soon as I heard that story about the sea-child."

"But you know the song too!" whispered Pitiable, still amazed.

"You are not the only descendant of Charity Goodrich, my dear. My mother taught me her story, and the song, and said I must pass them on to my own daughters, but I was too plain for any sensible man to marry for myself, and too sensible to let any man marry me for my money, so I have no daughters to teach them to. Not even you, since you already know them. All the same, you shall be my daughter from now on and we shall sing the song together and tell each other the story. It will be amusing, after all these years, to see how well the accounts tally."

She smiled, and Pitiable, for the first time for many, many days, smiled too.

THE
SEA-KING'S SON

There was a young woman named Jenny who was the only child of her parents. Her parents were not wealthy as the world counts wealth, but they had a good farm and were mindful and thorough farmers; and since they had but the one child, they could afford to give her a good deal. So she had pretty clothes and kind but clever governesses and as many dogs and cats and ponies and songbirds as she wanted. She grew up knowing that she was much loved, and so she had a happy childhood; but the self-consciousness of adolescence made her shy and solemn. And she found, as some adolescents do, that she was less and less interested in the kinds of things her old friends were now most interested in, and so they drifted apart. Now she preferred to go for long solitary walks with her dogs, or riding on the fine thoroughbred mare her parents had bought her when she outgrew the last of the ponies. Her mother had to forbid her to stay in the kitchen through the harvest feast, where she would have gone on bottling plums and cherries from their orchards with her mother and the two serving-women till all the dancing was over; and at the next fair her mother sent her on a series of errands to all the stalls where the young people would be working for their parents. But Jenny only spoke to them as much as she had to, and came away again.

Her parents had hoped that she would outgrow her shyness, as she had grown into it, but by the time she was eighteen, they had begun to fear that this would not happen. They worried, because they wanted her to find a husband, that she might be as happy with him as they had been with each other; and they hoped to leave their farm in their daughter's hands, to be cared for by her and her husband as lovingly as they had cared for it, and given on to her children in the proper time. They worried that even a young man who would suit her well would not notice her, for she made herself unnoticeable; and they feared that it was only they who knew that, when she smiled, her face lit up with gentleness and humour and intelligence.

They decided that they would take her to the city for a season, and that perhaps so drastic a change in her usual way of life might bring her to herself. They had relatives in the city, and this could be done without discomfort. They told her of their plan, and she would have protested, but they told her that they were her parents, and they knew best.

But because of her knowledge that she was to go away, she carried herself with more of an air during the next weeks—it was an air of tension, but it made her eyes sparkle and her back straight. She looked around her at her familiar circumstances with more attention than she had done for years, as if this trip to the city were going to change her life forever. And she knew well enough that her parents hoped that it would, that they hoped to find her an acceptable suitor: and what could change her life more thoroughly than marriage?

They were going to the city a little after the final harvest fair of the year, when the farm could be left to look after itself for a while, with none but the hired workers to keep an eye on it; and when, as well, the best parties in the city were held, after the heat of the summer was over. The letters were written, and the relatives had pronounced themselves delighted to have Jenny for a season and her parents for as much as they felt they could stay of it. Her parents permitted themselves to feel hopeful; even the possibility that Jenny would fall in love with some city boy who loathed the very idea of farming seemed worth the risk.

But things did not turn out as Jenny's parents had planned. For at the harvest fair she caught the eye of a young man.

This young man lived in a neighbouring village, and was one of four sons, third from the eldest. His family too held a good farm, like hers, but they had four sons to think of. The first was a hard worker, and he would have the farm. The second was clever, and was to be apprenticed to his uncle, who was a clever businessman in the city. The fourth was grave and thoughtful, and would go into the priesthood. The third was beautiful. His name was Robert.

He knew he was beautiful, and all the girls knew it. Jenny knew it too. She had loved him for four and a half years, almost since the day that the blood that made her a woman first flowed, and her mother had explained to her what this meant, and what would happen to her on her wedding night. When she had understood, she had blushed fierily, and tried to forget. It had only been three days before that she had seen Robert for the first time, and had wondered at her own inability to think of anything else since, for such a thing had never happened to her before; boys were just boys, and their differences from girls had never been terribly intriguing. It seemed to her that her mother had just explained this too, and rather than feeling pleased and excited, she felt it was all too much, and was frightened. None of this she told her mother, who might have been able to reassure her; and she never told anyone of her feelings for Robert.

So she knew she loved this young man, but she had never done anything to draw his attention to her. But she was now eighteen, and he twenty, and he was beginning to realise that he could not go on merely being beautiful at his parents' expense, and that it was time that he put his beauty to what he had always known was its purpose: to find himself a wife who would keep him comfortably.

He had known about Jenny for as long as she had known about him, for it was his habit to ask about every girl he saw, and he had asked about her on the very day she had first seen him. But, vain as he was, he did not know that she loved him, for she was that clever at hiding it. He found her such a dreary, dim little thing that even though he did not forget about her, in the four years since he had first been told about her parents' farm and the fact that she was the only and much beloved child, he had not been able to bring himself to flirt with her. There were other, prettier, livelier girls that pleased him better. But this year, the year that she was eighteen and he twenty, he decided the time had come, and he had steeled himself to do what he had by this time convinced himself was his duty; and, looking for her at the harvest fair, had been astonished at the change in her, at the sparkle in her eye and the straight, elegant way she carried herself. Without inquiring about the source of the change, either to her or to himself, he found that his duty was not quite as dreadful as he had expected. He flirted with her and she, hesitantly, responded. She had seen him flirt with other girls. And he had to admit, by her response, that she might be dim but she was not unintelligent. And so to keep her interest he had to . . . put himself out a little.

He came to call on her at her parents' farm, and was charming to her parents. She had told him that she was being sent off to stay a season with her parents' relatives in the city, and while she did not tell him why, he could guess. She told him that they were due to leave in a fortnight's time. The day before they would have left, he asked her to marry him.

The warmth of her kiss when she answered him yes startled him; and again he thought that perhaps doing his duty would not be so dreadful after all, for if she was not as pretty as some, still the armful of her was good to hold, and she loved him, of course, as he expected her to.

She did love him. And she believed that he loved her, for he had told her so. She thought she would have known—for such was her acuteness about anything to do with him, and her mother had many friends who came joking and gossiping around, and she always listened—if he had ever proposed marriage to any of the other girls he had been seen with over the last four years. And if he did not love her, why else would he have proposed? For marriage was for life, and a husband and wife must come first with each other for all the days of it.

She knew, for she was not unintelligent, about the pragmatic facts of being a third son; but she was also innocent, and in love. She could not believe that any man would take a wife wholly on account of her inheritance.

Her parents saw that she was in love, and rejoiced for her, or they tried to, for they could not rejoice in her choice, and they were put to some difficulty not to let her know their misgivings. Their guess of the likeliest inspiration for his proposal was not clouded with love or innocence; and they too knew about his position as third son. But, they comforted themselves, they knew nothing against him, but that he was a bit over-merry in a way that they perhaps were wrong to dislike, for they were old and he was young; and they knew also that he was not much given to hard work; but this too might be on account of his youth, and his undeniable beauty, which had encouraged people to spoil him a little. Naught had ever been said truly against him. He was only twenty; perhaps he had realised it was time to settle down, and had made choice of their daughter by recognising her real worth, including that she might settle a husband she loved—perhaps he did love her, for that reason. Not for the sake of her parents' farm. Not only for the sake of her parents' farm, for they never tried to tell themselves that the farm had no place in his calculations. Many marriages, they said to each other, are built on less; and she loved him enough for both, and perhaps he would grow to love her as much, for he was—he was good-natured enough, they thought. There was no meanness in him, just carelessness and vanity.

But when he sat in their kitchen or sitting-room with them and their daughter, they did not like it that he did not seem to notice when she smiled, he did not seem to love that bright look of gentleness and humour and intelligence; he did not seem to see it. He petted her, as he might a little dog that sat adoringly at his feet, and her parents tried not to like him less for enjoying that their daughter adored him in such a way.

So it was; and so it went on. The wedding date was fixed, and the relatives in the city had had the situation explained to them, and had promised to come to the wedding themselves, and suggested that perhaps the young people could visit them some day. The plans for the wedding progressed, and Jenny seemed no less in love, and Robert grew no less kind to her, even if it was the casual kindness of a boy to a little dog.

The two farms lay on the opposite outskirts of two towns. The distance between was considerable, and when the young people wished to visit each other, thought had to be taken about time and weather, and who would do the work left undone. Both towns lay near a small cup of harbour, one on either side, each on a little rise of ground with the harbour at the low point between. It would have been much the quicker for anyone wishing to go from the one farm to the other to go down to the harbour and up the other side; but no one ever did go that way. There was still an old, broken road that led over what had once been a wide bridge for heavy trade and traffic between the towns at the head of the harbour, but it had lain untouched for three generations.

There is rarely much contact between sea-people and land-people, but for a while there had been a wary association between them in the vicinity of this harbour. No one remembered how it had begun, but for many years there was a limited but profitable trade in certain luxury items: the sea-people loved fine lace, for example, perhaps in part because it perished so quickly under water, and bright flowers preserved in wax or glass. The land merchants preferred pearls and narwhal horns. Neither side was able to trust the other, however, saying that each was too strange, too alien, that they could not—indeed should not—be comfortable in each other's company. This lack of confidence grew with time instead of easing, and no doubt trouble would have come sooner or later. But when trouble came, it was grievous.

Three generations of land-people ago, a greedy merchant had cheated the sea-people who had rescued him from drowning, and they had been angry. But when they asked the town councillors to right this wrong, the town councillors had said that as the merchant was of the land, like themselves, they would not decide against him.

The sea-people are no more cruel than those on land. But they had lost several of their own in the storm that had foundered the false merchant's ship, and they guessed—correctly—that the land-merchant's faithlessness was for no better cause than a desire to recoup financially. So then the king and queen of the sea-people had let their wrath run free, for they had asked for redress to be offered honestly and had been denied.

The water had risen in the harbour and beaten against its walls till all the ship docks were washed away. And the sea-people said: This is what you have earned, for your greed and your treachery, that this kind harbour shall never be kind to you again, and the merchant trade of which you have been so proud is denied you for as long as the sea-people shall remember you and your decision, and the sea-people's memory is long. If any shall set a boat in this harbour, it shall be over-turned; and if any shall set foot on the bridge at the head of the harbour, then shall a wave rise up and sweep them off and into the sea where they shall drown, as your merchant might have done.

And so it was. At first the towns, who had been rich and fat for a long time, could not believe it; and they set to work re-building the docks, and repairing their ships, and repaving the bridge at the head of the harbour, and they grumbled as they did it, and particularly they grumbled at the greedy mer-chant who had brought them to this pass. But in a year's time they had all but bankrupted themselves, all the merchants of both towns, and the banks that had loaned them money, and the outfitters that had provided the goods; and there were no longer any workers who would take jobs on docks or ships either, because there had been too many freak waves, too many sudden storms, too many drownings.

Over the three generations since then, the towns had shrunk back from the harbour, and looked inland for their commerce, and the farmers, who had once been considered very much inferior to the merchants of the sailing trade, were now the most important citizens. The merchants and bankers and outfitters either died of broken hearts or moved away; and the hired workers learned to cut a straight furrow in-stead of a straight mast, and the sailors mostly went north or south, although a goodly number of them, too, went inland, and became coopers and cordwainers. It was said that the original merchant who had caused the trouble changed his name, and took his family to the other side of the world, but that bad luck had pursued him even there, and he had died in poverty.

Jenny's family had been farmers on their farm for many generations, and were little touched by the change in their status. They were farmers who cared about farming, and what the people around them thought of farming seemed to them only amusing, because everyone must eat, and that is what farming is for. Perhaps they had a few more cousins on the town council in the three generations since the collapse of the sailing trade than they had previously, but this did not greatly change their outlook either, so long as the towns continued to provide markets and fairs, and enough hungry and prosperous folk to buy farm produce. There had never been any sailors or fisherfolk in their family, and they believed in their blood and bone that the sea was an unchancy thing at best, and better left alone. Even the tale of the sea-people's curse could not stir them much; it was too much what they would expect of sea-people, had they ever thought about it.

A system of longer inland roads sprang up to connect the two towns, for even without the harbour their people had too long been closely involved with each other to break off relations now. The new connecting road curved far inland, staying high on the ridge above the harbour so that the road might cross while the stream that fed it still lay underground, and as a result it was an hour on a fresh horse even between the two towns, and nearer three between outlying farms.

Once the betrothal had been officially set and posted, the parents of Jenny and Robert relaxed, a little, about letting them visit each other; and if Robert rode over to see Jenny in the afternoon, her parents expected to put him up overnight and he rode home the next day, and vice versa. There were some words spoken between Jenny and her parents, for her parents felt that it was not proper that she ride all that way alone, and sent someone with her, usually right to the gate of Robert's family's farm; and let her know further that they would still not allow this at all if it hadn't been clearly understood that there was a sister still at home as well as Robert's mother, and that Jenny would share the sister's bedroom. Jenny, scarlet with shame, said this was nonsense, and that furthermore it was unnecessarily tiring and tedious for whoever was sent with her; but her parents said that it was in this wise or not at all, and so she yielded, but with a less good grace than was usual with her.

It had been tacitly assumed by each family that the extra pair of hands would be put to use, in a little way to make up for when the pair of hands they were used to having available weren't there for a long afternoon and overnight; but because the parents of each child were very cautious with the parents of the other child, they did not exchange any words about the relative usefulness of their two children. It would have been very awkward if they had been less cautious, since Jenny could lay her hand to almost anything, indoors and out, while Robert seemed capable of almost nothing without so much explanation that it became easier to do it yourself—or so Jenny's father said to Jenny's mother, more than once, in exasperation. Jenny's parents had begun to try to teach Robert the running of their farm—much of which should have been familiar to him already but mysteriously seemed not to be— and tried to believe that all would be well, once the boy was married and settled.

It was but two weeks before the wedding, and the final frenzy of preparation was beginning. It was not to be a grand wedding, but it was to be a large one, with many people staying through the day and into the evening, and much food eaten, and plenty of musicians for plenty of dancing. Jenny's parents could not but notice that there was a growing edge to her excitement that was not . . . what they would expect or want in a bride-to-be, and all their previous fears about Robert rushed upon them again. Her mother tried to talk to her, but she would not listen; and the odd edge to her excitement grew more pronounced; till at last her mother, desperate, said: "Child, you know we love you. We will not ask you any more questions that you do not wish to answer. But if—for any reason—you wish to call the wedding off, for pity's sake, tell us, and we will do it for you."

Jenny rounded on her mother then, in a way she never had, and screamed at her, and said that her parents were determined to destroy her happiness, that they did not need to tell her again that they did not like Robert, that of course she wanted the wedding to go as planned, and to leave her alone!

Her mother, shaken, pulled away from her daughter, turned and left her, and Jenny threw herself sobbing on her bed.

Jenny's mother said to her husband, "There is nothing we can do. Something is wrong, dreadfully wrong, but we must let her bear it herself, for she will accept no help from us."

They left her alone that day, shut up in her room, and went on about the farm work and the wedding preparations with heavy hearts.

And Jenny, after several solitary and gloomy hours, crept out of her room and down the stairs, and to the barns. She saddled her mare, Flora, and led her down a soft path where the mare's iron shoes would not ring and give them away, and mounted and rode off. Jenny looked back after she had run off her first misery with a gallop, and saw that her long-legged wolfhound bitch had followed her. She scolded her, and Gruoch's ears drooped, but she peered at her mistress up under her hairy brows, and clung to Flora's heels, and showed no sign of going home as ordered. So they went on together, the three of them.

It was twilight when Jenny reached Robert's farm, and his family was not expecting her. She paused at the gate. She knew why she had come, but she did not know what to do about it, and, knowing she did not know, had put off thinking about it, and now she was here and had to do something. At last she dismounted, and led Flora through the gate—while Gruoch oiled her way between the rails—and closed it behind them; and then she tied her mare to the fence and went on alone, her wolfhound still at her heels. She went down the path towards the farm buildings, as she usually did, although usually she rode, and at the sound of hoofbeats some member of the family would come out to meet her, for they were looking out for her. But they were not expecting her now, and she and her hound made no sound of footsteps.

It was spring, and there was much to do, for it had been cold and wet till late this year, and some evenings everyone worked on in the fields till dark. She should be home, now, doing the same. The buildings seemed deserted, and she wandered among them, a little forlornly, feeling that she'd come on a fool's errand. It was all very well, what her mother said—what her mother had offered—but it was not that easy; and as she thought this, her eyes filled up again, and tears ran down her cheeks. As she took a great, gulping breath, she thought she heard something. She turned and walked towards the nearest barn. It sounded like someone giggling.

The door was only a little ajar, and it was almost dark inside, for there was not much daylight left. But there was a hatch door left open at the far end of the barn, high up in the loft, and a little of the remains of daylight came through it, and fell on a heap of golden straw. Robert was lying there, with a very pretty girl. The very pretty girl had no clothes on.

Jenny gasped, for she could not help it. She had, slowly, over the six months of her betrothal, come to understand that Robert did not love her, and this, when she had finally faced it, had caused her much grief. She felt that she had been foolish, and did not know where to turn; it had not occurred to her that her parents were wise enough even in such things to ask them, for she knew they loved each other, and had never thought of anyone else from their first courting days. She had felt, obscurely, that she had failed them somehow by loving a man who did not love her. Nor had she wanted to call off the wedding even now; not clearly, at least; for she knew she did still love him; perhaps she was only hoping for miracles; but she thought perhaps that he might have some . . . reassurance for her, that he might have something for her, even if it was not love, if she asked him. But she did not know how to ask for what she wanted, for what she would accept in place of love. She did not know what she would accept instead of love because that was what she did want, and what he had promised her. She had come over here, dumbly, thinking to find Robert, perhaps, alone; perhaps something would come to her that she could say to him.

She was very young, and very innocent. She had not, at

her worst moments, expected anything like this. She knew what her own warm blood, when his arms were around her and their mouths met, meant; this was one of the reasons she could not bring herself to call off the wedding.

And so she gasped. Robert heard the sound, soft as it was, and stood up, throwing himself away from the pretty naked girl, leaping away from her, whirling to put his back to her as if she had nothing to do with him. He was still dressed, but both his shirt and his breeches were unlaced. His mouth dropped open; for this moment even his gift of ready, flattering speech had deserted him; for a moment he forgot he was beautiful. "Darling—" he said at last, or rather, croaked; and Jenny put her hands over her ears, and turned and fled. He took a step after her, but the wolfhound paused in the barn door and turned back to him, bristling; and he heard her growl. He stopped. The wolfhound slid silently through the door, after her mistress, and disappeared.

Jenny blundered among the familiar farm buildings like a hare among hounds; she was weeping, and felt that she would die at any moment. But she came, as much by accident as anything, around the corner of the first of the buildings, and looked up to see her grey mare glimmering in the twilight. Flora was anxious, and stamped her hoofs, swung her quarters back and forth, and swished her tail. Jenny made towards her, conscious now too of the tall wolfhound at her side, and she opened the gate in spite of her shaking fingers, untied her mare and led her through, and carefully closed and latched the gate again as any child raised on a farm knew to do by second nature. Then she mounted, and Flora leaped into a gallop without any message from Jenny.

Jenny did not mean to take the dangerous way. She thought she might die of sorrow and betrayal, but there was nothing in her healthy young spirit that could make her wish to kill herself. But in her trouble the only haven she could think of was the warm safe place she had known all her short life: her parents, her parents' farm, the farmhouse with its rosy warm kitchen and her bedroom with the quilt she and her mother had made themselves. She could not bear not to go there as quickly as possible; and the angry unfair words she had last spoken to her mother pressed on her too. She had to take them back. As quickly as possible meant the old road across the bridge at the head of the haunted harbour; but she had no thought for sea-people, or old curses, or anything, only that it was a little over an hour home this low way rather than three hours the high roundabout inland way.

She knew, of course, that the bridge was never used, but everyone from the two towns was familiar with bits of the old road that led to and away from it; the newer roads that had replaced it struck off from it. Since its bridge was shunned, it had to be; but the road itself was not fearful. As the last of the old people, who remembered their parents' friends' deaths by drowning, themselves died peacefully in their beds, the custom of not using the road remained while the specific details of the proscription on the bridge faded.

Furthermore, she had not seen Gruoch turn Robert back at the barn door. The possibility that he might try to follow her was more awful than any ancient malediction. So she set Flora's nose down the valley.

The mare had already had one journey today, and she was fretted by her mistress's mood. She went on as fast as she could, but she was tired. Jenny, who loved her, knew this, even now when she was half-distracted with her great trouble, and pulled up once they were out of sight of Robert's farm, and let the mare breathe. They went on again, but more slowly, and the twilight was really only the end of dusk, and full night came upon them almost at once. The mare began to stumble. Jenny dismounted and led her; and discovered that her mare stumbled not only from weariness, but from the roughness of the road. They were now on the last bit of road to the bridge, which was never used, and the cobbles had been torn up from sea-storm and land-frost, and the moon was not bright enough to show their way clearly, because streaming horses' tails of cloud dimmed her light.

But a little wind came up, and blew the wisps away, and the moon grew brighter. The implications of what had happened began to clarify themselves in Jenny's unhappy mind as well, but the focus of her worry for the moment was her parents, who would not know what had become of her, and would be the more anxious about her disappearance after the scene with her mother. Already she was adjusting to the fact that she no longer had a betrothed; that she would not be wed in a fortnight's time. She did not know that her sudden, desperate weariness was partly on account of that adjustment. She only thought that she had had a long journey, and that she was very unhappy, and that her parents would be worried about her. She still had not remembered the sea-people's curse.

Her wolfhound set foot on the bridge first, and a tiny ripple of wave curled beneath it, like an echo, and subsided. She was walking at Flora's shoulder, and it was the mare's front hoofs that struck the bridge next, before her own feet;

and she had just time to notice the same ripple of wave rise and begin to fall before she stepped on the bridge. But as soon as she stood on the bridge herself, it was no ripple but a wave that rose and fell upon the bridge, drenching her mare and her hound and herself. When the wave drained away, back into the harbour, there was a man standing in front of her. He gleamed strangely in the moonlight; there seemed to be something very odd about his skin. She saw him at once as human, even if the moonlight seemed to sparkle off him in flakes and facets, for he had the right number of limbs and the right order of features; and she assumed he was a man because his outline seemed to her more male than female, broader shoulders than hips, a muscular neck and square jaw beneath the wet hair that fell to his breast. But while she could not see that he wore any clothing, she could not see that he had any genitals either. And then as he held his hand up to bar her way, she saw, in the moonlight's strange little iridescent ripples, that there were webs between his fingers.

"You may not pass," he said, and his voice was deep, deeper than any human voice she had heard; almost she had difficulty understanding the words; it was as if the wind had spoken. Or like the roar of a big sea-shell held next to the ear. A cousin had brought her family a huge sea-shell once, as a curiosity, and it lay on the mantelpiece with other useless objects the family was fond of, the pipe-rack a nephew had made, though Jenny's father had never smoked; the grotesquely hideous sampler that some great-great-great-aunt had made in her childhood which had mysteriously metamorphosed into a family heirloom. Her parents' sitting-room rose up in her mind's eye, and she shivered with loss and longing, for in this first great sorrow of her life, it seemed a thing more wonderful than a silver man who had formed himself from a wave.

"You may not pass," he said again as she stood dumbly, but she thought that there was a reluctance to his words; perhaps it was only the odd echoing quality of his voice. "No land-person may set foot on this bridge and live, and I must drown you."

She was still thinking of her parents' sitting-room, and she remembered then the cousin telling the story of the sea-people's curse when he had brought them the sea-shell. And she shivered again, for she found she was sorry to die; she realised she would not have died of love, and despite her weariness a flame of anger rose in her, that she should die for so stupid an error as loving a man who did not love her. For a moment her anger warmed her, and she stopped shivering.

The sea-man turned away from her, and she thought all these things in the crack of a second, as she saw that a wave as swift as the first that had drenched them was arching up over them now; and she knew that this one would fill her mouth and her lungs, and drown her. "No, wait!" she said, and put up her own hand.

The sea-man stopped, almost as if he were glad of the excuse, and turned back to her; and the wave curled back instead of forward, and fell again into the harbour, and a few drops only rebounded, and twinkled on the bridge. Her heart was beating quickly, and she knew she had no case to plead; she knew the curse as well as any child born of these two towns knew it; she had only forgotten it, because it had not seemed to her important. Her present position was her own fault. But perhaps she might spare those dear to her something.

"I beg you to let my mare and my bitch go free," she said, her voice shaking, for it was all she could do not to fall on her knees and beg for her life, now that she understood that she was to die and that she wanted to live. Her fingers clutched Flora's saddle-skirts to keep her on her feet, for the shivering had seized her triply hard as soon as she spoke. "Spare them and send them home as they are, dripping with sea-water, that at least my parents may know what has happened to me."

The sea-man looked at her, and his eyes gleamed in the moonlight much as his skin did. "Tell me about your parents," he said.

She took a long, rough, choking breath, for she knew that her self-control could not bear her much further. But gallantly she began to talk of her parents, not so much thinking that if he listened then she might live a few moments longer, but that she might have as her last thoughts some memories of her parents, who had truly loved her. She said that she was their only child, and she told him about the governesses, and the dogs and the ponies and the cats and the songbirds, and the quilt that she and her mother had made that lay on her bed, and she did not even notice that she wept again as she spoke. Then she went on to tell him about the man who had been her betrothed, and how much she had loved him, and how she had at last understood that he did not love her, and how she had gone to his farm to—talk to him, though she did not know what she would say, and she had there found him . . . with another girl. A pretty girl, and she touched her own ordinary face, and did not realise that it was wet with tears and not sea-water. She could think of no more to say, and fell silent.

Silence stayed a little while, broken only by the sound of

the ripples of sea-water caressing the barnacled stones the bridge stood on. The sea-man had turned a little away from her again, looking down the harbour to the sea-mouth.

At last he turned back to her. "I am the king of the sea-people," he said. "It was I whom the merchant cheated, and I who declared this curse on these towns and all their people, who would not give me justice only because I was of the sea instead of of the land. My wife begged me to be less harsh, but I was young and furious, and revelled in my own strength to get revenge. And I was angry for a long time, and for the first few years I enjoyed pulling down the docks and drowning land-people, in the memory of ours who had died, for I did not differentiate one land-person from another, just as they had not cared anything about me and mine but that I was not of them.

"But that was a long time ago, even for sea-people, and I have grown old, and I have had less and less joy in guarding this harbour and this bridge.

"In the meantime, my wife and I have had a son. And as I listen to you, I think what it would mean to me, if his horse and hound came home some day, gouged by the weapons of the land-people, so that I would know what had happened to him, and know that I would never see him any more. And I understand, now, why my wife would have made me hold back my wrath, and not say my curse.

"No one has set human foot on this bridge for many a long year, now. You are the first.

"And I cannot drown you. If this is a loss of honour for me, then so be it. I am no longer young, and I have learned about things other than honour, or perhaps I have learned something about honour that has less to do with pride. Mount up your mare and ride home, and let the weariness and sorrow of this sea-king go with you, and be driven into the dry ground by your horse's hoofs."

She stood, staring, her mind numb with trying not to beg, and her body numb with the cold of the night and a drenching in sea-water.

"Go!" he said again. "Mount and ride! And ride quickly, for the land-people, I now remember, cannot bear the touch of the sea, and grow sick from it, and I see by your trembling that this sickness touches you already. It is something I have no charm for. Go!"

But as she scrabbled at her mare's stirrup, she was shaking too badly, and could not get her foot in; and even when she had her foot in place, she had not the strength to pull herself into the saddle. The sea-king took two steps towards her, and seized her by the waist, and lifted her into the saddle. As he released her, one of his webbed hands touched hers, and she felt a shock, and before her eyes rose up a glamour of sea-palaces and a land beneath the sea where the people of this king lived, and it was very beautiful. But perhaps it was only fever, for by the time her mare brought her home to her desperate parents, she was deep in delirium, babbling about waves and sea-men and moonlight on strangely iridescent skin, and no word at all of Robert, and her parents did not know what to think. For they remembered the curse, and the smell of sea-water was strongly on her, and they wondered if perhaps the curse had changed, and that now the sea-king for his vengeance took only the minds of those who crossed him, and not the lives.

But the fever broke, and the delirium shrank back like a tide on the ebb, and did not return. Jenny lay blinking at her familiar ceiling, with the familiar quilt under her fingers, and when she turned her head on the pillow, she saw her mother sitting there, watching her. She asked what day it was. Her mother hesitated, and then said, "You have been sick for seventeen days." She could see her daughter counting, and saw the relief on her face when she counted past her wedding day and knew that it was past; and that told her mother what she wanted to know, and she too was relieved. But then the full reality of the conversation broke upon her, and she burst into tears and ran out of her daughter's bedroom and into her own, where she woke up her husband to tell him the news, for they had taken it in turns never to leave Jenny's bedside for the last seventeen days. And the news was better for him than seventeen nights of good sleep would have been.

The youngest maid servant was in the upstairs hall when Jenny's mother rushed across it, and heard her mistress crying, and for a dizzy, awful moment half-guessed the worst. But she couldn't bear the thought of being the messenger of such ill tidings, so she tiptoed closer till she could hear the joy in her mistress' voice as she spoke to the master, and then fled downstairs herself to spread the glorious news to the rest of the household.

Jenny recovered only slowly. It was another week before she set foot outside her bedroom, yet another week before she ventured out of the house, and then only as far as the kitchen garden. The day after she had taken her first steps out of doors, her mother told her that Robert had been asking for her. He had come several times when she was ill, the first time the very day after she had come home wet and delirious, and he had been most anxious to speak to her. Her mother and father had been polite to him, but they were sorely preoccupied with Jenny's health, and thought nothing at the time of the peculiarity of his manner, for they had no attention to spare. But her mother had seen the relief on her daughter's face when she heard that seventeen days had passed during her illness. And so now she told Jenny only the brief fact of Robert's continuing attendance, without saying that he had become more insistent, in this last week, since she had admitted that Jenny was recovering. Without saying that when people asked about a new wedding date, she had been noncommittal in a way that let people guess there would be no new wedding date. She would have put off speaking of Robert at all, and spared her daughter's convalescence a little longer, but that she feared he would find her one day when she was alone, without her parents to intercede, mediate—send him away for good. What she wanted was that Jenny be well and strong and happy again. So, briskly, even perfunctorily, she told her daughter that Robert wished to see her.

Jenny went still in a way that was not just the natural lethargy of the invalid, and the cat in her lap woke up from its boneless sleep and gathered itself together again into four discrete legs and a tail, and looked up into her face. "I would prefer to avoid him," she said, and that was all.

It was a month before Jenny could ride again, and she still tired easily; so it was two months, and high summer, by the time she felt able to make a journey of more than half an hour from her parents' gate. She did not tell her parents where she was going; and she took Gruoch with her.

She rode to the bridge at the head of the harbour between the two towns.

She had told her parents little of what had happened. She had let them think she had somehow gotten lost and wandered near the sea-shore before she realised what she had done, and been drenched that way; she let them think that what she had said in her fever dreams of angry, vindictive sea-men and tender, weeping sea-women were only the result of her belated recollection of the curse, her own terror of what might have happened to her if she had not turned her mare away from the harbour in time.

She had not told them that even after her fever left her, she had gone on dreaming of a land beneath the sea, where the water was the air, but silvery and swirly, and the people walked on the sea-bottom with a curious, graceful, rippling stride, and there were horses with long slender legs and foamy manes and tails like little girls always wanted their ponies to have; and there were great grey-green hunting hounds not unlike her own dear Gruoch; and even the biggest trees had flexible trunks, and bowed and turned in the heavy air with slow elegance, trailing their frondy leaves, and that the fish nested in them like birds.

She rode back to the bridge, but she halted a few steps from it, suddenly unsure of herself. The sea-king had let her go, despite his promise to drown every land-person who touched the bridge or set boat in the water or dock-post next to the harbour shore, for as long as his people's memory should last; and perhaps to thank him was the worst thing she could do. The thanks of a land-person might be the last thing he wanted, the thanks of a land-person he despised himself for sparing.

At the same time she remembered how his face had looked when he mentioned his son and his wife, and she remembered that when he set her on her horse, he had used his strength cautiously when he might have been harsh with her. But she feared that she remembered these things for the wrong reasons. Perhaps her desire to thank him was only an excuse to see him again, to see the person who lived in the land she dreamed of. And she felt ashamed of herself.

But as she stood hesitating on the bank, looking at the stones of the bridge but not daring to set foot upon them, the water below the bridge boiled up as it had done once before. This time the sun was sliding down the sky but nowhere near setting, and the long rays of afternoon set the wave on fire, and rainbows fell from every drop of water.

The wave did not wet her nor her horse nor her hound this time, and when it drained away again, a different sea-man stood on the bridge. He looked very much like the sea-man she had seen before, but not so much that she did not recognise the one from the other; this one was younger and plainer and had no bitterness in him.

She said before she could stop herself: "You are the sea-king's son." She said it as he was saying: "You must be Jenny."

"Yes," they said, again simultaneously, and both smiled; and each saw how the other's rather ordinary face lit up with gentleness and humour and intelligence.

"I wished to say thank you," said the sea-prince, and Jenny looked at him blankly, feeling that they were still speaking simultaneously, although she had said nothing more aloud.

He smiled again at her puzzled look. "I was born after my father's curse was laid on this harbour, and I grew up knowing that my father was weighed down by some sorrow that grew heavier each year; but I did not know what it was, for neither my father nor my mother nor any of the court would tell me. My parents would not because they would not, and their people would not because my parents forbade them, and they loved my parents enough to obey, no matter how much I teased them. But my father told me the story at last, just these few short weeks ago, with the breaking of the curse when he let you go free.... And I have not been able to put the thought of you out of my mind since, and so I determined to meet you if I could.

"But could I? I have been haunting this bridge lately as closely as it has been haunted in all the long years of the curse; and very lonely I have found it too. Not even the fish come into this harbour voluntarily, and my horse once tore his bridle free where I had tied him, and ran home, which he has never done; and my favourite hound will howl, however often I tell him to be still. I thought perhaps I was deluding myself, that there was no purpose in my coming here; but I could not believe this, I felt sure that you would have to come here again, you would come here at last." He took a deep breath, and she noticed that there was a slight hissing or rattling in his breathing, but she forgot this at once because he smiled again as he looked at her. "You *did* come," he said, and sounded as delighted as a boy who has just had his first pony ride.

She felt more ashamed of herself than ever. "I told myself that I wanted to thank your father for sparing me, but when I got here I thought that that was not the reason I had come at all." She went on slowly: "I have dreamed of a land under the water, and of a people who live there, with silver-blue horses and grey-green hounds, and fish that nest in the trees. I have dreamed of this every night since I stood on this bridge, and your father set me on my horse and told me to ride home to my parents."

He looked surprised. "That I cannot explain; I do not know of anything like that happening before. Although it is true that we have stories saying that you of your shore-bound land and us of ours were once the same people, and lived as neighbours and friends, and not merely fellow merchants, with no bonds of kindness, in the way that ended so badly for us all. And I know there are people among us who dream of the land, as you have dreamed of the sea, but I have always thought it was just a kind of longing, a wish for adventure, or an escape from something that troubles them." But Jenny turned away at his last words, and "Forgive me," he said at once. "My parents have long tried to school me in thinking before I speak, and say that I will be a disastrous king if I do not learn better manners. I have talked to you too much in my head, you see, these last weeks, waiting for you; I did not tell anyone about wishing to meet you. I think my father and all his people want nothing about this harbour to be part of their lives, not even a memory of its existence. And now I can't stop talking.

"Your dreams, whatever their cause, are true ones, although there are lands in other parts of the sea where the horses and hounds are sunset-red or spotted brown and black and green, and some where people have fishes' tails instead of legs, and speak a language we do not know." His voice did not have the deep, fierce echo of his father's, and although his accent was strange to Jenny's ears, like his father's, the son's voice had a merriness to it, like bubbling water, and the faint rattle of his breathing only made it more like, and more charming.

He told her stories of the sea-lands he had visited till it was time for each of them to go home. "I am glad I came," said Jenny, without thinking; and the sea-prince said at once, "Will you come again?"

"Yes," she said, still without thinking.

"Tomorrow?" he said, hopefully.

She had to think then, if only to consider if she could escape for another afternoon; and she thought she could, and she thought not at all about her motivations. "Yes," she said.

This time she meant to watch him, but when the wave rose up over the bridge, the light from the setting sun upon the shining sleek water blinded her, and she shut her eyes; and when she opened them again, he was gone, and there was only a little pool on the bridge to show that anything had happened. If there had been anyone there to wonder, it would have seemed very strange, for there was no wind to whip a wave up over the bridge's side like that, and leave a pool on its broken surface.

It was not till she was riding home that she remembered that she did not know his name.

And she rode back to the bridge the next afternoon at the same time, and by now she was aware that she was not thinking about her motivations, but she only noted this and continued not to think. And there was someone on the bridge already, waiting for her, and he no longer looked at all like his father the king, but only like himself. He stood up at her approach, and walked off the bridge to meet her, and all the thoughts she was not thinking briefly overwhelmed her, and she stayed in her saddle a moment longer, fearing to climb down out of the safety of her own world and into a strange one. But he put his hand on her stirrup and his other hand to her mare's bridle, and Flora dropped her nose and let him do it, which was not her habit with strangers, even the ordinary, dry, flat-skinned, clothed sort. And so Jenny stepped down and faced him, and he smiled the smile that lit up his ordinary face with gentleness and humour and intelligence.

"What is your name?" she said.

"Dreiad," he replied.

They met many afternoons after that, and her parents only noticed that she seemed to be growing rosy with health again, and were willing to let her mysterious absences go unquestioned. And perhaps his parents felt similarly willing to let their son pursue whatever it was that so manifestly made him happy.

Dreiad told Jenny more stories of the lands under the sea, and she told him about her parents' farm, and what she could of the lands beyond them, for she had travelled little. She had only been to the city where her relatives lived once—it was a two-day journey from the farm—when she was still quite small, and her chief memories were of how tall the strange eerie creatures with black iron claws for feet, which her parents told her were lampposts, looked to her, taller than trees, with the great glowing, flickering globes set on their summits; and how enormous the kerbstones were she had to step up and down on from the road. There were no kerbs on country lanes.

At first she had supposed that since Dreiad could breathe air as she did, he was as free of the land as she was and only chose to live in the water, and was shy about telling him the things she knew, when he could see for himself and draw his own conclusions. But he told her it was not so. "I cannot go even so far from the sea as visit your farm myself," he said. "I cannot let the land-air dry my skin or I will die." And, several times during the course of any one of their afternoon conversations, he did wade back into the water and splash himself all over.

It had occurred to them both that being thrown up on the bridge by a wave was a little spectacular for everyday use, especially if they wished to keep their meetings a secret. The harbour itself was avoided by everyone, but there were many people going about their business not so far from all view of it that Jenny and Dreiad could be sure no one would notice anything worth investigating. Jenny felt that small dazzling daily rainbows on the haunted bridge might well arouse curiosity. So now they met on the sea-shore, some distance from the bridge, and usefully around a curve at the mouth of the harbour where in three generations of disuse a young wood had grown up. Behind it there was a small meadow where Jenny tethered Flora, and Gruoch tried out various trees for sleeping in the shade of.

Jenny grew accustomed to Dreiad's strange, ripply, silvery skin; it was much like fish-scales, although not quite like, and she had seen fish rarely enough in her life, and never thought of their scales as pleasant or unpleasant to look upon. But she found Dreiad, as the days passed, very pleasant to look at, and she forgot that he was scaly, and damp, and remembered only that his smile made him beautiful. As they grew to know more about each other, their differences became both more dear to them, and more shocking. They teased each about the language they shared, that (Jenny said) land-people had taken with them as they adapted to life in the sea; that (Dreiad said) land-people had learned to use even in the unforgiving air, which constantly dried out the mouth and throat and lungs, which even land-people acknowledged had to be kept moist. The idea of dairy cows was absurd to Dreiad: "Milk is for baby creatures! Your mother suckled you, did she not? And then stopped as you grew bigger. Cow milk is for baby cows!" She brought him a piece of cheese, but although he tasted it, he made a wry face and was not converted. But Jenny found the green juice that the sea-people ordinarily drank, which was some decoction made of underwater grass, too terrible even to sip at.

They rarely touched, for his skin was clammy on hers, and hers uncomfortably hot to him; and when they realised they had fallen in love with each other, this became a sorrow to them, and they teased each other less about sea and land, and their conversations grew awkward. Jenny's parents began to worry about her again, for she looked a little less rosy and a little more haggard, and they wondered if perhaps Robert had waylaid her sometime during her absences from the farm, and was attempting to win her back. They asked her about this, but she said "No, no" impatiently, and with that they chose to be content for a little longer.

It did happen occasionally that Jenny and Dreiad could not meet for a day or two; their lives had been full and busy before they met, and squeezing several secret hours every day from their normal occupations was not possible. Neither made any protest when the other said that they could not meet the next day, but they always parted sadly on those days, and Jenny, at least, began to ride home pondering how what had begun might end, and yet not willing to ponder. For the moment his company was enough and more than enough, in the way of lovers; but she knew the time was coming when this would no longer be true, because he was of the sea and she was of the land, and she knew that even the thinking of it made that time grow closer. Dreiad had never said that he loved her, any more than she had ever said she loved him; but she knew that he did, because there was so much in each of their natures that reflected the other, in a way that was new and strange and wonderful. And nothing at all like her days with Robert had been. Nothing at all. Nothing. Nothing.

It was an afternoon when Dreiad had told her with an odd suppressed excitement that he could not meet her the next day. She had begun to ask him what his excitement was about, and he had begun to put her off—and so she stopped asking; but as a result they looked at each other with embarrassment and had not known how to pick up their conversation again. Even with the knowledge of having hurt her, Dreiad could not quite hide his excitement, whatever it was; and this hurt her too, that there should be something that gave him such pleasure that he could not tell her of. And as a result she began to doubt herself, to doubt the truth of his unspoken love; after all, she had believed—for much longer than she had known Dreiad—that Robert had loved her, and he had filled her ears with the telling of it besides.

It cannot end in any way but unhappiness, she thought. He will marry a sea-princess, for his parents need an heir; and I am not even a land-princess. I suppose, when the harvest is over, we will go to the city, as we were to do last year, and they will find me a nice young man to marry. The idea was so bleak, she could only look at it glancingly. But they were right about Robert; I should have listened to them—I should have let them speak. They will be able to find me someone who is kind, and keeps his promises, and I will listen to their advice. It will not be a bad life.

She drew on reserves she did not know she had, for she had never had cause to learn to put herself aside to be bright and merry for someone she cared about. But after they parted, for all that Dreiad had looked long into her eyes before he walked back into the sea again, and promised as eagerly as he had ever promised to meet her the day after tomorrow, she went home very unhappy.

She did not even hear the approaching hoofbeats, nor had she paid attention to Gruoch's sudden look of interest and warning. When she did hear them, and knew it was too late to turn aside, she ignored them, keeping her face resolutely down, determined to pass without acknowledging the rider whomever it was. But this proved impossible, for a once-familiar hand reached out and seized her mare's bridle, and Robert swung his horse around to walk next to hers, clumsily, for he was still holding her rein, and his leg ground against hers in the saddle. It was a heavyish blow, and his stirrup leather pinched her calf above her low riding boots and beneath the thin cloth of her skirt; but that was not the reason she cringed away from it, sending such a message to her sensitive mare that Flora curvetted away, fighting the strange hand on her rein, and threatening to kick. Robert had to let go.

By the time Jenny had her mare under control again, she

realised there was no point in running away, although this had been her first thought. Gruoch was moving in that painstaking, measured way that a hound expecting the command *Go!* moves, and while Jenny did not believe that even with such a command her gentle bitch would leap for Robert, she was careful to keep her own gestures placid. She patted her mare's neck, but Flora was no fool, and did not drop her head, but kept her neck and ears stiffly upright, and pranced where she stood.

"Jenny," said Robert, and all of his twenty years' experience of playing to his audience was in his voice. No one could have stuffed the two syllables of her name more full of anguish.

How could I ever not have known? she thought. She risked a glance at his face, and saw anguish beautifully arranged there too. It was a splendid performance, but it neither moved nor amused her. She felt low, and stupid, and humiliated.

"Forgive me," he said. He was already a little dismayed by her unresponsiveness. He was so accustomed to being able to get what he wanted by careful handling and dazzlingly distracting displays of charm that he had forgotten that some people are simpler in their habits and more straightforward in their reactions. Since there was a little real anguish in him—although it was about the loss of the farm more than about the careless error that appeared to have lost him her—he felt that he was expressing genuine pain.

That, at least, was easy enough to answer. "No," she said, and turned Flora's head; but he thought he knew what the roles were, now, and he kicked his own horse to block her passage. Flora reared, not liking any of this at all, and spun around twice on her hocks, and Robert would have liked to do something heroic, but he was not much of a horseman. Jenny brought her mare down alone, and the effort steadied her, and she realised she was going to have to hear Robert out. She would not enjoy it, but she could bear it.

She was not interested in his explanations of a momentary madness, of the depth of his real passion for her, of how his— aberration—was in fact caused by the agony of the delay of their wedding; here she actually curled her lip, and he hastened on. He even shed tears, and she watched, fascinated in spite of herself. He called her cruel, first still in anguish, and then, as he realised he was getting nowhere, in anger. How dare she set her paltry will against his? She wasn't even pretty.

He exhausted himself at last, and she risked letting Flora go forward. The mare danced sideways as they passed Robert's horse, but he had run out of drama, and let them go. She wanted to put Flora to the gallop as soon as they were clear of him, but she was afraid that he would read in this a flight worth pursuing; and so she let her mare break only into a trot, and worked to keep it leisurely, although Flora fussed at the bit, and her ears lay back. Gruoch loped casually beside her.

She never saw Robert again.

She went to bed early that night, but there was little rest for her in the long continuous dreams of the land under the sea; and now she was seeing her sea-prince arm in arm, as lovers should be, with a sea-princess, who had golden-green hair that lay in curls behind her, suspended on the silvery, ripply water that was their air. She saw them kiss, and she thought her heart would break; and it had broken once already. She did not know if she could recover, this second time, so soon after the first. She woke in cold, grey dawn, imagining her prince telling her of his betrothed, she the land-girl of whom he was so fond, just like a sister to him. He would offer to let her meet the sea-princess, and the sea-princess, who had a good heart, would ask that Jenny be godmother to their first child.

She almost did not go to meet Dreiad the next day, but she had promised, and they had never yet broken promise to each other; and what she feared had nothing to do with promises. So she went, but she knew that her eyes were shadowed, and that smiling made her face hurt, and she did not know what she could give him as an excuse, for she had promised herself that she would not tell him the truth. If he was happy, she wanted him to be happy with no hindrance from her. She did not think of telling him of the meeting with Robert as a reason for her depression of spirits, for she had forgotten it herself.

But as it happened, Dreiad was too full of something else to notice her mood: too full of the same suppressed excitement she had seen in him two days before, only it was much stronger now, it was as if he moved carefully for fear it might burst out of him without any decision from him to yield to it. They must already be betrothed, she thought drearily.

He held out a hand as if to take hers, and then dropped it, remembering; she had made no answering motion, having not forgotten. "I have something to tell you," he said.

"Yes?" she said, and was pleased to notice that her voice was calm, even cool.

He looked at her in a little puzzlement, as if first taking in that perhaps not all was well with her; but the excitement bubbled up again and would not be stoppered. "I went to visit someone yesterday, which is why I could not be with you.

This is someone I have been looking for for some time, someone who could answer my dearest wish."

She nodded, her hands clasped at her belt.

"And I have found her!" He laughed as if he could not help himself, but then, looking at Jenny, the puzzlement came back for a moment. "Can you not guess?" he said, but in a quieter voice; and again his hand reached to touch hers and withdrew, and again hers had made no motion to meet his.

She made herself smile. "Yes, I think I can guess," she said, but the tone of her voice was wrong and he heard it, and the puzzlement deepened, and the excitement sank out of his eyes and some uncertainty crept in, and distress with it.

"I—" he said, and paused. "I was so sure you would be as pleased as I. It is the answer, you see. Or I hoped it was."

She did not hear his words, but she saw the distress and was sorry. She was breaking her promise already. She tried to smile. "Tell me," she said.

But the excitement had left him, and he stumbled over what he had to tell her. "She lives far away, and at first I only knew the rumour of her, and I couldn't ask openly, of course, but everyone is accustomed to my having strange fits of curiosity about this and that and I didn't tell anyone why I wanted to find her, of course, and I was able to at last, without telling anyone, I mean. I had to tell her, of course, but it won't matter, soon. . . . I mean, I thought it wouldn't matter. . . . I thought. . . ." He looked at her, miserably.

His misery touched her, for she did love him. And her hands made the same gesture that his had, twice, wanting to reach her, touch her. Her hand reached towards him and, remembering, retreated. "Tell me," she said again, her voice stronger. "I do want to know."

"It's only that she told me how you may visit under water," he said in a rush. "Visit *me.*"

It was so completely not what she was expecting that her mouth dropped open; and when he saw that she had not guessed what he had to tell her, he laughed for pure relief. "She is very old, and will not tell you her name; I believe nobody has known her name for centuries; she is very old even by our standards. And she says that it is not that she doesn't want to help anyone, it's just that almost everyone has such silly ideas of what they have to have help with, and she got tired of sending silly people away, and so now she is very hard to find in the first place. She says sometimes the silliest people are the most stubborn, and she wonders if some of the people with the problems she really could help with simply decide that it is their fate and stop trying; but then maybe if that is their attitude, it *is* their fate. But when I found her, and told her about us, she was perfectly willing to help, but she said it was an unusual situation and she could remember only one other case, but it was a long time ago, and she would need time to remember what she knew about it. That's why I couldn't tell you last time. I wanted to wait—just in case she couldn't remember, couldn't help us, though I was pretty sure she could, she had all but promised that she could."

Jenny was responding to his excitement without, still, really taking it in. All that she understood clearly was that this *she* was not his betrothed sea-princess, and that Dreiad was calling himself and her, Jenny, *we.* And so she listened to the tone of his voice and was happy. But when he came to the end and drew breath, she still didn't know what she was happy about.

"She's really very nice," he said, finally, "and it's funny, because she likes to talk. It's not that she doesn't like people or anything. I'll take you to meet her. You'll like her too."

Jenny couldn't speak. She stood, smiling, her misery evaporating like fog in sun.

"Well," he said, beaming at her. "Will you come?"

"Come?" said Jenny, still thinking, *He calls us* we. It was too absolute a thing, the division between land and water, the division between her and him. By tomorrow she would have figured out a way to see even this as merely a putting off of the inevitable, putting off their eventual, absolute parting; he was offering her a visit to his land, like the visits he could make to hers. That was all. That was why she still resisted taking it in, because of what would follow.

"With me," he said. "To my home." And then his self-possession broke, and his hands reached for hers and seized them, and he said, "Oh, Jenny, I love you so!" Her hands had reached too, to seize his the sooner, and the clasp was as if their two hearts met, for neither noticed that one was too warm and too dry, and the other too cool and too wet. He drew her into his arms, and wrapped them around her, and hers went round him, and she laid her face against his cool wet shoulder, and his damp hair brushed her flushed cheek.

But after a moment, solemnly, he took a step back from her, though he kept his hands around her waist. "It is a risk for you," he said.

"I care for no risk," Jenny said, and realised that she meant it; at this moment she could have slain a dragon, defied any number of sea-kings and their curses. "What is this risk?"

"You must believe that I love you," he said, gravely, looking at her.

She laughed. "Do you love me?" These words had never passed between them before: the fact that they could not touch each other felt as if it precluded such words, negated the feelings behind them—till now, till just now, when he had told her that he loved her, when he had told her that he had learned of a way that she might visit his underwater country. And yet she knew that she was still of the land; if she stayed in his arms for long, much as she wished to be there, she would grow cold and faint; already she felt colder than she had, despite the warmth of joy.

"Yes," he said, and while he tried to say it solemnly, his eyes lit up with the excitement she had taught herself to fear. "I love you."

"Then I believe you," she said, joyously.

And he kissed her.

His kiss was cool, and damp, like his skin; but when he dropped his arms from around her and took her hand, it did not feel so cool or so damp as it had done only a moment before. He led her down, into the water, and her wet clothes bound her legs, and she paused: and Gruoch had leaped in after her, drenching them both with spray, and she felt the drops pour down over her face and found them refreshing. Gruoch thrust her nose into Jenny's hand and shivered; and Jenny stroked her head and said, "You must wait for me here, little one, for I will return"; and she knelt down in the cold sea-water and looked deep into her bitch's eyes, and she could see Gruoch giving up whatever it was she needed to give up, as a good dog will do for the person it loves, and Jenny stood up again while Gruoch waded back to the shore. She looked over her shoulder then, but Jenny pointed away, and the tall hound trotted to where Flora stood tied in the shade of a tree, happy to browse over the summer grass without care till her lady returned and set her saddle on her back and asked her something she understood. Jenny watched Gruoch lie down—back obediently to the shore—and then she turned again to Dreiad, and put her hand in his, and walked deeper and deeper into the sea, till the water closed over her head.

She gave a great gasp, and felt the cold water rush into her lungs; but she did not drown. And they walked down the shoaling sea-bottom to the centre of the harbour, which was very deep indeed, and her hair drifted up from her head, and her clothes swirled around her, and she found that they chafed her, and then she felt Dreiad's hands on her, loosening them. For a moment she fought him, but he did not realise it, for he thought she was only fighting the constriction of her useless clothing; and then she understood what he was doing, and shed her clothes willingly, and found she was the same neutral, hairless, faceted, silvery color that he was beneath her clothes, here, as she was, under the sea, for such was the magic of the kiss of the sea-man who loved her.

He took her clothes carefully from her, for if they had been set adrift they would have been taken by the water eddies, and tossed and tangled here and there; and he folded them, deftly, in a way she could not have done, under water as she now was, and laid them on the sea-bed, and put a rock on them. "We will find them for you when I take you back," he said, "for you will need them again then; and we do not want to lose them, or have them wash ashore and be found by someone who recognises them."

And he took her down into the deeps of the sea, and taught

her how to choose walking on the sea-bottom or swimming like a fish, and how what on land were merely lungs for the taking in and pushing out of air now became a kind of swim-bladder that she could adjust as she chose, although the effort of it was strange to her, and her chest hurt afterward, as a strained muscle does when it performs some feat beyond its strength. And he took her to the great palace where his parents lived, and they made her welcome, and it turned out that she was less of a surprise to them than either she or Dreiad expected, for the sea-king had noticed the direction his son took when he set off on his mysterious absences; and the story had got back to him as well of his son's search for the old sea-woman who knew many tales of things and many charms that had made the tales possible, and while he did not know what Dreiad had asked her, he had guessed at what it might have been, and he had guessed right.

And Jenny went riding on the tall slender-legged sea-horses with the foamy manes, and chased fishes like hares through the bowing trees behind grey-green hounds; and he introduced her to his cousins, who were sea-princesses with great curls of golden-green hair that lay behind them on the silvery water that was their air. And also they rode to visit the old sea-woman who had told Dreiad of the charm to permit Jenny to visit under the sea; and the two women were delighted with each other, and found each other easy to talk to; the sea-woman reminded Jenny of her mother and her mother's friends, and the conversations they had, of cooking and midwifery and the doings of their neighbours.

And her prince took her back up to the land, where her horse and her hound awaited her, and kissed her once more, and she was an ordinary land-person again, dressed in dripping-wet clothes; and she had a tricky time of it, that night, getting herself back indoors and dry before her parents saw her.

The next day they did it better, and after he kissed her, she waited till the itchiness of her clothing grew unbearable, and she undressed on the beach as a silvery sea-person, and tucked her clothes into the empty saddlebag she had thoughtfully hung to her mare's saddle that day, that no one might notice anything amiss, did anyone notice a horse and a hound near this haunted harbour-shore where no one came. And Gruoch watched from under the tree where Flora was tied, and did not try to stop Jenny walking into the sea this second day; but she greeted her again anxiously when she came out.

On the third day, Jenny said to her sea-prince, "If I kiss you, can I bring you to my parents' farm, and introduce you to them?"

His smile lit up his face even more wonderfully than it had before, and he said, "Yes, if you love me."

She laughed, and kissed him, and gave him the clothes that she had borrowed from the back of her father's cupboard, and there then stood before her a tall young man with big long-fingered hands that stuck out too far from the ends of his sleeves, and a nice, ordinary, kind, open face. And she took him home.

She decided that the only thing she could tell her parents was the truth; for however much they would wish not to believe her, they would believe her because she was their daughter, and so she could take them down to the shore after she told them the story they would not want to believe, and they could see her prince turn silvery, and walk into the water, and they would believe her then because they had to.

And so this is what Jenny and Dreiad did; and her parents did not want to believe them, but they did accompany the two of them to the shore, and saw them kiss, and saw the silveriness break out first across the forehead of the young man with the open honest face, whom they had liked at once, and watched it creep down his cheeks, and then across the backs of his hands under the too-short sleeves; and they saw him undress, and walk into the water till the surface of it closed over his head. And they believed, because they had no choice.

But it was only the two of them who could come and go in each other's worlds, for it was only the two of them who loved each other in the way to bring out the charm. But both sets of parents knew what was before them in their children's eyes, and were not surprised when Jenny and her prince came to each of them in turn and asked permission to marry. Neither parents would have wished their child to marry someone of so distant a country that none of their family or people could visit it; but both sets of parents loved their only children deeply, and would not stand in the way of their happiness: and the two families met on the shore of the harbour, and liked each other, and that was a help, for they found themselves supporting each other's feelings as they would have done for good friends in the ordinary way of things; and thus found that their feelings were much alike. And on that same shore Jenny and Dreiad were married, and began dividing their time between land and sea.

Some time between Jenny and Dreiad's betrothal and marriage, news came from a farm on the far side of the other town, that a third son named Robert had married a very pretty girl whose pregnancy was slightly too advanced even for her loose wedding gown to disguise; and that he had been apprenticed to her father, who ran a not unsuccessful brewery, although his beer was not well thought of by anyone who could afford better.

The story of the land-girl and her sea-prince of course got out. But all the big sea-trading merchants had left the two towns long ago, and there was no one nearby who wanted to take up the sea-trade again. Somehow the townsfolk had come to believe in the last three generations that it was not merely the sea-king's curse but their own blindness that had caused their downfall, which meant that they took the removal of the curse much as the sea-king himself had, as a relief of guilty responsibility. But there were a few farmers who had had fisherfolk as great-grandparents; and some of these came hesitantly down to the harbour again, and set sail in small boats newly and carefully built on the harbour shores. And the small boats sailed beautifully, and caught just enough fish that the fisherfolk's families were content and well-fed, and not so much that any city merchant came sniffing around to organise them and make a proper profit. And between the breaking of the old curse and the making of this new marriage, the sea-people and the land-people found themselves willingly drawn close; and so the sea-people swam to the surface to say hello when they recognised a familiar hull overhead, and sometimes offered advice about where the fish were; and the land-people greeted them politely, and listened to their advice and were glad of it. But these same land-people, when stories of their friendship with their sea-people brought curiosity seekers to the newly lively towns on either side of the once-haunted harbour, had nothing to say, and turned blank faces and deaf ears to all questions from both casual and prying outsiders.

Jenny's parents' farm grew in a long wide strip from its original place on a little rise behind the southern town down to the shore near the harbour mouth. It grew this way in no particular wise except that it was a track used so often that at last Jenny and Dreiad and her family laid a path, a queerly shining grey path, to the water's edge; and in the clearing they had to do to lay the path, they found earth that the farmers among them decided was too good not to use, and so fields sprang up on either side of that path till the farm really did stretch down to the shore in an odd haphazard way. But the farmers were right about the earth, for crops put in those path-side fields grew easily and abundantly.

Jenny and Dreiad had twelve children. Two of the twelve were sea-people, and had an especial care for the fisherfolk of the harbour their mother had been born near. Two of them were land-people, and took over the farm when Jenny's parents died, and married land-people who were also farmers; and the farm was held by their family for hundreds of years, and for many generations after Jenny, its members were astonishingly long-lived; although they now produced as many fishers as farmers. Jenny herself lived, while not a long time by sea-people's standards, still a very long time indeed by land-people's accounting of such things.

And the other eight were of both land and sea, and could live on either the one or the other; and if on land they did look a little silverier than ordinary land-people, and if in the sea they looked a little rosier than ordinary sea-people, still this made no one think less of them, for all of them had open, honest faces that lit up with gentleness and humour and intelligence when they smiled.

SEA SERPENT

"I am Mel."

"I have heard of you."

"You are Iril." (Not a question, a statement.)

"Yes."

"You will take us across the water." (The same.)

"How many?"

"Twenty and twenty men. Some gear."

"Eight large coppers."

Mel took a bracelet from his wrist and tossed it on the ground in front of where Iril sat. The gold was as thick as Iril's small finger.

"You will come with us into the hills and show us how to build rafts so that we may float the stones downriver to the water," said Mel. "That done, you will ferry the stones across the water and help us to float them as far as may be up into our own hills."

"Stones?"

Mel half turned and considered the space before him. A

shape made itself, shadowy, like frozen smoke, its height twice that of a man and its width a long pace through each way. Iril measured it with his eye, unsurprised. As he had said, he had heard of Mel. How could he not have, from the travellers he ferried across the estuary? Much of their talk these days was of the great new shrine to Awod, the Father-god, that this man Mel was building up in the hills to the south. Such a shrine would need huge stones for its central ring. The best stones, the stones with power in them, came from across the water.

"How many such stones?"

"Ten this first year."

The shape faded. With his crutch Iril hooked the bracelet towards him, picked it up and weighed it in his hand.

"Twenty and twenty men is not enough."

"You will bring your own people also."

"How many days into the hills?"

"Three days. Silverspring."

"*Those* stones?"

"Those stones."

Iril tossed the bracelet back at Mel's feet and looked away. For twenty and twenty and seven years he had carried women north across the estuary on their pilgrimage to the ancient shrine of Tala, the Earth-mother at Silverspring, where Siron was priestess. Tala had been greatest of the Old Gods, just as Awod was greatest of the New. So there was enmity between them. Iril took no side in this contest. He served Manaw, the Sea God, who was both Old and New. The sea does not change.

Mel took another bracelet from his arm and dropped it

beside the first. Then a third. All watched in silence, the men of Iril's kin to his right, the women to his left, and Mel's own followers behind him.

There was a half-built hut behind Iril's men. Mel gestured and they moved aside. He considered the hut. Between a breath and a breath it burst into flames, not shadows of flame as the stone had been shadow. The hut burnt and became embers and did not remake itself.

Iril nodded. He had heard of Mel.

"No man can find the path to Silverspring," he said.

"I will open the path," said Mel. "If I fail, you will keep one bracelet. But I shall not fail. Those times are over."

Iril looked to his left, at his eldest son's first wife. She met his gaze but gave him no sign. He looked back to Mel.

"No," he said.

Mel turned and studied the men of Iril's kin. He beckoned one forward. Jarro came like a sleepwalker. He was Iril's third son, ten and five years old only, barely a man, but he could dream the wave. Iril's two elder sons, Farn and Arco, were expert raftmen. They could take a raft north on the ebb, even in rough weather, and then bring it smoothly back, riding the flood-wave. But neither of them, as children, had ever shown the signs. Neither of them now, however much leaf they chewed, could fall into a half-trance and then dream the wave, become part of the moving water, know it as a man knows where his own limbs are in the dark. Almost as soon as he could talk, Jarro had prattled on waking about the wash of the tides along the estuary. Then he had lost the gift, as growing children did. But one day, when he was a man, he would chew leaf and dream the wave again. If he had been a distant cousin, he would still have been more precious to Iril than any of his own sons. Mel had never seen him before.

"Shall I show you what he will become if you refuse me?" he said. "Now in shadow, as I showed you the stone? But if I choose, in truth, as I burnt the hut?"

Iril did not look at Jarro, nor at the women. He dragged one bracelet towards him and put it on his arm.

"My terms are these," he said. "When the stones float, I will take the second. When they leave my care, the third. Furthermore, we bear no weapons. We take no side between tribe and tribe. We carry and deliver. All that has to do with water is in my charge and at my command. All that is on land is in yours."

"So it shall be," said Mel. "My terms are these. You will float the stones to this shore, and then up our river as far as may be, so that I may have them in place by Seed-in. They have powers that I will lay asleep, but for this they must travel all together."

"That will take thought," said Iril.

"It must be done."

"These stones weigh many, many men. Are you able to make them less?"

"They are what they are. They will weigh their own weight."

"The river from Silverspring. How wide? How deep?"

Mel considered. The air around him wavered as if heat were rising through it, and then he was standing on untrodden grass beside a small river running along a mountain valley. Iril could see the shapes of huts through the left-hand mountain. The slopes of the valley were clothed with ancient woods. He nodded and the scene vanished.

"We will cut timber for the rafts there," he said. "Cable and thongs we will need more than we have, and also twenty and twenty and ten float-skins for each stone."

Mel considered.

"I have sent for this stuff," he said. "Do we cross to-day?"

"I have one raft waiting, unloaded. On the morning ebb I can take over ten and six men, and some gear, and return for another party on the evening wave. Thus we could all cross in five ebbs, which is three days. If we must all travel together we must wait for rafts to come downriver, or build new. Either will take many days."

"We start this morning," said Mel.

It was an easy passage. Iril, propped on the low platform at the centre of the raft, scarcely needed to gesture to the two sweep-men. They knew their work, using the curve of the main current that touched the southern shore of the estuary just below Iril's village and then, guided by the intricate and endlessly shifting pattern of mudbanks beneath the water, swung almost all the way across to the northern shore. Not that a stranger, however skilled a raftman, would have been safe if he had tried it. This was no ordinary ocean tide, falling steadily from high to low. Here twice a day the waters of the outer sea were hauled into the estuary between the narrowing arms of land and held there by the weight of the tide behind them. Then, when the tide reversed itself, they were sucked swirling out, often falling within the space of a milking time by the height of six grown men. On the stillest day the race of the main outflow was a muddle of hummocked waves, but if a raft was set rightly among them, the current would carry it clean across to the other shore, with only an occasional stroke of the sweeps to hold it true. But if Iril had misjudged his course—in places by no more than the width of the raft itself—he might well have been caught in an eddy which would have carried him half way back to the southern shore and then perhaps out to sea, or at least left him stranded on a mudbank in mid-estuary.

Iril made no such mistakes. He had been riding the ebb tide and the in-wave for more than the lifetime of most men. He walked with a crutch since his leg had been caught between two logs when he was a boy, as his father's raft had broken up in a freak squall. His father had been lost, with all who were on that half of the raft, but Iril had brought his half safely home.

They landed and ate. Then Iril, helped by his middle son, Arco, hobbled up to a low red bluff from which he could see right across the estuary to the mist-blurred shore beyond. Mel came with them. The tide had gone, leaving a waste of glittering grey mudbanks patterned with channels through which the river waters still flowed to the sea. Iril pointed and said a few words. Arco grunted and returned to the landing place, but Iril took a leaf from his pouch, chewed it, settled down on the grass, curling up like a dog, and slept. Mel stood in silence. Sometimes he was there, watching the raft being readied as the waters began to return. Sometimes he was elsewhere.

Towards sunset Iril snorted in his sleep and woke. Hauling himself upright on his crutch, he touched Mel's elbow and pointed down the estuary, without apparently having looked to check that what he was pointing at was indeed there. The leaden waters glimmered with the gold leavings of the day. Across their surface ran a level line, as if they had been ice which had cracked from shore to shore. Iril hallooed down to the raft, already waiting in the shallows. The men poled it clear of the shore.

"Small wave, this season," explained Iril.

He felt no anger against Mel for the burning of the hut and the threat of horror to his son, nor fear of him either. He had been threatened before, by kings among others, and had when necessary given in to their threats, but both he and they had known that there were limits to their power over him, because in the end they could not do without him and his kin. Who else could dream the wave? Who else could ride it?

This wave, which he had called small, was about half a man's height. As the tide returned, the narrowing estuary forced it to hummock up, because there was nowhere else for the mass of water to go. It came silently, foaming only where it rummaged along the shoreline. At one point the water surface was at *this* level, at the next it was at *that.* The difference was the wave.

When it reached the raft, it pushed it ahead while the sweepmen paddled gently to keep the carefully shaped stern-board at the exact angle to spill the propelling water away on the near side and so nudge the raft sideways along the wave. The raft was picked up and swept towards the southern shore in a sweet easy movement, like that of a skinning knife lifting the hide from the flesh beneath. For a while it followed the course of the main channel, but the underlying current made little difference. Only the wave mattered, as it carried the raft across the estuary on an almost straight diagonal that re-crossed the main channel at the end of its long curve and fin-ished up a little below Iril's village. There the raft would be beached to let the wave go by, wait for the still-rising tide to refloat it and be poled up to the landing stage on the last of the inflow. When it was well set on its course, Iril's middle son came up the hill and helped him down to the huts, but Mel stayed where he was, gazing south. Sometimes he was watching the dwindling raft. Sometimes he was elsewhere.

They made a litter for Iril and carried him inland, leaving his sons to manage the regular crossings. Mel led them not by the pilgrim's road, but along minor tracks and across bare hill-sides, always making good speed. At evening he brought deer to the camp, which stood blank-eyed, trance-held, waiting for the knife. On the third morning they crossed a ridge and came down through dense autumnal woods to the valley and river that Mel had shown Iril when they had first met. With a pole Iril measured the depth of the clear, brownish water, re-peating the process as they travelled along the bank until they reached a waterfall with a pool below it. Feeder streams tum-bled down from either side above the fall, and beyond them the river was much less.

"Overland to this pool," said Iril.

"Good," said Mel. "The first stones will be here in three noons, the last stone not for four more. You may stay and make ready."

"My people will fell timber," said Iril. "I will come with you and see Silverspring while its stones still stand."

"You are not afraid?"

"No man has seen Silverspring. I have lived more than a life."

"Come, then."

Above the fall the forest closed right down to the stream. The track along which they had travelled ended in a wall of brambles. Mel considered the barrier for some while, until part of it became shadowy and vanished, and the trees beyond wavered and vanished also, leaving a clear path that ran on a ledge above the stream. In places boulders had been rolled aside, or piled to level the way. The slopes on either side became steadily steeper until track and stream ran through a defile which ended in a sheer cliff with the river welling out into a pool at its foot. Mel considered the cliff, again for some while, until it opened a crack in itself, a crevice not four paces wide, with cloudy sky beyond.

Iril was surprised by none of this. It was known that no man could find the way through to Silverspring. But he had also heard of Mel.

Beyond the crevice the valley widened into a huge volcanic crater in the heart of the hills. Its bowl was rimmed by bare black cliffs, with steep woods below them, but the bottom was a wide clearing of sheep-nibbled grass and strips of ploughland. At the centre rose a gentle mound, ringed half way up by a circle of standing stones. Below this circle, directly facing the crevice, was a dark opening from which the stream flowed.

Beside the woods on the left were a dozen huts, in front of which a group of women waited, some with babies in their arms. There were no older children and no men. They watched Mel and his party emerge from the crevice as if they had known they were coming. Mel ignored them and walked towards the mound. When he was about twenty and ten paces from the cave, a woman came out of its darkness and faced him.

She was short and plump, but moved with grace. Her face was pale, round, soft, her hair a greying black. She wore a dark green cloak which fell to the ground all around her. She was not what Iril had expected, and at first he thought she must be a servant, but then he saw that she must be Siron.

At her appearance Mel's people had halted, but Mel walked forward until he was a few paces from her. Iril growled to his bearers to follow, but they would not, so he slid himself down, took his crutch and hobbled on alone. Siron's gaze left Mel and caught him. He was aware that she could have stopped him but she let him come. As he neared, she considered him, considered his leg, the half foot that twisted sideways at the ankle. The years-long ache vanished. The foot straightened. Wasted muscle and smashed bone grew whole. For five paces Iril walked level, like other men.

Siron stopped him a little behind Mel's shoulder. Her eyes asked a question. He shook his head and tapped the bracelet on his arm. Many of her pilgrims came across the water. She would know that the wave-riders did not break a contract for any threat or gift. She looked away and his leg was as it had always been.

Mel spoke. Iril did not know the words but could hear the tone of command. Siron answered with a question. Mel spoke again, shortly, and then Siron for some while, a dignified pleading, mixed with some anger and much grief, until Mel cut her short with one flat sentence. She did not reply, but considered, and moved to one side.

Out of the darkness of the cave, low down, close by the stream, a head appeared, flat, scaly, dark green patterned with black, wider than a man's two spread hands. A forked tongue flickered from its mouth. The jaws gaped, showing fine white fangs. The body emerged in slithering windings, wide as a man's thigh and many paces long, with the tail still unseen in the cave. The head reared up, weaving from side to side, peering for its target.

Mel gestured with his right hand, held low. Iril sensed a movement close behind him, smelt a sharp reek, but did not flinch as a beast paced close beside him, cat-shaped but large as an ox, its fur yellow-brown blotched with black. Saliva dripped from the yellow, curving fangs, as long as walrus tusks. As it passed Iril, its tail twitched against his thigh, hard, like a rope's end. By that he knew it was no sending but a thing, itself.

The beast faced the serpent, tense, balanced, watching for the strike. The serpent's head swayed back and forth, probing. The beast moved, seeming to start its spring, but it was a feint. The forward flash of the serpent's head was too quick for Iril to follow, as was the beast's counterstroke, but then they were facing each other again, the beast apparently unharmed but the serpent with dark red blood oozing from a gash behind its head. It resumed its weaving, but the movement now seemed less certain, and when the beast took a half pace nearer it withdrew, turned back on itself and slithered into the cave. Siron followed it without a word, making a gesture as she passed into the darkness. The cave vanished, and the stream now welled directly from the turf.

Mel scratched his beast between the shoulder-blades and dismissed it. It stalked towards a group of grazing sheep, which moved nervously away, all but one that stood waiting blindly. The beast killed it with a blow and dragged its carcass into the trees.

Mel walked up the mound and round the ring of stones, laying a hand on each in turn and marking some with a smear of orange stuff which he took from a small pot. The women had vanished into their huts. Iril watched the men begin to dig, and to set up the tackle they would need to lift the first stone onto its rollers. They knew what they were doing, he decided. He signalled to the litter bearers, who came and carried him back to the pool below the waterfall. The crevice did not close up on them, and the track was clear all the way.

The pool was apparently close enough to Silverspring for the stones to be hauled to it one by one without Mel losing his control, so having seen to the floating of the first of them, Iril returned to his trade. There were others beside Mel who needed to cross the water, and it would be a moon and another moon before all ten stones were ready to float down to the estuary. The problem of how to build and manage a raft large enough to take them all across the water together filled Iril's spare hours.

Women travelled to Silverspring for the midwinter rite. Iril said nothing to them but took no fees. They came back shaken and disconsolate, saying that they had been unable to find the way, even those who had made the journey often before. The night after the last of them had gone, Iril chewed leaf and lay down in his cot to dream the wave, as he had done many nights since his return from Silverspring, trying to set his great raft on it in his dream, and feel how the inert thing might move in response to the moving waters. In the small hours of the dark the wave swept through his mind as it swept up the estuary. After a lifetime of practice he could direct his dream to any part of its passage, and know why the currents and eddies and cross-currents flowed as they did, and why they changed and reformed through the seasons, so that he and his sons could ride both ebb and flow through the year.

This night as he travelled with the surging tide in his dream, and set his dream raft upon it, he sensed something else close by, a great mass that was neither raft nor water, but moved easily in the current, of its own will, as a bird does in the wind. Many, many years earlier, a whale had stranded in a lagoon below the village after a wild high tide, and when it had died, there had been prodigious feasting. Never had any man seen so great a beast. Could this be another such? It seemed yet larger. Though he had merely sensed it, and in a dream only, Iril knew it was there.

He was not the only one. He woke and saw Jarro squatting by his bedside, waiting for him to open his eyes. He grunted, enquiringly.

"Something behind the wave," said Jarro. "Big. It came in the dream."

"Who gave you leaf?"

(It was not good to get the habit too young, as Iril himself had been forced to do.)

"I ate no leaf," said Jarro. "The dream came, like when I was a child. The thing was there. It was not wide, but long, long."

Iril frowned. His own easy childhood dreamings were lost

beyond recall. But he felt he could remember every moment of the night, a few nights after his father had died, when he had first chewed leaf and lain down to dream the wave. How clearly that dream had come, and with what a mixture of terror and exultation. Leaf was rare and expensive. Wealthy men chewed it for their own pleasure. Chieftains gave it to their warriors before battle. But for Iril, as for other dream-workers and seers, it was a necessary tool because it freed the hidden dream. Yet Jarro had dreamed the wave without it, and seen the thing behind the wave more clearly than Iril had himself.

Next ebb, though there was no need, he crossed the water, taking Jarro with him, and climbed to the bluff. Iril chewed leaf.

"Watch," he said, and as Jarro settled cross-legged, he wrapped himself in furs against the thin, sleety north-easter and lay down to dream. As he slept, the water sifted seaward in his mind, dwindling through its channels until the mudbanks emerged to reek in the sun. Then the tide returned and crept back over them until it lay level from shore to shore.

All this time Iril sensed nothing strange or new. The water was mere water. But shortly before half tide, when the main surge came and the wave was formed, Jarro woke him.

"It is there, Father," he said. "It waits."

"You also slept?"

"No, Father. Waking, the dream came."

Without leaf? Without sleep? Iril had had both, but already for him the dream was weakening. Vaguely the forming wave stirred in his mind, with something even vaguer beyond it. He hauled himself up and stood, watching the water. A raft was waiting to cross, with his sister's son in charge. A large load for this slack season: a horse dealer with five ponies, still half wild; a pot merchant from Hotpool, returning with empty panniers; two cousins journeying to the oracle at Glas, hoping to settle an argument that might otherwise turn into a blood feud. The estuary was ruffled by the crosswind, but the moon was well into its wane, so it should be an easy crossing on a middling wave.

The wave, imperceptible lower down, reached the sudden narrowing at Owl Point and hummocked itself up. Its hairline formed across the grizzled surface. Iril called, his sister's son waved, and the men poled the raft out. The close-tethered horses bucked and squealed. The wave neared, a good steady one, barely flecked with foam. It picked the raft up, moving it forward and sideways so evenly that the horses calmed a little. Nevertheless Iril's tension rose. He had chewed leaf too often since his return from Silverspring, and its power had built up in his bloodstream until even fully awake he was dimly aware of a continuing dream, and of the tide flowing in his mind. With the same uncertainty he now sensed the thing that was not water, huge, unknown, coming invisibly up behind the wave. He could not tell where, but because of its size, he guessed it must be in the main channel. Even at half flood, nowhere else was deep enough.

The raft slid on. Before and behind the wave the wrinkled water remained unchanged. Iril shook his head and muttered. He was old, he had chewed too much leaf, he was starting to dream untruths. That had happened to his grandfather. He must ease off, or he would build his great raft amiss and so fail in his contract. He was shaking his head again, as if trying to shake the fraudulent dream out of it, when Jarro spoke. In the grip of the trance, Iril had forgotten he was there.

"Now!" he gasped, horror in the single word, startling Iril into full awareness.

And then the thing happened. They saw it sooner than the men on the raft. Iril's sister's son, up on the platform, had his eyes on the line he must travel, while crew and passengers were below the wave crest and the thing began a pole-length behind it.

A shape like a branchless tree shot out of the water, rushing in on the raft and at the same time curving forward and over until the men there saw it suddenly towering above them. Heads tilted, arms were thrown up, the raft lost its footing on the wave and slewed as the thing struck down, not at the raft itself but into the water beyond it. Now the arch spanned the raft and closed on it. The head emerged behind the sternboard, shooting on and over to make a second coil, now gripping the raft, hauling it back through the wave, tilting it, spilling all that was loose into the churning water, while the head emerged for the third time, hovered a moment and hammered down onto the timbers, blow after blow, smashing the structure apart in an explosion of sunlit foam.

Iril, appalled, whispered prayers to Manaw for his men and passengers, though he knew that no one would live long in such water at this season, whether the serpent found them or not. But the shock had cleared the dream vagueness away and he watched with steady eyes, studying the thing as he might have studied an unexpectedly altered sandbank. Its head was much like the head of the serpent that had come from Siron's cave, only enormously larger. Its body too was much like the body of that serpent, but as thick as the trunk of a large tree. Its length was hidden, but Iril could see how the water was churned for many pole-lengths along the main channel, and how in places solid humps arose as the hinder end threshed in response to the writhings up front.

When the raft was demolished the thing swam on up the channel and doubled back, with a pole-length or so of its neck held clear of the water. From time to time it struck down at something it saw. At one point it rose with a man's body caught round the waist between its jaws. It thrashed him to and fro, like a dog killing a rat, and swallowed him whole. It continued to cruise the channel for a while, but at last slid under the surface and disappeared.

Mel had said, "If you strike trouble, send for me." Iril sat on the grass, bowed his head and made a mind picture of Silverspring, of Mel standing beside the now broken ring of stones. When he looked up, Mel was in front of him, with the estuary and the snow-mottled hills of the far shore just visible through his cloak and body. Iril told him aloud what he had seen. Mel whispered in his mind, "I will come." The shape vanished.

Only the horse dealer came living to the land. When the serpent had struck, one of the ponies had managed to tangle itself with its neighbour, so the dealer had loosed its tethers and had looped its halter rope round his wrist. The impact had tossed both man and beast into the water, still tied to each other. The horse in panic had struck out for the shore, and the man had managed to haul himself up alongside it and cling to its neck, where its body heat had perhaps helped keep him alive a little longer. The luck of the secondary currents behind the wave had carried them shorewards. Watchers at the jetty had seen this, and four of them had taken a light raft out and reached them. By this time the man was unconscious and trailing again at the rope end, but they'd cut him free and brought him ashore, with the horse still swimming beside the raft, and dried and wrapped and warmed him at the fire, and he had revived.

When he could talk, he confirmed what Iril, seeing it from a distance, had thought. The thing was like a land serpent, but unimaginably huge. It was not smooth-skinned, like an eel, but had dark, blue-grey scales and vertically slitted eyes. That was all he had had time to see, hearing the yells of alarm and looking up over his shoulder as the head struck down.

That night Iril took no leaf. He made Jarro move his bedding closer to his own, and as the wave formed, woke himself and reached out and felt for Jarro's arm. The flesh was stiff and shuddering with nightmare, so Iril woke the boy and held him in his arms like a baby as the wave went by, and again in the faint light of dawn as the ebb began and the monster returned to the sea.

Jarro slept late, and when he rose he was heavy-eyed and pale, but he said, "To-night do not wake me, Father. It is better that I watch this thing, and learn its ways."

Mel was there in the morning in his own body, though it was three days' march to Silverspring.

"Siron caused this," he said. "I did not think she had the power."

"Can you counter it?" asked Iril.

"My power is from the Fathergod. It is of air and fire, the creatures of daylight. Hers is from the old Earth-mother. It is of water and under-earth. I have wondered why she has made no move to delay our taking the stones, though she would have known that I could overcome her."

"She could perhaps have dried out the river."

"She would not do that. The river is holy."

"Then you can do nothing about this serpent."

"Nothing directly. I will think what else. Let us see if it appears again to-day."

It did not, nor the next, though both Iril and Jarro, dreaming the forming wave, sensed strongly on all four tides that the same large thing was following close behind it. The attack of the serpent had not been seen from the southern shore, so on the third day Farn brought a raft over on the ebb to find what was amiss that none had returned on the wave. Fortunately for him and his crew, the tide was still high, so the monster had the whole estuary to patrol, and missed him. With him came Iril's nephew. This man, always a boaster, insisted that he would test the passage by crossing back on the wave, and persuaded two others to go with him. The serpent rose as before in the main channel, coiled round the raft, and smashed it to pieces with hammer blows of its head. None of the men came ashore.

Farn said, "This thing cannot come into the shallows. We can pole the stones singly up along the shore as far as the river mouth, cross there on a low tide, and return down the southern shore."

"How many days?" said Mel.

"Two moons or more. We could move at high tide only. The water must cover the mudbanks each time."

"Too long. The powers I have laid asleep in the stones will begin to stir at bud-break. I must have them in place by then."

"If you were to take them back to Silverspring and wait another year . . ." suggested Farn.

"No," said Iril. "We have a contract. And something else. This serpent, if we sneak the stones round by the water's edge or take them back to their place, will it leave these waters, do you think?"

"Not while Siron chooses to keep the way barred," said Mel.

"We live by this water," said Iril. "It is our field. The wave is the ox with which we plough it. How shall we live if these are taken from us? If people fear that the serpent may return, will they use our rafts to save a few days' journey? What are a few days out of a life? By the axe of Manaw, I will take the stones over, or else die. And I will also overcome and destroy this serpent that has killed my sister's son, and my men and passengers. I, Iril, say this."

The men sitting around the fire muttered praise. Nobody asked how it should be done.

Iril gave orders and worked all night with the men while they built a light raft, buoyed with skins, with no platform, so that it would float either way up. For the moment it did not lie level in the water, having extra float-skins on one side, near the sternboard, with a slip rope up to the post where Iril would stand. Jarro crouched by his side to watch as with his own hands Iril shaped the inner edge of the sternboard. When the raft was on the water, he levelled it with a net of boulders lashed above the extra floats. The sun rose over the glistening mudbanks of low tide.

"Give me leaf," said Jarro. "Let me dream the wave as you go."

"You are too young," said Iril. "You dream well without it."

"No," said Jarro. "There is something more to dream. I do not know what. Give me leaf, Father."

Iril passed him the little leather pouch and watched the boy retire to their hut. *Yes*, he thought. *To-day may well be the last time I ride the wave. If so, Jarro must see how I fail.*

With two sweepmen, heavily greased against the cold, and with safety lines round their waists, he took the raft out on the morning wave.

Being so light it travelled fast, and Iril sped it along, slanting the sternboard to its limit against the wave-foot. All rafts had different quirks, and he had only this short stretch over the shallows to learn this one's bad habits. For the moment his mind was wholly on that, but just before they swept into the main channel, he experienced a sort of internal blink, a flicker, as if something voiceless had spoken to him. *It is there. It waits.*

There was no time for astonishment or wonder. As the raft lurched into the rougher waters of the channel the serpent reared behind them and arched over as before. Seen this close, its hugeness and speed were not the worst of it. There was a ferocity about it, a malice, an unstoppable focussed power as it performed the single act for which it was made. Iril watched in silence. When its head plunged back into the water, he yelled. The sweepmen flung their weight against the shafts. Iril tugged at the slip rope, releasing the extra floats, then clung to his post. The sweepmen crouched and gripped the loops that had been tied in the deck, ready for this moment.

The raft spun. The weight of the boulders tilted the shaped edge of the sternboard into the wave. The raft dipped further under the mass of water, stood on its side, was swallowed by roaring foam, and finally rose clear of the coiling body and well behind the wave, floating in the long side-eddy for which Iril had been racing.

The sweepmen loosed the net of boulders and heaved them over, levelling the raft once more. Then they took their sweeps and worked with all their strength to use the flow of the tide behind the wave to carry them over the mudbank on the upstream side of the channel. Iril twisted to and fro, watching his course and studying what the serpent did.

Its head had emerged while the raft had been buried in the wave. By the time he could see it again, it had completed its second coil, and only as it now reemerged discovered that it had caught nothing. Still it lashed down at the place where the raft should have been, several blows, before it started to look around. Even then it did not seem to perceive the raft and for a while continued to search the water close around it. At last it withdrew its neck and disappeared.

Another of those flickers—*It comes back!*

A sudden ruffling of the surface confirmed that the serpent was racing back along the channel to where the raft had come out of the wave.

By now the men had laid their sweeps aside and were poling their way across shallows. The serpent's head emerged and peered round. It saw the raft and turned. When it felt the check of the mudbank, it reared high out of the water and struck forward, but still fell a good pole-length short of the raft. Iril told the sweepmen to back water, and then tempted it, judging his distance. Once it almost stranded itself and needed violent wallowings to get clear, but the tide was still rising and he dared not stay long. It continued to rage up and down, looking for a way round the obstacle, long after

Iril had guided the raft over the next channel and into the more regular shallows along which they could pole their way home, using where they could the secondary currents of inflow and ebb. It was a weary distance, but every now and then that secondary awareness flickered into Iril's mind and showed him the serpent patrolling the deeper water. Now that he had leisure to think about it, he understood what had been happening to him, and his heart lightened with the knowledge that the task he had set himself was a little less impossible.

They came ashore late in the afternoon. Jarro was waiting on the jetty, dizzy with exhaustion and unaccustomed leaf.

"You spoke in my head," said Iril.

"You heard?" muttered Jarro. "I was not sure. I was with the serpent in the water. I felt his anger. With its eyes I saw you on the raft. I called to you in your mind but I heard no answer."

"You did well," said Iril. "I give you great praise, my son."

He turned to Mel.

"This is your gift?" he asked.

"Not mine," said Mel, "but we have loosed strong powers in this place, I and Siron. Look . . ." He gestured towards the estuary. "You have seen when two strong currents meet in your water, how the lesser waters around them shift and change. So with the boy. He has dream-powers. He is young. Those powers have not hardened. He is changed."

"Such waters are very dangerous," said Iril. "Not even I can tell how they will flow."

"No more can I," said Mel.

The men feasted and praised Iril and the sweepmen for their deed, but Iril shook his head and turned to Mel.

"What do you know of serpents?" he said.

"Let everyone be silent and still," said Mel.

He considered, and after a little while a viper came gliding into the firelight. The men shrank back, but Mel picked the snake up and loosed it into his lap, where it shaped itself into coils and lay still. He stroked its head with a fingertip.

"A small mind," he murmured. "A simple pattern. What it does, it does, that being its pattern."

"I think it does not see very clearly," said Iril.

"What moves close by, it sees well. Things still, or at a distance, hardly at all. It hears ill also, but its smelling is very keen. And it feels the tremors of the earth with its body, a footfall, or prey moving close by."

"What smells arouse it?"

"Warm flesh."

"How is its seeing in the dark?"

"Very dim. I speak only of this viper. Other serpents may be otherwise."

Mel put the snake down and it slid away into the dark.

Iril went to his cot and slept, dreaming whatever dreams were sent. He felt the wave go by, but his mind did not move with its onrush. Next morning he climbed with Farn to the bluff above the landing place.

"I do not take you," he told Jarro. "It is not good to cram a young head with old memories."

He did not tell him that he was afraid, afraid for his son in a way that he had never been for himself.

Farn built a small fire, on which Iril threw leaf. He told his son to feed the fire and see that no one, not even Mel, came near. Then he sat down, cross-legged, and, breathing the smoke, put himself into a waking trance. His eyes gazed out across the estuary but he did not see the shining mudbanks, nor the tide that crept over them, nor the passing wave, nor the level flood, nor the rush and tumble of its going. All day he remembered moons and seasons, mudbanks and channels and currents that had come and gone and made themselves again. Between dawn and sundown he remembered twenty and twenty and seven years of tides. In the evening he woke himself, and his sons carried him down and set him by a roaring fire and rubbed the life-warmth back into his limbs.

Mel came.

"Can it be done?"

"With the right wave, perhaps. That may come at the new moon, if a strong south-westerly should blow."

"There will be that wind."

Iril stared at the fire, but his mind saw the dead lagoon on the southern shore where the whale had stranded. That had happened at a new moon, with a gale from the southwest. So, then, a raft, of normal length, but narrower, its sternboard shaped thus ... no platform, but rails to grip ... a third sweep, over the stern ... small decoy rafts, and fire and oil and kindling ... fresh-killed pig in small pots ...

Mel had seen into his mind.

"I can give you a salve to hide the odour of your own bodies," he said. "And a cordial against the cold."

"Good," said Iril, and in a louder voice, "I need six men. Perhaps none will live, but there will be great praise."

The ring of listeners stood, every man. Iril chose from among the older ones, who had less of their lives to regret, but none of his own sons. If he died, they would be needed, each in turn, to take on his contract with Mel, and try to defeat the serpent.

Mel left next day, and Iril set about building his new raft, longer than the first, but again with the inner corner weighted and then buoyed with extra floats, and again with a strange-shaped sternboard. As each wave surged up the shoreline, he experimented with small decoy rafts. When the main raft was finished, he blindfolded his six crew and made them learn various tasks by touch, and rigged cords to each of them from the place where he would stand so that he could signal to them in the dark. He talked long with his sons about other possible devices against the serpent, and also about how the great raft to carry the stones, already being built, should be finished, and its sections linked to flex with the water surface and yet move all of a piece so that the full moon wave could float the immense weight over.

Most nights he chewed leaf, but gave Jarro no more. Yet still as he slept and the flood-wave moved through his mind, he heard and from time to time the flicker of Jarro's mind, telling him the serpent's doings.

Three days before new moon Mel returned, bringing a salve and a cordial, neither magical, because he could not tell how much his powers would be diminished on water. Next morning he went up to the bluff and stood and considered until a gale blew up from the southwest, with sheeting rain and thunder. Iril watched the day wave pass, a whitely churning wall, curled over into spume at the crest. He could remember few taller. He watched the outrush of the tide, its torrent piled into ugly shapes by the contrary wind. At the rising half tide his sons carried him up in the dark to the bluff. He made Jarro stand by his side, and this time gave him a little leaf to chew. Mel came too, and by the almost continual lightning they watched the wave go by, huger yet, roaring above the roar of the storm, its crest streaking away before it under the lash of the wind. It was hard to sense anything through such tumult, but yes, perhaps, two or three pole-lengths behind the wave, like a huge shadow . . .

When the wave was gone, Iril bent and bawled in Jarro's ear.

"What did you see or feel?"

"It is there," said Jarro confidently, his voice suddenly loud in the silence that Mel had made around them. "It is stronger than the wave."

Iril turned to Mel.

"Such a wind again, to-morrow night," he said.

"It will be."

"The rain? The lightning?"

"As you choose."

"Then none."

They returned to the huts and slept. Iril did not climb to the bluff again to watch the day wave, but while it roared by lay half-tranced on his cot, dreaming what those huge tides might have done to the pattern of mudbanks. By mid-afternoon the rain had ceased and the wind settled to a steady southwest gale. He woke and went to the landing place to see to the loading and trimming of the raft. At dusk they ate well—this might be their last meal, ever, so why not?—and talked of doings on the water long ago, and the astounding idiocies of passengers. Jarro sat with his brothers, silent, his head bowed, and did not eat at all. Already, though the return tide had barely begun to flow, and even without the leaf Iril had given him, he was beginning to dream the wave. Before the meal was over, he rose. Iril heaved himself up on his crutch and hobbled beside him as he moved like a sleep-walker towards their hut. In the doorway Iril put his a hand on his arm and stopped him.

"Be with the serpent," he said. "I will do what I do."

"I am with it now," Jarro said in the voice of one muttering in his sleep. "It is far west, waiting in deep water."

He turned and groped his way into the hut.

Next, the pig was slaughtered and its pieces sealed into pots. Iril and the men he'd chosen smeared their bodies with grease, mixed with Mel's salve, and at half tide poled out and well upstream from their usual starting place. There they put down anchor stones. Iril chewed a little leaf.

They waited, tense but patient. The night was solid dark. Now a yellow light glimmered from the point below the landing place, where a watcher had fired a pile of dry bracken to signal the passing of the wave. The men loosed the anchors and poled a little further out while the sweepmen headed the raft upstream until the polemen, up at the bow, could steady it against a mudbank as the wave came on. Now above the wind they heard its deep mutter, swelling to a growl, to a roar.

"Way!" bellowed Iril, and the four men flung their weight on the poles to start the raft moving, the lead man on either side calling his pace to the one behind so that they could now march together back along the deck, driving the raft upstream. All this they had practised blindfolded. They were ready for the sudden heave of the raft as the wave surged against the sternboard, and the bank against which the poles had been thrusting slid away beneath them. They laid the poles down and lashed them, their hands knowing the knots without sight or thought, and then crawled to their stations on either side of Iril and gripped the loops of rope set there for them.

Only now, with the pressure of action over, did they truly sense the force of the thing that drove them. They had all ridden many, many waves, but none like this, this immense weight of ocean hauled up by the big moon, piled yet higher by the two-day gale, and now forced to cram itself into the narrowing funnel between the northern and southern shores. Not even Iril had known such a wave, this thundering wall, three times the height of a man, curving up behind the stern-board to a crest that hung almost over them, invisible in the starless dark, but heard in the shriek of the wind that whipped the spray from it, and the wave itself sensed, not only by Iril but by all of them, as a huge, cold, killing mass, driving them on.

But the raft, lying slant on the wave-foot with light foam creaming along the sternboard, seemed to move in a pocket of stillness in the lee of that wall, just as Iril had foreseen in his dream trance. With his left hand he gripped the safety rail, with the signal cords fastened to either side of it. With his right he managed his sweep, not to guide the raft but to sense the wave that drove it, feel the angle at which the raft lay to it, as well as any change within it. For a while he kept the angle low, as he was aiming for a different section of the channel than on his trial venture with the serpent. When they reached it, then would be the need for speed.

So they swept on in the roaring calm. All knew the dangers of these waters, had seen raft-fellows washed away and lost. Tension keyed but did not confuse them as the long moments passed. Iril waited, fully awake, his senses merely sharpened by the morsel of leaf he had taken. The wave spoke to him through his palm on the sweep shaft, while through the soles of his feet he understood the slither of waters beneath the raft. As the tremors minutely altered, he charted channels and mudbanks until he sensed the long curve of the bank that guided the main current. Almost at once Jarro's thought flickered into his mind.

It is here. I am with it. It comes!

Iril pulled twice on the cord that led to the loop gripped by the first poleman on his left.

The man tapped his mate on the shoulder. Together they crawled to the decoy rafts, broke open a pot of pig meat, slipped the skins off the stack of oil-soaked timber on one raft, opened their fire pot, dipped in a taper and thrust it into the stack. As soon as the flames bit, they slid the decoy overboard. By the time they were back in their places, the decoy was trailing along the wave-foot at the end of its cable with the timber blazing.

Now they could see, but at first only the glare of the flames and the glimmer of their reflection from the wrinkled surface of the wave. Then, as their pupils narrowed, they saw the wave itself, its towering closeness, the round of its wall curving back and then over to the glittering wind-shredded crest. The decoy rode lightly, tilted towards the sheer of the wall. Iril watched it only long enough to check that it was well set, then signalled through the cords to the sweepmen, him on the left to pull and him on the right to hold water, thus widening the angle of the sternboard to the wave, spilling more of the impelling force from its back edge and sweeping them faster along the line of the wave.

Half hypnotised, the crew stared at the light and the endlessly self-renewing wall, but Iril turned the other way to watch the small, pulsing curl of foam where the fore-end of the sternboard met the wave, telling him that the balance of the raft against the wave-foot was now at its limit. He could travel no faster. If he tried, the board would dig into the wall, the wave would crash down on them and they would be lost.

Now! whispered Jarro.

Out of the corner of his eye Iril saw the mouth of a pole-man open in a cry unheard above the roaring. The man pointed, up and beyond. Iril grabbed and jerked the cord that led to him—he'd told them that if the serpent appeared, they must not move. The man froze. Carefully Iril turned his head.

Directly over the decoy, black as the night but iridescent where the flame-light touched it, the serpent's body arched from above the wave crest. The head was already plunging to encircle the decoy. As it reached the water, the poleman there loosed the anchor-stone that held the tow rope and flung it overboard. The two rafts swept apart. For the space of three heartbeats they saw the flame recede, and then the stone reached the cable end and dragged the decoy under, and they were in darkness again.

Now Iril could only guess how long it might be before the serpent stopped hunting among the ruins of the decoy and came after them again, as he was sure it would. This was why Siron had sent it. He waited for Jarro's flash of thought, but it did not come. Half way along the southward sweep of the main channel, he signalled for the second decoy to be launched. As before, the glare of the flame seemed at first too much to bear, but eased and became the centre of a sphere of light with the raft at its edge, sliding in that weird stillness along the wave-foot with the roaring black waters behind and below.

Yet again they waited, tenser than before, but still the serpent did not appear. Iril began to fear that they had too thoroughly tricked it and they would have faced this danger for nothing. The crossing itself was pointless. They could never in this way bring over the great raft that was to carry the stones. That must come by day, with twenty and twenty men with poles and sweeps, who could be called to or signalled to by sight. It must come slowly too, on a moderate wave, easy prey . . .

No. The serpent must come now. It must know that its true target was still upon the water.

Before the timber was half-burnt, some flaw in the wind let a dollop of spray fall and quench it. Iril signalled for the tow rope to be loosed and the third decoy readied, but now there was a delay as the men had not expected the order so soon. A poleman came to check, bellowing above the wave-roar. Then he had to go back and tell the others, not hurrying, so as not to become entangled in the signal cords. Time passed that could not be spared. Any moment now, the channel would start its eastward curve, and shortly after that, it would be too late. At last, as the light flared and the decoy drifted away, a flicker from Jarro.

There!

One sharp cry, like a yell of sudden pain. And then something else, flickering still but continuing like the reverberations of that yell, not in the language of thought, but pure feeling, a furious cold lust, a hunting rage, hunting him, Iril, smelling him through the blind dark, sensing him by the tremors of the water round the raft. The mind of the serpent. And then it came.

It attacked this time along the line of the wave. Its head rose from the upcurve beyond the decoy, arched forward and plunged back in, close behind the main raft. As it did so, it struck the tow rope hard enough to jar the whole structure. Water foamed over the sternboard as its angle against the wave faltered. Iril and the sweepmen wrestled with the bucking sweepshafts to set it true. The man who had been waiting to loose the towrope kept his head and heaved the anchor rock over. For a moment the raft teetered on the edge of foundering, but as the wave drowned the decoy, it regained its angle and swept on in the dark.

This time Iril was sure that the serpent must have seen them, lit by the flames of the decoy only just beyond where its head struck down. Even as it went through its pattern of coiling round its prey, crushing it, hammering it to bits, something in its slow brain was telling it that this was not what it had been sent for. By the flicker in his mind he could sense the process, the lust of destruction turning to disappointment, to hatred and pursuit renewed. Well, if it came, it came, and who chooses to die in the dark? The moment was almost right. Down the grain of his sweep Iril could sense an alteration in the layer where the wave's root moved against the steadier underlying water, telling him that the raft had now reached a point where it would never have been on any normal, slower crossing, still well down from the landing place and close against the outer edge of the eastward curve of the main channel. He twitched his signal cords for the last time. The man with the firepot crawled to the timber stacked at the forward end, peeled the skins from it and set it blazing. Now, once again, they could see. So, when it came, would the serpent. The raft itself was the final decoy.

The sweepmen stayed at their posts. Two polemen tied spare floats to their waists and clutched them under an arm, then waited ready. The other two brought floats to Iril and the sweepmen and tied them on for them, then went and took their own and also waited, one of them where Iril could see him, to keep watch back along the wave. One-handed, Iril eased a small flask from his belt, unstoppered it with his teeth, and gulped at the burning liquid. Mel's cordial. He had not dared touch it till now, not knowing how it would interact with the leaf-juice and muddle his perceptions. It seemed to run through his veins like midsummer sunlight. He was grinning with the joy of conflict as he tossed the flask away.

There was no warning from Jarro. The serpent's head rose close behind the raft, shooting up in a low, tight arch and plunging immediately down. Iril yelled to the sweepmen, but before they could react to bury the sternboard in the wave, the raft jarred against the serpent's neck, slewed, and stood on its side. Its upper edge slammed into the arching body. By the last light of the fire Iril saw a man's body, arms and legs spread, sailing across the black sky with his float dangling behind, and then the wave came crashing over him and he was smothered in the hurl of water.

He made no effort to fight it, but found and gripped the neck of his float and dragged it under his arm. His head shot into air, was buried again, twice, and rose clear. The darkness was absolute, the water a violent churning chaos across which the gale roared, whipping the wave-tops to lashing spume.

He clung fiercely to his float but let the rest of his body relax and move where the water willed. Below the confusions of the surface he sensed a steadier movement, a strong, persistent surge, and knew that he was once again being carried by a wave, a secondary one, set up by the mass of moving water behind the main advance. Soon he could tell from the lash of the wind-blown spume that he was no longer travelling up channel, but slantwise across to the southern shore. So he, at least, was where he had intended they should come, being swept between the series of mudbanks that funnelled in towards the dead lagoon. Before long this wave would crash across the bar, flood the lagoon, surge on to swamp the low meadows beyond, and then withdraw. Well, if he was on it, so might the serpent be, still absorbed in its destruction of the raft and its hunt among the wreckage. Iril adjusted the float under his left arm and with his right arm and legs began to work himself lengthways along the wave, away from the serpent's searching, and clear of the main surge as it thundered over the bar.

The moment came in a battering and bellowing of water. Iril thought he heard a man's voice cry out in the tumult, but had no breath to answer. He had lost his grip on his float, but the cord had held and he regained it with a struggle he could not afford. He surfaced behind the wave and could hear its dwindling roar as it left him.

Well, the thing was done. It was over. Either he had trapped the serpent, or he had failed. There was nothing more he could do.

Realising that, the spirit seemed to leave him. For all this last moon he had driven his old carcass, both mind and body, beyond what it could bear. He had chewed too much leaf, breathed too much leaf-smoke, slept too little, dreamed the wave too often. Perhaps Mel's cordial had tipped him over the edge. It had at any rate lost its potency. His whole body was becoming inert with cold. The wind seemed less. Mel had said it would be so, but it was no help. He had no strength left, no will. His damaged leg had left off aching and was dragging numbly, like a log. Still he tried to swim, muttering prayers to Manaw, losing his sense and starting again, like a man praying in his dreams.

Where was Jarro? Safe in his bed on the northern shore, but . . . was he still dreaming the wave, following the serpent as it was swept through the tumult of waters? Why no warning from him of the last attack? Why nothing now? It was only his body in the bed, while his mind ventured among the spirit waters—dangerous as a tide-rip, Mel had said.

Speak to me, my son!

Nothing. Nothing from Jarro. But again through the dream of his exhaustion, the flicker of the serpent's hunt-lust, smelling out the traces his body had left in the water, sensing the feeble movements of his swimming—all this though his lifetime of dealings with these currents told him that he was no longer in the lagoon, but over the flats to the east of it, where the serpent could not come. He shut his mind to it, managed to switch the float beneath his other arm and forced himself on south, resting longer each time between the feeble strokes.

He was still swimming when his hand hit solid matter, vertical, softish, a wall of wet earth. Letting his legs sink, he found he could stand chest deep. The footing was too firm for a mudbank. Turf, a flooded meadow. An old man-made bank to the south of it, built to protect the fields beyond from such high tides. Half swimming, half hobbling, he felt his way along it until he came to a stone boundary wall and was able to climb onto that and thence to the top of the bank. He started to crawl along it. Even if he had had his crutch he could not have walked.

His cousin's son, not a wave-rider but a farmer, came out to look for him with two of the farm slaves carrying torches. Mel had sent the man a dream telling him where Iril lay, and had then woken him and spoken in a clear voice in the dark of his hut, telling him to go and find him. They carried him home unconscious, and his sons' wives rubbed him with salves for the rest of the night in front of a great fire, massaging the life-warmth back into his body.

While he still slept, men came to say that the serpent was raging in the lagoon, trapped by the falling tide. The wind had died clean away and the next tide barely lapped the bar. Two of Iril's crew had come exhausted to the village, one was found unconscious on the shore, and one dead. The other two were not seen again.

When Iril woke, they carried him down to the lagoon to watch the serpent die. This it did with slow, agonised writhings, having threshed the lagoon to stinking mud which it could not breathe. Dead, it immediately rotted, the skin bursting apart and black, stinking stuff oozing out, smoking as it reached the air. Those that breathed the smoke dropped to their knees and vomited, while the gulls that came for the carcass meat fell out of the air and died.

Iril's eldest son brought a raft over on the next day's wave, to check that the passage was now clear. With him came Jarro, who had slept for a day and a night after the storm, with Mel watching by his bed all that time. He was still almost too weak to stand, and needed to be helped up to the village. But next morning he insisted on going to see where the serpent had died. Iril went with him. They stood and looked in silence at the poisoned lagoon. Bubbles still rose to the oily surface, their vile reek wafting on the wind.

"I was there," said Jarro quietly. "I was trapped with the serpent. After the first decoy, it happened. The serpent lost you. It did not follow. I sought its mind. I spoke to it. 'There!' I told it."

"I heard your thought, my son."

Jarro nodded.

"The serpent followed you. It came fast. I tried to call to you, but I could not. I was caught up into the mind of the serpent. I thought with its thought. I felt its hatred. I felt its hunger. I joined in its hunting. I hunted you, my father."

"No shame," said Iril.

"It was trapped in the lagoon," said Jarro, still in the same quiet, half-dreaming voice. "It raged, and I raged with it. It suffered, and I knew its pain. It began to die, and I died too. Then Mel came. He came by the spirit paths and found me and set me loose."

For a long while Iril said nothing. There was horror in his heart to think how near he had come to killing his own son. And even though he lived, who could tell what the terrors of the adventure might have done to the boy? No, not a boy. Not any longer. He could tell, by the tone of his son's voice, by the way he had told his story, that in a night and a day Jarro had put his boyhood behind him, just as Iril himself had, in the squall in which his own father had died. And like Iril, from now on and for all his life Jarro would carry the scar of the event.

"You did well, my son," he said at last. "No man could have done better. Together we did this, you and I. We killed the great serpent."

"No, Father," said Jarro, "I did little to help."

"Not so, my son," said Iril. "You did what no other could have done, venturing along the spirit paths. The serpent lost me. It did not follow. I would have failed if you had not reached into its mind and spoken. Who before this has heard of such a deed? Mel himself could not have done it. He cannot dream the wave. That is our gift, ours alone, yours and mine. By the axe of Manaw, I say again, *we* killed the great serpent."

Normal traffic resumed. The ten stones were rafted down from Silverspring and the rafts linked together into the structure Iril had planned. He crossed the water to see that all was well, and to make any necessary adjustments and adaptations, but he let Farn take command when the full moon came and the whole great raft was floated over. Iril came as a passenger, saying he was still too weak for the work, though to others he seemed as strong as he had been before. It was a simple crossing on a big, clean wave. Siron sent nothing to hinder it. Once across, the raft was taken apart and the separate stones floated along the shoreline and upriver.

That done, they held a praise feast for Iril. Mel himself came, not a shadow or sending, and spoke marvellous praise, and praise for Jarro too, telling what he had done among the spirit paths. It was praise such as would be told for many generations. He left next day for the high ritual that would inaugurate the stones in their new home, and all the men except Iril went with him.

Iril's sons came to him, and stood side by side before him.

Farn said, "Come. There will be a place of honour for you, a place among the Major Chieftains."

Iril said, "I am too old and weak for such a journey, and my leg is very painful."

Arco said, "Perhaps Mel will heal it."

Iril shook his head.

"A contract is a contract," he said. "But I have done a thing no man ought to have done."

He took from his arm the three gold bracelets that Mel had paid him and gave one to each son.

"Go with my blessing," he said. "And take my place among the Chieftains."

He watched them walk away, noticing with pleasure how his two elder sons, mature men with wives and children, now accepted Jarro as their equal.

The day after they left, the women gathered in a long line, Farn's first wife leading, and danced solemnly though the village, three times, with many twists and windings. They sang in grieving voices, words Iril did not know, their secret language. Then they gathered in silence into a circle. One after another round the circle each took a pace forward, and knelt for a while, as if listening, then rose and went at once to her own hut.

That evening Farn's first wife came to Iril's hut with a salve.

"This is for your leg," she said. "It will ease the pain."

"Nothing can ease the pain. All has been tried."

"This is new. Siron showed it to me. She said, 'Say this to Iril. No curse of mine is on him.'"

"When did you see Siron?"

"This morning. Did you not see her? We danced and sang for her and she said farewell."

"Farewell?"

"Yes. She has gone. Those times are over."

WATER HORSE

When the Guardian of Western Mouth chose Tamia for her apprentice, no one was more surprised than Tamia herself.

The Guardian's choice was surprising in more ways than one. Everyone in Tamia's inland village paid the Guardians' token as all the islanders did, and "please the Guardians" and "as the Guardians hold back the sea" were sayings as common there as anywhere. But Guardians' apprentices came from the fishing villages, or at least from the villages that lay near the shore, outside the ragged ring of the Cloudyhead Mountains, with a view of the sea. Many inlanders never saw the sea at all; "Mountains are the right horizon for me" was a common inlander remark.

Every islander, inland and seaward, had heard that the Guardian of Western Mouth was growing old, and that she still had taken no apprentice. Although of course the Guardians always knew what they were doing (it was one of the things they learned in the process of becoming Guardians), still, it was very odd, how long Western Mouth had put off taking an apprentice. Some of the voices saying this rang and echoed on the phrase *very odd*, with a curious, intent, almost greedy intonation. But no one in Tamia's village had been interested in contemplating who might finally be chosen, as it would not be one of them.

Tamia was her mother's eldest child, and the only one by her first husband, who had died in a hunting accident. Her second husband, Tamia's stepfather, tolerated Tamia's presence in his household because she was quiet and useful. Tamia had never asked her mother what she thought about her husband's attitude towards his stepdaughter. She had been afraid to ask since she had seen the look on her mother's face when the midwife put her second husband's first child in her arms. Tamia had been six. She had spent the year since her mother remarried trying to be helpful. She had known that her stepfather didn't want her, but she had hoped he might change his mind. After Dorlan's birth—followed by Coth, Sammy, Tinsh, Issy and Miz—she grew accustomed to the idea that he would not. At least, with so many little ones to look after, there was never any shortage of work for Tamia to do.

Tamia was happiest looking after her family's animals. They had two cows, one to provide milk for themselves, and the second for her mother to make cheeses to sell; and six sheep, whose fleeces they sold to the weaver and whose lambs they sold to the butcher. As soon as Tamia was tall enough to steady the most phlegmatic of the ewes between her legs, she began learning to shear; but her stepfather took the lambs to the butcher. They also had a small flock of chickens, and only when Tamia was collecting the eggs were none of them missed.

And, until Tamia was twelve, they had had a pony, Columbine, who pulled a plough over their little quarter-hectare of cropland, and who was hired out, with her plough, to other farmers of smallholdings. Columbine had been bought and trained to her work by Tamia's father, but it was the money on Columbine's hiring that enabled Tamia's stepfather to spend so much of his time arguing with the local council over how the town should be run, and how much the Guardians' token should be. "I feed and house seven children on the tiniest fraction of what we pay one Guardian every year! Magic is magic! It has no mouth to put food into, no back to be sheltered from storms!" was one of his favourite protests.

But Columbine had been old when Tamia's mother had remarried, and one cold winter morning when Tamia was twelve, the pony had lain down in the shed she shared with the cows, and refused to get up again. She died that night, with Tamia's tears wet on her neck, because Tamia had refused to leave her. Tamia caught a severe head-cold as a result, and had to go to bed for a sennight, and her stepfather was very angry. But Tamia had lost her best friend, even if she had been only a pony. It had been Tamia who fed and brushed her, and tended her tack, and led her to her other jobs, and fetched her home again. Columbine settled down as soon as she saw her work ahead of her, but she could be positively balky if anyone but Tamia tried to lead her through street traffic.

When Tamia had been a little girl, she had thought the Guardians must be gods, or at least like gods; by the time she entered her teens, she knew they were enough like ordinary people to need to eat and sleep and protect themselves against the winter, and that certain traders brought them what they needed, paid for by the token levied against every islander from birth. (The Guardians had simple tastes—so went the stories—in food and clothing; in everything, in fact, except their desire for gold; but it was considered bad luck to discuss this. Even Tamia's stepfather was carefully unspecific about where most of the yearly token went.) She also knew that occasionally some Guardian descended from the mountains to one or another of the seaside villages and wandered among its inhabitants for a day, for reasons known only to themselves, frightening everyone they said "Good morrow" to, even members of the local council. Tamia wondered how you recognised a Guardian. She had seen Guardians' traders occasionally, had seen how they seemed to carry silence and mystery with them; but then, in a village as small as hers, every stranger was recognisable as a stranger, and treated as such.

But Tamia hadn't liked listening to her stepfather speak against the Guardians' token, nor to her neighbours debating when Western Mouth would choose an apprentice. It seemed to her rude. So she stopped listening. She had almost forgotten about Western Mouth's apprentice when the trader came to their door one evening.

Tamia knew him and his pony by sight, but she had never exchanged words with him—though she had, once or twice, with the pony. He knocked on their door at twilight, when Tamia and her mother had their hands fullest, putting children to bed. Tamia heard her stepfather open the door, and speak sharply to whoever stood there, and spared a fragment of her attention to wonder who it was, as she sought nightgowns crushed into dark corners, faced torn-to-bits beds, and grabbed small shrieking bodies attempting to flee the inevitable. Her stepfather would welcome any of his friends, and her mother's friends knew better than to stop by at this time of day. Who could it be?

Her stepfather had to say her name twice before it registered, and then Tamia found she had no voice to respond with. "Yes, Stepfather?" she managed at last; and the child in her arms stopped struggling in surprise. Everyone in the family, even the littlest, knew that Tamia was of no importance.

"This man has a message for you."

Tamia set Miz on her own legs, and stepped timidly forward. "Good evening," said the trader. "I beg pardon for disturbing you. I have a message for you from the Guardian of Western Mouth: that if you are willing, she would have you to apprentice. She would be glad to see you as soon as you are able to come."

The trader paused, but Tamia was having trouble taking it in. Her fourteenth birthday had been last week, but little attention had been paid to it; her mother had wished her happy birthday, and given her a kiss. Fourteen was traditionally the age that Guardians took their apprentices. She stared at the trader's hat, and the long curling red feather that hung down from it. His pack leaned against the door-post, and she could see the pony in the door-yard. Its ears were pricked towards her, as if waiting for her to speak. The trader went on, gently, softly, as if his words were only for her, and it did not matter if any of the rest of her family heard him or not. "Do you know the way to Western Mouth?"

Tamia's village lay at the edge of the foothills of the

Cloudyheads. It was the last village on one of the main traffic routes from the centre of the island to the sea, reached through a narrow gap in the mountains about half a day's brisk walk distant. It was not a very promising gap—there were better routes both north and south, but they were much farther away—and it was passable enough that Tamia's village had a good trade in dried ocean-fish and seaweed for finished lumber and hides, and what surplus crops the steep flinty farmland produced, and that Tamia's mother's cousin, who had married a fisherman, could come for a visit now and again.

A little north of that route was a narrow path that broke off from the main way and darted fiercely uphill, joining the long trail or series of trails that finally linked all the mountains in a ragged circle, but here made its way along the eastern edge of the Flock of Crows towards the Eagle, the tallest of the western Cloudyheads. Tamia had never seen anyone use that track, nor did she remember anyone telling her where it went, but she knew that it would lead to Western Mouth the way she knew that cheese was good to eat, or that the old man who lived at the edge of town and raised spotted ponies could give you a love-charm if you asked, and if he felt like it. It was just something everyone knew. "I—I think so," she said to the trader, although her voice did not sound like her own. "It is the path running up towards the Eagle, is it not?"

"Yes," replied the trader, and nodded his head to her respectfully, making his red feather gambol across his forehead. "At the last turn you must make to reach the Eagle, there is a trader's sign"—and here he took a bit of wood out of his pocket and showed her the sign scratched on it. And then he turned and picked up his pack and left them. That brief nod of his head seemed to hang in the air of the cottage after the man had left, as if a pole had been stuck in the floor at that place, and a banner tied to its top, declaring Tamia's emancipation. Tamia ducked round that place, as if something there blocked her way; she half-imagined the sparkle of a tiny pennoncel there, out of the corner of her eye. It was long and curly and red. In the silence she returned to Miz, who had stood staring, mouth open, one arm half in its sleeve and the other hand caught under her chin by her nightgown's collar, and began to pull her straight. The other children sighed and moved; there was a wail from Issy, who often wailed. "When will you go?" were her mother's first words. "Tomorrow is washing-day."

"Then I will leave the day after tomorrow," replied Tamia.

She hugged the cows and sheep good-bye; they looked at her in mild surprise, and carried on eating. The chickens would be glad to be rid of her, because they would be able to keep more of their eggs to themselves. She said good-bye politely to her mother and her half-siblings; her stepfather had left unusually early that morning to bother the councillors. Then she set off towards the Eagle. The journey would take her a day and a half, and her stepfather had complained so much about the necessity of letting her have a blanket to sleep on that she had promised to send it back again with the first trader who visited Western Mouth after her arrival.

If Western Mouth didn't simply send her home again, apologising for the mistake.

She made good time on the first day, and was well up into the lower slopes of the mountains by the time she had to stop because it was too dark to see her way. She had nothing to make a fire with, and ate a little cold food, and wrapped herself in the thin blanket, and leaned back against a tree, reminding herself firmly that bears never came this far west, and wolves were only dangerous to humans in the hardest winters. She found a few gaps in the leaves to look up at the stars through. She thought she would not be able to sleep—at this time of night she was usually trying to put children to bed—it was all too strange; but she was tired, and even the tree-roots couldn't keep her awake, although her dreams were uncanny, and full of water and wind.

She was very stiff in the morning, and cold, and for the first hour or two she walked on with the blanket still wrapped round her shoulders. But she warmed up at last, and began to step out more freely; and it was before noon that she turned off the track that ambled round the inner edge of the Cloudyheads and struck upward towards the Eagle, according to the little trader's sign scratched by the way. The slope was even worse than it looked, and she had been climbing steadily for over a day already. Soon her lungs felt as if they might burst, and her thundering heart beat against her ribs as if it would break out. She couldn't imagine how a trader might walk up this path, carrying a heavy pack, nor his pony, carrying even more, toil behind him. She kept her head down, both to watch her footing and to prevent herself from seeing how much too slowly the crest of this hill came towards her; but she did not see any boot- or iron-shod hoof-marks.

She wondered whether her heart pounded so only on account of the steepness of the path, and if some of it were not her fear of the Guardian. She wished she'd thought to ask what the Guardian of Western Mouth was like. But she had had no opportunity; it was not a question she could have asked with her stepfather standing beside her, and by the next morning the trader had gone.

At the point just before most of the side of the mountain sheared away in a deep dangerous cleft, and when you had passed it, you had left the Flock of Crows and now stood upon the Eagle, she stopped, and leant against a tree, and looked back the way she had come. She knew about this place, where one mountain became another, although she had never been here before. It was spectacular, and mkre than a little frightening, even though the path that bit into the mountainside to run over its head was wide enough to be re-assuring in anything but the worst of storms. She thought that the forest she could see at the Eagle's foot was the far side of the forest her village lay against. The village sat in the bottom of a little valley surrounded by foothills; there were other little valleys north and south and east over the foothills, where there were other villages—it was said that at the centre of the island was some truly flat land several leagues across, but Tamia didn't know anyone who had been there—and west, still invisible around a swell of mountain, the route to the great and dangerous sea, which the Guardians protected everyone from.

Why had this Guardian chosen her? She could protect no one. She had never done a very good job of protecting herself.

When her heartbeat stopped banging in her ears as if her heart were trying to escape her body, she pushed herself away from her tree with a sigh, and walked on. The last bit, up the

Eagle's side, was much the steepest. Her tiny bundle of personal belongings weighed on her shoulder like a stone, and the roughness of the folded blanket now chafed her where it touched her damp skin; her head ached as much as her legs did; and sweat ran down her forehead and into her eyes, although the day was not warm.

The twisty uneven path spilled out onto a wide flat meadow so abruptly that she staggered. As she put her hand out to balance herself, a hand grasped hers, and steadied her. "Good day," said the woman who had seized her. "You must be Tamia."

Tamia knew the words were merely courtesy. Only someone invited by a Guardian would dare visit a Guardian; Tamia was now near the top of the Eagle, where Western Mouth lived, and Guardians—except for their apprentices—lived alone, so this person must be the Guardian she had come to meet; and while she had never met this or any other Guardian, this one must have known who she was, to have asked her to come ... her thoughts tailed away in a muddle. There was that inconvenient question again, pressing up to the front of her mind and making her stupid, making her incapable of so much as saying "Good day" in return: Why had the Guardian chosen her?

She had not expected the Guardian to be small and round— a full half-head shorter than Tamia, who was not yet grown to her full height—nor to have short charcoal-and-chalk-white-striped hair that flew wildly round her head like the clouds Tamia knew as mares'-tails, and black eyes bright as a bird's. But she knew at the same time, without any doubt, once she had looked into those eyes, that this woman was Western

Mouth, the Guardian who had called Tamia to apprentice, and that she had been waiting for her.

The woman smiled—a smile just for Tamia, as the trader's nod had been just for her—and Tamia, not accustomed to smiling, smiled back. "Since you want to know so badly, my dear," the Guardian said, "it is for many of those things you are worrying about that I chose you. I want someone whose worth is plain to me, but not to everyone else, so she will not pine for what she has lost; and I want someone who has your cleverness, and deftness, and perception, and who is accustomed to looking around for things to do, and finding them." She said this half-laughing, as if it were a joke of no importance, or as if it were so obvious it did not need repeating, like that cheese was good to eat or the man who raised spotted ponies could also make love-charms. She added more seriously, "Perhaps you would like to sit down and rest, and have a cup of tea and look around you, and we could have the rest of this conversation later."

Tamia barely heard the end of this. Of course she could not sit down and rest, and drink the Guardian's tea, on false pretences, when the Guardian—for some reason—thought she was welcoming her new apprentice, and Tamia knew she was not. Tamia thought, The things I am accustomed to looking for are floor-sweeping and child-minding and animal-tending things. Not Guardian things. And no one has ever called me clever, or deft, or perceptive.

Perhaps the Guardian saw some of this in her face, for after it seemed that Tamia would make no answer, the Guardian went on: "I have been here alone for a long time, and I have forgotten that some of the things I know not everyone knows. Oh, the high, grand Guardiany things—I know you don't know them yet. But you will have to notice the other things for me, because I will not, and tell me to teach them to you. My first command to you is that *you must tell me* when you don't know something. There is no shame to not knowing something—no, not even after the fifth time of asking and being told! There are many things much too hard to learn in one telling, or in five. Even in the beginning. And even the easiest of the easy ones, there are so many easy ones, you will forget some of them sometimes too. You won't be able to help it. But you are to learn to be Guardian after me. You do understand that, do you not?"

Tamia gulped, and nodded.

The Guardian looked away from Tamia for a moment, and Tamia thought sadly, Now it comes. Now she will tell me the thing that I know I cannot do, and I will have to tell her so. But the Guardian only said: "And—are you willing?" The woman seemed suddenly smaller, and less round, and her eyes were not so bright, and her hair fell against her skull, like ordinary hair. "I will not keep you against your will. If you would prefer to return to your village, you may go—and with my thanks for making this long walk to speak to me yourself, instead of sending your answer with the trader. I might have come to you, but I have never liked mountain-climbing, and I'm getting old for it besides; and I did want to see you face-to-face—even if your decision went against me."

Tamia blinked, and listened to the woman's words again in her head, cautiously, and realised she meant them, meant just what she had said. "Oh, no! No, I do not want to go back." She did not mean to add, "They are glad to be rid of me! Especially since I have been called to the Guardian, which is a great thing for them to be able to say," but she did, because there seemed to be no way not to tell this woman the whole truth.

The woman was looking at her thoughtfully, the faintest line of a frown between her eyes. "I could send you to another village—I could send you with enough of a dowry, a dowry from a Guardian, that you would be able to marry comfortably."

Involuntarily Tamia heard her stepfather saying, Magic does not have a mouth to put food into, a back to shelter from storms! She shook her head to clear it of her stepfather, and looked around. There were trees surrounding the meadow, and the final peak of the Eagle rose above them, and the clouds overhead looked like galloping horses, as clouds often did to Tamia, and what Tamia had left yesterday was lost behind the many windings of the narrow path. She thought about what the Guardian was offering her—she stopped herself wondering why she was offering it to her, or she would stick there and never go any further in her thinking. She raised her hand and tapped herself on the breast, feeling the solidity of her own body, the faint hollow echo when she struck high on her breastbone; and she thought, No, I am not dreaming. The sweat of her climb still prickled down her back, and stuck her hair to her forehead.

She thought of being able to marry someone like Bjet, or Grouher; of having a house of her own; she thought about having yelling babies of her own; she thought about washing-day in her mother's home. She thought about having her own smallholding, and a pony to plough it that did not have to be hired out to other farmers for the money it would bring.

It would be a great thing, to come from somewhere else with a dowry a Guardian had given her. It would be a great thing, and perhaps, if she were lucky, it would make her great with it. But she would never belong to the place that took her in. Better, perhaps, to be a Guardian; and for the first time since the trader had brought the news to her stepfather's door, her heart lifted a little, and her mind sat up and looked around and thought, Hmm, to be a Guardian, how interesting. How . . . exciting.

Something odd was happening to her face; her mouth couldn't seem to decide whether to turn up or turn down. The small round woman was smiling at her quite steadily. "It's beginning to sink in, is it, my dear? You bring it all back to me, looking at your bright young face—I was where you were once, you know. I couldn't begin to imagine why the Guardian had chosen me, and I thought it must be some mistake. It isn't, you know. We Guardians make mistakes—are you too young to remember what happened to poor White North and Stone Gate?—but we don't make mistakes about picking apprentices. You might say we can't, any more than you can wake up in the morning without having a yawn and a stretch and going to look for breakfast. Which isn't to say that you can always demand or predict what breakfast is going to be. Will you tell me what you are thinking, my dear? I might be able to help."

Tamia looked round again, and this time she saw the little house with a peaked roof close to the edge of the clearing nearest the Eagle's final summit; a great hollow yew twisted around one corner of the house, cradling a dark invisible haven in its bent limbs; and there were stones of various sizes laid out in a pattern in a wide, shallow pool of water that lay round both it and the house. The water glittered, and something like tiny stars twinkled on the biggest stones. "I am frightened," Tamia said to the Guardian. "But I would rather stay here, with you."

The Guardian's smile turned a little wistful. "It is wise of you to be frightened. Being a Guardian is . . . well, it is hard work, but you are not afraid of hard work. It is things other than hard work too, and you will learn them; and some of them are frightening." She patted Tamia's shoulder. "That's a hard thing to hear right off, isn't it? But it's as well you should know at once. Mind you, many more things are not frightening, and I'm afraid I must tell you that very many of these are no more—and no less—than boring. Appallingly, gruesomely boring. As boring as washing-day, and cleaning out chicken-houses.

"But oh! I am glad you have chosen to stay. It does not happen often that an apprentice refuses the position, but it has happened. Four Doors, who is the oldest of us, remembers it happening once when he was an apprentice. It has taken me a long search—and fourteen years' further waiting— to find one someone who would suit me. I am grateful not to have to begin the search again." She laughed at the blank look on Tamia's face, and took her arm. "Come see the house. I have your room half-ready; I thought you would like to do the other half yourself. And perhaps you will finally let me make you that cup of tea? It is true that I have forgotten much of what it is like to be fourteen, but *I* think you need a rest."

✦   ✦   ✦

Weeks passed in a kind of enchanted blur. Tamia had never worked so hard in her life—but she had never eaten so well, dressed so well, slept so well—been so interested in everything—nor so noticed in her life either. The good food and the clothing, and the knowledge that she could go to bed early any evening she was too tired to stay awake—and in her very own room, shared with no one!—were merely glorious; the being noticed was rather odd, and unsettling. She wasn't used to it; and then, to be noticed by a Guardian ...

She loved the Guardian almost at once; but that also meant she wanted, that much more than if she had only liked or admired her, to please her, and so she went in terrible fear of doing something wrong, of making her unhappy—it was too hard to imagine her angry to fear making her angry. And she couldn't believe that she didn't daily, hourly, prove to the Guardian that she was not as clever or as quick or as hardworking as the Guardian needed her apprentice to be.

"How long, d'you think," the Guardian said matter-of-factly one day at lunch, "before you will stop waiting for me to realise I've made a dreadful mistake and send you away? I told you that first afternoon that this is not the sort of mistake Guardians make, and I have seen nothing since to make me suspect that I've just erred in a new, tradition-confounding way, and will go down in the annals of history as the only—well, the first, anyway—Guardian to have made a mistake in choosing her apprentice."

Tamia kept her eyes on her plate.

"Eh?" said the Guardian. "How long?"

Tamia raised her eyes slowly, but kept her face tipped down. She knew that tone of voice; it meant the Guardian

wasn't just talking to make conversation. She was really waiting for an answer. Tamia didn't have an answer. "I don't
know," she said, very quietly, to her plate.

"Well, I would like you to find out, and give me a date.
Because it is very tedious to me, and I can't imagine it is giving you much pleasure either. Try assuming that you belong
here—just as an exercise, if you like. Like making rainbows or
slowing down every thousandth rain-drop or turning clouds
into horse-shapes is an exercise."

Tamia grinned involuntarily at this last reference to her
new favourite game. She glanced over at the water-garden
that lay around the house and the old yew. It was a beautiful
bright day, and warm in the little pocket of valley where the
Guardian's house stood, although there were mare's-tail wisps
blowing overhead, and the tree-tops were singing in the wind.
The Guardian and her apprentice were having their lunch
outdoors. Ordinary flat grey stepping-stones led through the
water from the foot of the house-stairs, and next to the yew
tree stood a tiny table and two chairs. Making rainbows and
tweaking rain-drops and doing things with clouds began
with rearranging the stones in the water-garden, in their shining bed of gold grains, fine as sand, and strangely shaped gold
pebbles.

Tamia stood up slowly, and walked to the edge of the pool.
There were a lot of stones she still did not know the uses of,
but she was beginning to develop a feel for the ones that had
uses; it wasn't quite a hum, like a noise you heard in your
ears, and it wasn't quite a touch or vibration you felt against
your hand when you held it near them, but it was a little like
both together. She walked slowly round the edge of the

water-garden, looking at various stones, and the way the tiny irregular fragments of their bed caught the shadows and turned them golden. Near the corner of the house she came to an area where there was no pressure at all against her ears or her skin or her thought from any of the stones. She knelt down and, after a moment of holding her open hands above the surface of the water, picked up two. The water was cool, as it always was, although the sun had been on the water-garden most of the morning. She held the two stones quietly for a moment. These would do. No, better than that. These were good ones. They gleamed with atoms of gold too small to see; only their twinkle gave them away.

She came back round the corner of the house, and knelt down near the little table where lunch was laid, in a curve of the pond-edge that allowed them their island. She ran her fingertips along the pebbly edge, drew them into the water; then she made a tiny hollow in the pond-bottom—which was no deeper than the length of her fingers—and felt gold flakes swirling up and adhering to her skin; and then she placed one of her stones in it, wriggling it round till she felt it, intangibly heard it, go *mmph*, like a well-fitted horse-collar settling against the shoulders it was made for. There was a tiny burst of light, and the twinkles of gold on her fingers and on the stone she had chosen disappeared.

Then she did the same to her other stone, and sat back on her heels, and watched as the air and the water around the two stones changed, and she felt the change float and expand, almost like scent, and wreath itself around her, almost like smoke. This was the first magic she'd ever done without the Guardian telling her how. "I—I've tried—I've done—" she said in a voice rather higher than her usual one. She swallowed. "I'm ready now. I will—I will now stop waiting for you to send me home."

"Thank you," said the Guardian, and she moved off her chair, and knelt by Tamia, and put her hands just above the two stones, as if feeling heat rising off them.

Tamia had been with the Guardian nearly a year when the Guardian said one morning, "It's time you had a look at the sea. The way I want to go, it's a long walk, we'll take lunch—and perhaps tea." She tied up food in two bundles, and they set out, towards the Eagle's peak behind their small meadow.

They often went for long prowling walks along the shoulders of the mountains, following deer trails when there were deer trails, and even rabbit trails when there were those; the problem with rabbit trails was that they were made by and for creatures no more than a foot tall. On some of their walks there was a good deal of scrambling. But the Guardian showed Tamia what plants had leaves or berries or roots that were good to eat—or at least nourishing; or possessed healing properties. And they always looked out for stones that might fit in the water-garden, though they had to wait for the traders to bring them new supplies of the gold that their magic used. Tamia now knew the name of the trader with the red feather in his cap—Traetu; and his pony, Wheatear, for the long curly hair-whorl on his neck, like a stalk of wheat bent by the wind.

Tamia talked to the traders—and their ponies; she also greeted and was friendly with the deer, and the rabbits, and the foxes, and the hrungus, and the birds that visited their meadow or that they met on their walks; and the Guardian said to her thoughtfully, "If you were not so suited to our work, I would wonder if I had called you to the wrong craft; for the wild creatures love you, and no Guardian in all the long list of our Guardianship has ever had a familiar animal."

Tamia shook her head. "It is only that my best friend—before you, dear Guardian—was a pony."

But they had never climbed the peak of the Eagle. Tamia, like many inlanders, had never seen the ocean; and she had been too busy and too happy in the last year to think about it, although in the back of her mind she was aware that what she was here for was to learn to protect her land from the ocean, to become a member of the Guardians, who built and patrolled the boundary that kept the land safe from the water. She had no very good picture of what the ocean might be like; she knew that fishermen travelled upon it in boats, like the inlanders sometimes travelled on their ponds and streams and lakes; but when she thought about it at all, she thought of it as a kind of nightmare thing, perhaps a little like a sky full of storm-clouds.

When, in the early afternoon, they finally stood on the top of the Eagle and looked around them, she was amazed. This great, dazzling, every-colour-and-no-colour expanse was like nothing she had ever imagined, let alone seen; and she thought of the cousin of her mother's who had married a fisherman, who described the sea with a shrug as "A lot of water you can't drink," and she could not understand how anyone could think this way. But then, she had probably never stood on the Eagle's head with the wind in her face—and the Guardian she was apprenticed to standing at her side. The salt smell of it was very strong. She knew the smell from her village; sometimes on wet, foggy mornings when the wind was coming steadily from the west, a faint tang of it was just noticeable as the fog was pushed farther inland to shred itself on tree-tops. It had never seemed to her any more interesting than any other smell. But where they stood, with the wind bucketing around them, this tallest peak of the Eagle seemed to lean out towards the shore while the Cloudyheads on either side seemed to draw back in alarm, the water was on nearly three sides of them and the land seemed little more than a memory behind them. Here the ocean smell was wild and tantalising and full of mysteries.

This is the best, Tamia thought. There is nothing better than this. Not even doing my first magic by myself—not even meeting Southern Eye and Four Doors when they came to see my Guardian, or talking to the traders when they come here, not even Traetu, who told me my Guardian wanted me and will always be my favourite—this is almost as good as being my Guardian's friend. She glanced at her Guardian, who looked away from the sea long enough to meet her apprentice's eyes, and Tamia was sure, as she had been sure many times before, that the Guardian knew exactly what she was thinking.

After a little while, the Guardian said thoughtfully, "This island is a strange place; I believe there is no other place like it in all the wide world, though there must be other places just as strange. It is our strangeness to be a threshold between land and water; and the boundary between us is striven for, and fought over, and it shifts sometimes this way, and sometimes that. Perhaps there are Guardians on the other side of the boundary, as we are the Guardians of this; perhaps it is only on account of our angle of vision that it seems to us that the forces of water desire to overwhelm us. Perhaps whatever lives in the deep of the water does not understand that if it succeeded in bringing the dry lands under its sway, it would kill a great many people and plants and animals who love their lives, for I assume plants and animals love their lives too; perhaps it does understand, and does not care, for we are mere land-dwellers. I do not know. But I do know that it is over this one island that the war is fought, and if once we yielded, then all those lands behind us—farther from the boundary we protect—would immediately come under threat; and they have no Guardians. We are the Guardians, and here we hold the line."

Tamia listened to her Guardian, because she always did; but she was still in thrall to the great beauty of the ocean, and did not understand. It was not until half way through her second year as the Guardian's apprentice that she saw her first great storm.

There were dangerous storms every winter, storms where people and animals might be lost, if they were unlucky. But she had only seen one or two storms as great as this one when she lived in the valley, storms that uprooted trees and drowned sheep in the fields, that levelled houses, and might occasionally do the same to whole villages. "Island weather," everyone called it, and the old people nodded sardonically after it was all over and the losses were never as great as first they appeared, and said to people like Tamia's stepfather, "Are you so sure the Guardians do not earn their tokens?"

But she could not have guessed how much wilder and

more fearful such a storm would be near the crest of the Eagle, and, as a Guardian's apprentice, what it would be like to be one of the people trying to help throw back the deluge that threatened to drown their land like a fishing-boat in a sudden squall. She knew about rain and wind, about the prying fingers of storm under the eaves, the whiplash of sleet and the terrifying lift of a strong wind, if you were so unfortunate as to be caught outdoors in it; she did not know, when she lived in the valley, about the high mad voices in it, and the faces that almost shaped themselves from the roiling mists, nor the clinging of wetness that looked like rain, and first ran down your body like rain, but then seemed to wrap itself about you like a bolt of heavy cloth, and pull you under.

She did not know that the stones in their own water-garden would hide in the cloud- and fog-shadows scudding across on the pool's surface, would elude them by the rain in their eyes and the pounding of the wind against their bodies, by the sudden inexplicable water-spouts in the garden itself, which created deep scoured trenches in the sandy floor of the pool, where the stones they had so painstakingly placed then rolled and tumbled. She did not know that the flakes of gold that lay in the sand or floated in the water would become sharp as flints, and cut at her, that the golden pebbles would become dazzling, dizzying, vertiginous, that the rainbows that often hung round the water-garden would turn a muddy, treacherous brown, and twist around her, hampering her, tangible as vines. Tamia knelt and crawled at her Guardian's side, straining to hear her Guardian's shouted words through the shriek of the wind, knowing without being told that the water was being called to rebel, to rise up in mastery and dominion over the land, and that while the stones in their own garden dodged away from them, shifted in their places and slid into unexpected holes, that the water was winning.

Several hours they waded and crept and floundered through the water-garden, the gritty stones slipping through Tamia's cold fingers, her forearms and forehead sore from sand rubbing against skin when she tried, uselessly, again and again, to wipe the wet from her eyes, while she expected at any moment to discover that *she* had become the tiny gap in the wall through which the conquering water would at first seep, and then trickle, and then blast and roar.

But storms like these were very rare. And Tamia, who had nightmares for months after this one, was glad of it; because for the first time since she had made her first magic in the water-garden, she wondered again if perhaps her Guardian had made a mistake about her after all, that she was not strong enough to be a Guardian. But there were no more savage storms, and Tamia's other lessons went well, for she was not, as her Guardian had said on their first meeting, afraid of hard work.

The second year passed more quickly than the first, and the third quicker yet. She saw Southern Gate again, and Four Doors several times—"Four Doors is always a wanderer, whoever it is; the Four Doors when I was an apprentice was just the same, and my Guardian told me that the two she could remember before that one were wanderers too"—and White North once took Tamia away for three days, on one of those Guardians' walks through the villages of more ordinary folk. "I should take you myself," said Tamia's Guardian, "but I told you I'd grown too old for mountain-climbing. White North will look after you. You should see the people you guard occasionally, and remind yourself of what their lives are like, especially when you're still young and unused to this work; it makes what we do here more real." Tamia hadn't liked being away from her Guardian—and had not enjoyed the looks on the faces of the villagers they met—but White North was a pleasant travelling companion, and her Guardian was right, the experience had made her feel for the water-garden much keener. She had gone walking once more, this time with Four Doors, early in her fourth year as apprentice.

But some time during that fourth year Tamia began to notice, although she fought against noticing, that her Guardian was slowing down. She went to bed earlier in the evenings, and while she rose as early as she had when Tamia first came, it seemed to take her longer to wake up, and Tamia took over more of the ordinary checks and guards and sightings and alignings of the Guardian's tasks, and she bid the old yew good-day and good-evening, and when she went for walks—or rather, when she was sent on them, for she would not voluntarily leave her Guardian alone—she went by herself. But when the Guardian spoke, she was the same Guardian she had always been, and so Tamia tried to ignore the rest.

Soon after the beginning of Tamia's fifth year as apprentice, her Guardian fell ill.

Tamia found her, one afternoon, returning from gathering mushrooms on the gentle slopes of the Dove, slumped by the water-garden. She had fallen into the edge of the pond, and the first, horrifying thing Tamia noticed was that she had fallen with her cheek propped against one of the stones

Tamia had placed during the first magic she had ever done by herself; and because of this, her Guardian's nose and mouth had been held just clear of the surface of the water.

Tamia did not allow herself to think about this for long. Her Guardian's face was a strange, chalky-grey colour, her breath rasped, and her body lay in a twisted huddle. Furthermore, the wind down the mountain was cold today, and her left side lay in the pond. Tamia had dropped her basket halfway across the meadow, and had run to her Guardian; but even when she raised her head and shoulders onto her own lap, she could not waken her; and the sound of her breathing was dreadful.

Tamia did not remember how she got her up the house-steps and indoors, but she managed it somehow. She pulled her Guardian's wet clothes off, and towelled her dry, and wrapped her in her warmest dressing-gown, trying to be as gentle as possible with the heavy inert weight of her beloved mentor, trying to fight against the battering strength of her own fear. She noticed that the left side of her Guardian's body was chilly and stiffer than her right, but she thought this was only on account of her having lain in the water. She lit a great fire in the hearth, and made up a bed for her Guardian near it, and then sat by her side, holding her hand, trying to make her own mind less blank, less frozen with dread and grief, more able to think what she must do.

At last, near dawn, it seemed to Tamia that her Guardian's sleep shifted a little, and became more like normal sleep. She put an arm round her shoulders and raised her up, and tried to make her drink a little water; and her Guardian seemed to half-rouse, and her lips closed on the rim of the cup. When

Tamia held it up higher, the liquid trickled out of the left corner of her Guardian's mouth; but Tamia saw her Guardian's
throat move in a swallow, and for the first time since Tamia
had found her lying in the pool, her own mind came out from
under the deep shadow where it had lain.

There were ways for the Guardians to send messages
among themselves, but Tamia did not yet know them, for messages were tricky, and ill-handled could disturb or confuse the
intricate network of protection which was the Guardians'
chief task. No trader was due to visit them for weeks, and in
her Guardian's present condition, Tamia could not leave her
long enough to look for help. The first day passed while Tamia
continued to sit at her Guardian's bedside, and fed her water
and broth when she could, and cleaned her up when her
body failed her in other ways, and spoke softly to her so that
her mind, if it had been cast adrift by whatever had seized
her body, might hear her voice and find its way home.

Another day passed, and another. Tamia had to leave her
Guardian's bedside to brew more broth, to dip up more water
from the well; even to sleep, and eat, and wash herself, and to
do the laundry, that the Guardian might always have clean
sheets to lie on. But Tamia was not without hope, for while
the Guardian had still not opened her eyes and recognised
her, sometimes her right hand moved towards the cup that
Tamia was holding, and sometimes, while she drank, she was
almost sitting on her own.

On the fourth morning, Tamia went outside, down the
house-steps to the water-garden, and paused there, for the
first time since she had found her Guardian stretched out at
its edge. The last few days she had crossed the stepping-stones

quickly, intent on some errand. The water-garden had had to look after itself in the much greater need to look after her Guardian; Tamia had barely remembered to wish the yew tree good-day and good-evening. But the water-garden could not look after itself; and besides, Tamia had thought of something she might try—a message she might be able to send.

This was much harder than that first solitary magic she had done—lifetimes ago, it seemed now. But that had not been truly solitary, any more than any of the other magics she had done since had been, because her Guardian had been there. Even if she was indoors or on the other side of the meadow and could not see what Tamia was doing, she was always there if Tamia needed help. And what Tamia was doing now was something new, something she had not been trained to do.

She walked three times round the house before she felt the presence of any stones that might do for her purpose. When she knelt beside them, their presence seemed to waver, like the reflection of a disturbed pool; she had to wait till everything—including her anxious breath—had calmed. Yes, these would do. She chose one, two, three—oh dear—four, five, six and seven—this was too many. She sat with her stones in her lap and looked at them; the gold flecks blinked at her hopefully. Well, it was the best she could do. A real Guardian could do new things with her water-garden, things she hadn't been trained for, because she felt its water like a part of the tidal rhythm in her own body, the individual stones as thoughts she had thought or might one day think. But Tamia was only an apprentice. An apprentice's standard service to a Guardian was twenty years—and Four Doors, who liked to talk, had told Tamia stories of apprenticeships that had been thirty or fifty years. Tamia had had only five years. She would have to create a rough, clumsy magic because she could not create a subtle one.

The golden flash, when it came, was blinding. When her vision cleared, her seven stones lay in a sandy-grey bed, and the golden glitter even on the far side of the water-garden seemed muted. She swallowed with a suddenly dry mouth; but it was done, and she had done it.

She was so exhausted, she could barely drag herself up the house-steps again, and into the front room where her Guardian lay. There she dropped down beside her, clasping her Guardian's right hand, her head on the edge of the mattress, and fell asleep.

It was her first deep sleep in days, and she was woken out of it by a sense of uneasiness. It seemed to her that she heard her name being called, very softly, but over and over again, and that she should recognise the voice that spoke it, but she did not; and that there was something wrong with her name as it was spoken. . . .

She woke up, and found that her Guardian was holding her hand firmly enough to be giving her tiny squeezes as she repeated her name—"Tamia, Tamia"—but why did it sound so strange? Tamia said, or half-groaned, "Oh, I am so glad you are awake!" and bent towards her and kissed her, and then as she turned away from her to look for the tinder-box and kindle the lamp, she saw the rain streaming in through the open shutters on the far side of the Guardian's bed.

She lit the lamp first, and saw the pools of water the rain had left, and had a nasty, sick feeling in her stomach that the pools were too regularly shaped, and looked rather too much like the shape her seven stones made in the water-garden. She closed the shutters and then flung all the rags she could find in the pools of rain-water, just to disturb their shape, till she had time to go round them one by one and mop them up properly. She blew on the red heart of the drowsy fire, and stirred it, and fed the tiny flame that wavered into being (rain stung her face like embers, hissing down the chimney); and then she went to the water-ewer, and was glad to find that it was still half-full, because it was now quite dark out, and drawing water in darkness and heavy rain would have been unpleasant.

She brought the lamp nearer the bed, so she could see her Guardian's face; and reassured herself with the warmth of her hand that the Guardian had taken no chill from Tamia having let the fire almost go out. "Guardian, you're better!"— and a little joy and relief slipped out in her words; but she knew there was still something badly wrong. "Guardian—"

"Tamia," her Guardian said again, and now, in the lamp-light, Tamia saw that her mouth was not working the way it should, and that one whole side of her face looked slack and limp. The Guardian saw the shock register in Tamia's face, and patted her hand with her own good hand; for the weakness extended all down one side of her body. Trying to speak very carefully, she said, "I know—a little—about what has happened. Something that happens sometimes to old people."

But Tamia put her hand over her mouth and said, "Don't talk. You must eat something, now that you're awake. You must get stronger. And then—then we'll know better what to do." She turned away before she could read the expression on her Guardian's face, and when she sat down again with some hastily reheated porridge, her Guardian allowed herself to be fed like a little child, and Tamia learned quickly to slip the spoon in the side of her mouth where it wouldn't all help-lessly dribble out again.

The rain continued over the next several days. It was early autumn, when the change of weather often comes quickly and strongly, and when storms are common. The winds that caromed around their little meadow seemed wilder and more directionless than usual, even for autumn; but Tamia delib-erately did not think about this. She had mopped up the rain-water pools, and while she opened the shutters as often as she could for daylight, however grey, and fresh air, however damp, she kept sentry-watch against the rain spotting the floor. Her Guardian drifted in and out of sleep, but Tamia hoped it was only sleep now. She ate obediently, and tried to help when Tamia washed and turned her, so she would not grow sore from lying in the same position too long; and she regained control over her body functions. And she allowed—because she was given no choice—her apprentice to rub the dead side of her body, and to move that leg and foot, and bend the arm, and curl and uncurl the fingers.

Every time Tamia went near that side of the house, indoors or out, she felt what she had done to the water-garden pulling at her.

As the days passed, the rain fell harder and the wind blew stronger, till Tamia could rarely open the shutters at all, and during the days as well as the nights the world seemed very dark. Even with the shutters closed the house rattled and creaked, and the wind and rain battered the walls like fists, and little draughts crept in and played with the lamplight.

The cloud-cover hung low and thick and menacing over their meadow, and Tamia only went outdoors long enough to draw water from the well, and to greet the yew tree, and ran back in again. She began to wonder if she might not be able to collect enough water by setting bowls and basins on the stepping-stones, and then she would not have to linger so long beneath this bleak and accusing sky. When she had lived in the valley she had hated stormy weather, when she could not go outdoors; but now the pressure of the gloomy hostile weather seemed the proper backdrop to her fears. The water-garden throbbed like a bruise.

"Something wrong—this weather," said her Guardian; Tamia shrugged. She was more interested in gently flexing her Guardian's ankle. "Water-garden?"

Tamia frowned a little at the foot she was holding. The seven stones meant that the rest of the garden felt so different, she had not dared touch anything else; but she was determined that her Guardian should know nothing that might trouble her, if it could be done by Tamia not telling her about it. She had been sure that her seven stones would be noticed by some other Guardian. Well; apparently she had guessed wrong. It had been almost a fortnight. Perhaps she should remove them; the bruise feeling was growing stronger, and every time she walked across the stepping-stones now, she got a headache as well.

Perhaps the weather was so savage outside their meadow that no one could come to them. Tamia's eyes strayed to the larder. They were already running low on lamp oil but they had some weeks' food left; and then a trader must come. . . .

The last thing she expected was the apparition that burst

through the door late that night, in the middle of the worst storm yet. It was a tall male apparition, wringing wet, and it found Tamia with its eyes and roared at her.

She had been sitting, as she sat every evening, by her Guardian's bed, holding her hand. It was nearly time for her to go to her own bed, dragged out from her own little room to the other side of the hearth, so that she could hear her Guardian easily in the night. The bellow of the storm tonight was curiously soporific; and she had been thinking about nothing in particular for some time when the door was flung open, and a wave of water hurled the tall figure in upon them. The water, as it fell on the floor, arranged itself into seven small pools like seven stones in a water-garden.

"What have you done, girl, are you *trying* to drown the world?"

Tamia sat where she was, open-mouthed in shock; barely she felt her Guardian stir herself for a great effort, and sit up, leaning on her good arm. The force of the man's gaze held Tamia motionless; she felt it burning through her, and she thought, When it reaches my heart, I will die.

But her Guardian said, "Water Gate! You let my apprentice go, or I will fry your entrails for my supper!" It was the longest sentence she had spoken since she had fallen ill.

Tamia was released so suddenly, she fell off her low stool and onto the floor. Dimly she heard the conversation over her head, her Guardian's exhausted voice, speaking in broken phrases now, and the slurring, which Tamia had grown accustomed to, so strong, she could hardly make out the words; and the man her Guardian had called Water Gate, his voice dropping down in sorrow and grief as he understood what had happened. And then they talked of other things, but Tamia did not listen, drifting in and out of some cold grey place where the wind howled.

At last Tamia felt Water Gate's hard strong hands, under her arms, pulling her gently but irresistably upright. He did not put her on her backless stool, but leant her against the edge of the Guardian's mattress; and he brought her a cup of her own broth, and wrapped her hands round it, and held them so while she drank. And then he said to her: "I beg your pardon most humbly, and I am ashamed, as Western Mouth has told me clearly I should be. It is true that I should have known that what Western Mouth's apprentice has done was through desperate need.

"But you see, apprentice of Western Mouth, you have torn a hole in the close-woven fabric that divides the earth of our world from the water of the next; and through that rent the water is pouring through. And you, apprentice of Western Mouth, are the only person who can stitch it up again—if it can be stitched."

Her Guardian, looking grey and weak, said, "I am sorry, my dear, but what he says is true. He would tell me that I chose an apprentice too late; I would say to him that you were born too late, and what has happened has happened."

She paused, but Tamia was still too shaken by Water Gate's greeting to stir or speak. Rest, rest, she wanted to say to her Guardian, I know it cannot be good for you to talk so much. But she looked at her Guardian, and saw Water Gate move to sit next to her, one arm round her shoulders, holding her good hand in his other hand, and realised that he was giving her his strength somehow; and a little, feeble hope stirred in her, and she thought: I will not care that I have drowned the world, if he will help my Guardian.

"Listen, my dear," whispered her Guardian. "It is almost dawn. There will be a lull soon—Water Gate has arranged that. And when there is, you will take the bowl on the top shelf, the one at the back behind all the other bowls, and fill it with water from the well; and you will bring it to me here. Fill it as full as you can carry it; and then do not spill it. Not a drop." And then Water Gate let her lie down, but still he sat beside her, where Tamia had sat for over a fortnight, and looked into her face, and held her hand. Tamia told herself that he was doing for her what she could not do, but still a lonely and hurt little voice inside her said, He is a Guardian, a real Guardian, not a five-years' apprentice, why cannot he do it, and leave me with my Guardian? It is not he who should sit there. But her Guardian had given the order, and so she did not say it aloud.

She heard the storm die away, and she opened one shutter cautiously and saw dawn struggling to penetrate the clouds. She took down the bowl—she had never seen this bowl be-fore, though she thought she knew every bowl on the shelf, for the Guardians often used bowls in their work—this one tingled against her skin like the stones in the water-garden. She went outdoors to the well. The ground of their meadow was an ocean of mud; tufts of broken grass crowned the crests of the waves. She tried to pick her way carefully, but there was nowhere to put her feet that was any better than any other. She was muddy to mid-shin by the time she returned to the house, and she was so anxious not to spill a drop that she did not dare kick off her shoes before she went indoors.

"The storm will not return today," said Water Gate. "Go outdoors, and remove your seven stones. Take them out of the
water-garden entirely, take them away. And then spend time
setting the water-garden to rights; it will tell you how, for
Western Mouth has told me you are a good pupil. I will
finish the work for you later—if this world is still above
water—but for now Western Mouth and I have other work."

Tamia listened to him, expressionless and unblinking; and
then she looked at her Guardian for confirmation before she
did his bidding. And she looked back at him, after she had
looked at her Guardian, to be sure that he understood that she
did what he said only because her Guardian told her to.

Tamia gathered the seven stones from the water-garden,
and while she had put them in uncertainly, she picked them
up now knowing that they had done what she asked, and
that there was no fault in them, only in her not knowing how
and what to do. She fondled them gently, as she had used to
stroke Columbine, telling them thank-you, telling them that
they were her friends. She thought about Water Gate telling
her to take them away; and she piled six of them together in
a little heap in the heart of the old yew. The seventh, which
was slightly kidney-shaped while the others were round, she
slipped into her pocket.

She spent the rest of the morning doing what she could
with the water-garden. She found that she could do more
than she had expected, for now suddenly she began to see the
ribbons of energy that ran between the stones. Like ribbons,
they were different colours and different sizes, and some of
them were taut and some were slack and some were tangled,
and it was her work to make them all smooth, and woven

equally together. When she put her fingers in the water, the shining flecks of gold swam to her till her hands gleamed like candle-flames; and yet, as she worked, the golden flashes were small and gentle, and seemed to ride briefly on the surface of the water like sweet oil before they dissolved and disappeared. Tamia almost thought they had a faint tranquil smell, like salve on a bruise, and in some wonder she understood that the ache of the bruise-feeling she had had since she placed her message-stones was the source of her new understanding, and she began to think that she would mind if she had drowned the world, even if Water Gate could save her Guardian.

She felt noon come, rather than saw it, and Water Gate came outdoors, and set a plate bearing bread and rishtha and dried fish on the edge of the stairs, and went back indoors again. Tamia ate her lunch, and went back to the water-garden.

When twilight came, Water Gate came out of the door of the house again, and called her; and she walked slowly up the stairs, for she was very tired.

The bowl of water now lay on the table in front of the hearth. Tamia's eyes were drawn to it at once, though it looked no different than it had done that morning. But she had little more than a glance at it, because she went at once to her Guardian's bedside, and took her hand, and asked how she was. "I am sure you have worked too hard," said Tamia. "Have you eaten anything? Let me get you some supper."

"Water Gate will make us both supper," said her Guardian, "because we must talk."

Tamia looked over her shoulder in surprise, and saw Water

Gate holding a frying-pan in one hand and a wooden spoon in the other. He laid them down, opened the food-cupboard, and with a meticulous care Tamia had to acknowledge, began to look through their stores. He had a long, lean face and heavy lines down his cheeks and around his mouth, and shaggy black hair. He was not so old as her Guardian. She could see no trace of the wild anger he had almost killed her with the evening before, but what she saw instead was despair, and when he turned briefly and met her eyes, his eyes agreed that what she saw in his face was the truth, though he would have hidden it from her if he could.

"Listen to me," said her Guardian, and Tamia turned back to her. "There is a new sea-magic. A Horse of Water has come ashore, and gallops up and down the countryside, destroying whatever her hoofs touch, and when she shakes her head, the water-drops that fly out of her mane are sharp as arrows, and kill what they strike. White North, Standing Stone, Four Doors, Southern Eye, and Water Gate have all tried to stop her, and they have all failed. We are the last . . ." Her Guardian stopped, and seemed to consider, and sighed. "Water Gate advised me not to tell you, but I cannot think that is right. It is Water Gate who finally discovered how the Water Horse had entered. It was not your seven stones, little one. It was my weakness. Your stones only marked the entryway; and, my dear, it was the best you could have done as well as the worst, or Water Gate might not have come here in time—in time for our last effort, our last chance.

"The other Guardians have tried, and failed, to curb the Water Horse, to dissolve her, or to send her back into the sea from which she came, as she trampled across each of their lands in turn. But she broke White North's water rope, and drank up Standing Stone's pool, and Four Doors' mire did not stop her, nor Southern Eye's maze, nor Water Gate's . . . well, Water Gate did not succeed either, it does not matter how.

"We are all that is left, and I am old and ill, and you are but a five-years' apprentice."

Her Guardian fell silent for so long, Tamia thought she would say no more, and was about to slip away and offer to peel the grads, so she could keep an eye on Water Gate; but then her Guardian's hand gripped hers more strongly, and she said, "Water Gate, in his effort to find out why the Horse had been released upon us, went through your village. Do you remember, on your first day here, when you did not want to tell me that your family would be glad to be rid of you? Water Gate says that your stepfather has taken to telling everyone that it was a tremendous sacrifice to lose you and he only did it because it was what was best for everyone, and that not only is his voice no longer heard raised against the Guardians' token, but your family are the only ones in all the lowlands Water Gate visited who are not terrified by the storms and the Water Horse, because they believe that Western Mouth's apprentice will save them.

"So perhaps they are right, and us Guardians all wrong. Listen. You will take this bowl of water, and *do not spill a drop*. You will have to walk slowly, for the bowl is brimful, but walk as quickly as you may, for the Water Horse is not far away. You will wait for her at the deep crack of valley where the Eagle meets the Flock of Crows. You will see her come striding towards you. Wait; and wait; and wait again; and wait still longer. Wait till she is upon you, till you see her shining blue eyes and feel her cold watery breath. When—and not till then—she would crush you with her next step, then throw the bowl of water over her.

"And—we will either have been successful, or not."

Her Guardian closed her eyes, and again Tamia turned to creep away, but her Guardian said, "You want to be there a little after dawn. It will be a clear night, and the horizon will grow light enough for you to walk by well before dawn—if you are careful, and you know the way—tonight you must eat the supper Water Gate prepares for us, and then you must sleep." Her Guardian's eyes opened. "That, at least, I can still give you. I can give you a good night's sleep."

Tamia said, "I would rather spend the night here, watching, by your bed." She did not say "this last night" but she did not have to; if the bowl of water did not work, they would not see each other again. Tamia was still too young and healthy for her own death to seem real to her; but she could just imagine never seeing her Guardian again, and that seemed more terrible than death.

"No," said her Guardian, simultaneously with Water Gate, stepping silently up behind them, carrying plates in one hand and a bowl of steaming food in the other, saying also, "No." Tamia turned and glared at him, and his mouth turned in the faintest, ironic smile, as he accepted that his "No" was nothing to her.

But she obeyed her Guardian. Dutifully she ate Water Gate's excellent stew, and dutifully she lay down; and her Guardian was as good as her word—as she had always been— and sent her apprentice to sleep.

Tamia did not know what woke her, but she woke suddenly and completely. She raised herself on one elbow, and looked through the crack in the shutters; she could just see the outline of the trees and the Eagle against the sky. "It is time to go," said her Guardian, calmly, from the darkness.

Tamia dressed quickly, and found a chunk of bread by feel for her breakfast. By then the light had increased enough, and her eyes had adjusted enough, that she had no difficulty seeing the stone bowl on the table, and the gleam of the water it contained. She stooped over her Guardian, and kissed her, and said, only a little breathlessly, "I will be back in time for tea," and then she opened the door and turned back to pick up the bowl.

She had forgotten about Water Gate. He was standing at the top of the house-steps, looking out on the churned mud of the meadow. He turned to look at her. There was a tiny silence, and he said, "Good morning."

She ducked her head in acknowledgement, and then slipped past him and down the steps. As she set her foot on the first stepping-stone to cross the water-garden, she heard him say softly, "Courage and good fortune to you."

The need to walk so carefully that the water in the bowl never quivered, that no drop was ever at risk of sliding over the edge and being lost, was a useful focus for Tamia's thoughts. She could not afford to think about how frightened she was, because it might make her feet clumsy or her hands shake; and so she did not think about it. She had her mouth a little open, so she could catch her breath more quickly, for the way was steep, but she was careful even so not to breathe too hard, for her own breath might disturb the surface of the water she carried.

It was still some minutes before dawn when she arrived at the deep narrow ravine between the Eagle and the Flock of Crows. She looked down the stony chasm and thought of a great Water Horse so vast and powerful that she could run up that slope; and then she had to remind herself again that she could not let her hands tremble. She put the bowl down, and then sat down beside it, and rested her head in her hands. She wished she had thought to bring herself something more to eat; and then she realised she was too tensely expectant to be hungry.

And so she sat, and waited for dawn, but as she waited, she began to be aware of a curious noise, a little behind and below her. It was a low, rhythmic noise, with a kind of gasp or grunt in it. At first she had thought it was the pre-dawn breeze, moving suspiciously up and down the crags and disliking what it found, but it was too regular for that; nor was it like any birdsong she had ever heard, not even the korac, whose family groups all talking together sounded like tiny axes chipping rock. At the same time it reminded her of something— some memory of the time before she had lived with her Guardian. Just to give herself something to do for the last few appalling moments before dawn and doom, she went to investigate.

The moment before she saw the mare, she knew what she was hearing. She was accustomed to watching over, and occasionally helping, her stepfather's sheep birth, though only once had she watched a foal being born, at a farm next to one of the smallholdings that hired Columbine. That mare had made this same noise.

But it wasn't the same noise. The farm birth had gone just

as it was supposed to, and the foal had been born in one long slippery rush after the mare had lain and shoved and strained and grunted for not more than half an hour. Tamia knew, without ever having seen or heard it before, that this mare had been trying to push her foal out into the world for a long, long time, and was very near the end of her strength.

The mare's eye was glazed, and her neck and sides were black with matted dirt and sweat; but even Tamia's untutored gaze took in that she was a valuable animal who had been well cared for. "My poor lovely," murmured Tamia, kneeling beside her head, "why are you here, in the wild, instead of at home being tended to? Did the Water Horse break your fence, your wall, and drive you away, up into the mountains where you could not find your way home?" It was unlikely there was anything Tamia could do, now, and alone, but seeing the painful, waning struggle of this gallant animal troubled Tamia deeply, even though the end of the world would come striding up the steep crag in another moment. Tamia forgot all that, and searched in her memory of lamb midwifery.

She moved round behind the labouring mare. She could see one little hoof sticking out of the mare's vagina; it appeared and disappeared in rhythm to the mare's weakening thrusts. Tamia knew what she would have done with a ewe, although she had never had to do it without someone else nearby who knew much more than she did; and she wouldn't even know that much, except that sheep tend all to lamb at once, and sometimes the only extra pair of hands belongs to a little girl.

There was not even any water to wash in first. She knelt down, and slowly began to thrust her arm and hand up inside the mare's body, feeling along the slender foreleg of the foal, till she found the second, bent leg, the knee shoved implacably against the wall of the mare's birth canal. Slowly she shoved the foal back towards the womb again—the mare tried to resist her, but she was too weak. Slowly, slowly, *slowly*, her arm very nearly not long enough, trying to guess at what she could only erratically and incompletely feel, she rearranged the foal's legs, felt that its little head was still pointed in the right direction, and began to drag it towards air and daylight and life. The mare's contractions were only sporadic now; Tamia could no longer hear her groan through the noise of her own rasping breath.

Tamia was covered in blood and slime and mud; it was hard to keep a grip on the foal's forelegs, and her knees and her other hand kept losing their purchase on the muddy ground; there was a stinging cut on the palm of her other hand where she had slipped on a sharp rock. Her neck and shoulder and back were on fire with cramp. She had stopped thinking about what she was doing, merely automatically pulling harder when the mare's muscles helped her, pulling and pulling, awkwardly jammed against the mare's hip, her other hand at first scrabbling for a better hold on the unsympathetic ground, and then, as the foal's two forelegs emerged together, pulling with the hand that had been inside the mare. She had first knelt down trying to be aware of where the mare's potentially lethal hind legs were; she remembered nothing now but pull—pull—pull.

The foal was out. She looked at it numbly, briefly unable to recall that this was what she had been fighting for. The second sac had broken some time before; now she wiped its nose and mouth free of mucus, but it lay unmoving. I knew—I knew—

said Tamia to herself, but she took her skirt off, for lack of anything better, and began to rub the foal dry. She knelt over it, and rubbed it as if it were a bit of dirty laundry on a washboard; only to dirty laundry she had never whispered, "Breathe. Breathe. *Breathe.*"

The foal gave a little gasp and choke, and then a long shudder. Its head came up off the ground, and then fell back with a thud, as if dropped. Tamia held her own breath; it could still have been too exhausted—or too injured—by its long struggle for what it needed to do next; and she was at the end of her own dubious expertise. It thrashed a bit with its legs, and stopped. And then suddenly, with a surprising, almost violent energy, it half-rolled up on its side, looking wildly around, as if it couldn't imagine what had happened to it. Shakily it extended a foreleg; had a quick heave and flounder, and fell down. It lay gasping; and then rolled up again, and began to rearrange its forelegs. Tamia took a long breath . . . and thought to look at the mare.

The mare was still breathing, but only just. Her dim eye looked blind when Tamia bent over her; the spume around her lips and tongue had dried and was beginning to crack. Tamia cautiously stroked her rough neck; there was no quiver of skin, no flick of ear, no roll of eye—nothing. "Oh, no, not you!" said Tamia. "You've had a fine foal! You must wake up now and see him. You must lick him all over, so that you know you belong to each other, and then show him how to nurse. Oh, mare, don't leave him!"

The mare's breathing was so shallow, Tamia had to put a hand to her nostrils to feel it. She looked around distractedly; she already knew there was no water nearby.

No water. None except . . . *Do not spill a drop of the water. . . .*

She ran back to her bowl, scooped a few drops on her fingertips, and threw them into the mare's face. She just saw the light come on again in the mare's eyes, saw her nostrils flare, saw her raise her head and look round for her foal. . . .

And then the dawn came up over the rim of the mountains, and as the first rays of the sun struck her face, Tamia heard the great challenging bell of the Water Horse's neigh, and felt the earth shake underfoot with her hoofs. Tamia stood at the head of the narrow cleft in the mountains, with the tears streaming down her face, because she had thrown away her world's last chance of survival against the sea on account of her inability to let one ordinary mortal mare die, who would probably now die under the Water Horse's trampling hoofs, even as Tamia herself was going to die.

She waited, holding her bowl. The absence of the few drops she had wasted on the mare was not even visible; the bowl still looked full to the brim. But then again, perhaps it was not, because Tamia's arms were so tired and strained that she could not quite keep her hands steady, and the surface of the water peaked in many tiny wrinkles which moved and ran in all directions, and yet no drop fell over its edge.

She could see the Water Horse now, see the great, glorious, shining silver cloud of her, for she was very beautiful, even more beautiful than she was terrible. Rocks cracked under her great strides; trees split and fell when she lashed her tail; her hoofs were as big as boulders, her belly as tall as a roof-top, her tail as long as the road to the sea. She moved almost as quickly as thinking; almost Tamia did not have time to raise her bowl as the Water Horse ran up the valley towards her, her tail streaming rainbows behind her. Tamia clutched her bowl to her breast, to hold it level, and she loosed one hand from it, and felt in her pocket for the seventh stone she had placed and then removed from her Guardian's water-garden, the one that was slightly kidney-shaped; one of the stones that had, perhaps, invited the Water Horse into the world. Tamia slipped the small stone into the bowl of water, and the water's surface bulged up to meet perfectly the brim of the bowl.

She saw just a glint of the mad, glaring, beautiful blue eye of the Water Horse, and then she threw her bowl's contents at her.

There was a crash like thunder, and a wind came from nowhere and struck Tamia so hard that she staggered, dropped the bowl into the chasm, and almost fell after it. On hands and knees, she began to crawl away from the edge; and then the rain began, and drenched her in a moment. When she found herself unable to go any farther, pressed up against a shoulder of rock some distance from the cliff-edge, she merely hunkered down where she was, and waited. I thought it would be all over at once, she thought. I didn't realise I would have to be drowned by inches. Never mind. In the roar of the wind and under the burden of her own exhaustion and despair, as she waited, she fell asleep.

She woke to blue skies and birdsong. At first she thought she had already died, and that by some mistake she had been sent to the Place of Joy—for surely people who fail at some great task entrusted to them are sent to live cold below ground forever. But she sat up, and discovered that this hurt so much she hardly could, and thought perhaps this meant she was still alive after all. She used the rock she was next to to help lever herself to her feet. Then she heard the whinny, and looked down at herself, and saw that she was only dressed in her sodden shirt and petticoat. As she stood up, there was a tiny pattering shower of water around her feet. She sneezed.

There was her mare—she didn't mean to think of her as hers, the possessive just slipped into her mind—and a beautiful black colt with a few grey hairs around his eyes and muzzle peeked round his mother's rain-soaked rump at the strange object that had just turned itself from a rock into a something else. But his mother whinnied at it again, and walked towards it, so he decided to come along too, trying to prance, and very nearly falling down for his pains. He was still only a few hours old; all legs with a bony, bulgy little head at one end and a miniature-besom tail at the other, and a few knobbly ribs to bind them all together. The mare came straight up to Tamia, and pushed her face into Tamia's breast; and Tamia laid her forehead against the mare's poll, and cradled her nose in her hands, and burst into tears.

It was only after this that Tamia thought to look into the abyss where the Water Horse had raced up towards them, neighing challenge and destruction. A great long ribbon of water shone there, arched and sparkling like the gay silky threads of a grey mare's tail, and rainbows played beneath it, and the rocks on either side of the valley were green with moss, and there was a great pool at the foot of the cataract which was very slightly kidney-shaped, from which a stream ran singing along the bottom of the valley. The water sprang out of a cleft in the rock at the very peak of the crag, where the Flock of Crows became the Eagle; where Tamia had stood with her bowl pressed against her breast to keep it steady, and had wept, knowing that what she was about to do was no use, because she had disobeyed her Guardian, and spoilt everything.

Tamia turned slowly away from the valley, back towards the meadow where her Guardian waited. The mare turned too, and fell in behind her. It was not a long journey, but the way was steep, and all three were still very, very tired. All of them stumbled, and Tamia and the mare leant on each other, and the foal took turns leaning on first the one and then the other, although when he leant against Tamia, he tended to step on her feet, and then he didn't seem so little after all.

It was nearer sunset than tea-time when they reached the Guardian's meadow, but Tamia saw the little hummock that the teapot in its tea-cosy made, sitting on the table in front of the house, between the water-garden and the old yew. And then she saw her Guardian emerging from the shadow of the yew, limping heavily and leaning on a stick, but coming straight and steadily towards them.

"Oh, Guardian!" said Tamia, and ran forward, and threw her arms around her. "Oh, I don't know why I'm here! I did it all wrong! I am so glad to see you!"

"Yes, you did do it all wrong," agreed her Guardian, with great self-restraint, saying nothing about the odd-smelling dampness of Tamia's shirt-front now transferred to her own, "and I don't know why either of us is still here either. Perhaps because I am the one who gave you the water, and I would have done exactly the same in your position—except that I would not have known how to birth a foal." And in her Guardian's eyes Tamia saw what she had known for a long time, although she had not let herself know she knew it: that part of the reason her Guardian had chosen her as apprentice was because she would make just that sort of wrong decision, and if it lost them the world, then so it did. "We can only do what we can do," said her Guardian softly. "Sometimes it is enough, despite all." More briskly she added: "And that valley needed a waterfall, don't you think? Although I hadn't realised it till you did it. The Grey Mare's Tail. There will be stories about it, you know."

"But not the true story," said Tamia.

"That's as you choose, my dear," said her Guardian. "But I would like to tell it, if you will let me—and we shall have some trouble making Water Gate keep silent."

Tamia looked towards the tea-table; there were only two cups laid out, and two plates.

"Water Gate has gone, back to his home," said her Guardian. "He left a message for you: well done." She laughed at the expression on Tamia's face. "He was particularly impressed by your use of the seventh stone—although he would have made you put it with the others if he had known, and none of them in the yew either. He said to tell you, Not even Guardians know everything—and that Western Mouth had chosen better than he could have guessed. He added some rather unflattering things about me, but you don't have to hear them."

Tamia scowled, because no one was allowed to say unflattering things about her Guardian. But she was distracted by a grey nose thrust under her arm. She stroked it, and said sadly, "I suppose, if we tell the story, we shall be able to find out who she—they—belong to."

"They belong to you," said her Guardian. "Do you think any islander would deny a Guardian's token so chosen? Nor do I think these two would cooperate about being given back. We can find out who they used to belong to, if you would like to learn the mare's name, and your foal's daddy."

"I do not care about names or bloodlines. I can name them myself, and they are who they are," said Tamia. "But I would like whoever lost them to know that they are safe and well."

"Then that is what we will do," said her Guardian. The foal was sucking interestedly at her sleeve. "I have told you before that Guardians have never had familiar animals; I believe you are about to begin a new tradition." She removed her sleeve from the foal's mouth; he gave her a wounded look, and stepped on her foot as he turned away towards his mother, and milk. "*Ouch.* I hope I am not too set in my ways to adjust."

KRAKEN

They wore traveller's clothes, tight-laced against the sea wind, she all in grey, he in worn brown leather. They leaned on the taffrail and stared aft. Now they could see the pursuing sail, of which the lookout's cry had told them an hour ago.

"Can it be one of my father's?" she said.

"How should it have found us, with all the wide ocean to search?"

Now the captain came and watched with them for a while.

"That is no merchantman," he said. "And no warship either. She follows too fast. My lord, you had best arm yourself. My lady, will you go below?"

Keeping to shadows, without seeming to be lurking, moving as if she were going nowhere in particular, Ailsa drifted along the mountain spur. Far above glittered the bright sunrise. Once over the first ridge, she changed course and headed directly along the slope to the cranny where she kept the spare harness. While she fetched it out and sorted it through, she whistled once, twice, and again. Now Carn came surging towards her, circled a couple of times to show that he didn't need to have come at her call, but had chosen to do so, took the titbit from her hand and let her slide the harness over his head.

As she was fastening the cheek buckle, she heard the school bell ring, calling her for the last time. She did not falter. Nor did she smile as she used to when she was younger, from childish bravado, setting out on another illicit ride, worth the consequences for the fun of it. To-day was different. To-morrow the school bell would be silent for the holidays, and when it next rang, it would do so for others.

Why not wait for to-morrow, then, when she would be free to ride out as she chose?

For that very reason. To-day she would say good-bye to childhood.

Carn flicked his tail, impatient.

"Oh, all right," she said aloud.

She clipped herself into the harness, laid her body along his with her hip beside the big forefin, tapped her tail against his flank, and streamlined herself to the rush of water as he surged away.

Now she did smile. It was impossible not to. To Ailsa, as to all merfolk, riding a blue-fin who really wanted to go was the finest thing in the ocean. You didn't need to be a child to feel like that.

They returned to the taffrail, he in dark armour that had clearly seen service, she in a long green cloak. By now the following ship was hull up, half again both their size and speed. A black flag strained at the masthead. The captain, still watching, turned and frowned.

"My lady, you should be below."

"Are you going to fight?"

"What else can we do? If we surrender, they will still slit our throats. A lucky shot may bring down her mast."

"Then I will fight too. My lord has spare pistols. I know the use of them."

Blue-fin have three main paces—drift, pulse and surge. Carn was still at full surge, delighted to be going somewhere, anywhere. Ailsa twitched the bit in his mouth.

"Easy," she told him. "Easy. We've got all day."

He responded as much to her voice as to the bit and slowed to a steady pulse, heading up to just below the wave-roots, where the going was still smooth, and the water golden with morning. Later, when they were beyond pursuit, they would practise some wave leaping. Carn was still young, Ailsa's first blue-fin—as a child she had ridden the smaller yellow-fin. The waves today were just about right for schooling him, steady in their march, tall enough for him to get the point, but not so tall that he might lose confidence.

Merfolk have an innate sense of direction, and Ailsa knew where she was heading, south-southwest, out over the Grand Gulf, a vast empty tract with immeasurable depths below. Nobody had much business out this way, so it was here that she was least likely to be seen. She had kept the same course for almost an hour when she heard the thunder.

Thunder, on a day like this? And there was something odd about the sound. It had the right deep roll but came jarring through the water as if it had begun there, somewhere ahead and to the left, rather than spreading more vaguely down from the distant sky.

Again! And Carn had faltered in his rhythm, as he did

when surprised. And again. Ailsa turned him towards the sound. No, not thunder—too short a rumble, and too regular. A boom, a pause. Another boom, and pause. Another. Now straight ahead. After several more booms she began to sense the distance, a few hundred lengths only. And from above the surface, not below.

Half consciously she had kept aware of the pattern of broad stripes, light and dark, that marked the sunlit and shadowed slopes of the waves above, running slantwise to her path. She headed Carn to cross them square, picked one wave and, watching it intently, pulled him into a climb and flicked him to full surge, aiming a fin and a half below the moving wave crest. In the last few strokes she lashed her own tail in rhythm with his to add to the speed of the outstrike.

The idea was to leave the wave as high as possible, so that your two bodies were well up into the burning air while the blue-fin's tail still had water to drive against. Then you saw how many wave crests you could clear before the instrike. But the confusion of the moving wave roots through which you were aiming made it harder than it may sound, and this time Ailsa struck so low that they barely cleared the first crest. This was just as well, as it gave them a soft instrike, and she wasn't ready for it. She'd been distracted by what she'd glimpsed across Carn's shoulder at the top of the leap. Two great ships of the airfolk.

There were old wrecks littered around the mountain, but Ailsa had never seen floating ships before, except in books.

White smoke puffed from the bows of the pursuer. Thunder rolled across the water. The shot fell wide. They did not see the splash. On the after-

deck of the fleeing ship, sailors waited beside two small cannon, four to each gun. Another boom, and a splash astern and to starboard.

"Why do you not fire back?" said the woman. "And why so many of you? Are you not needed to sail the ship?"

One of the sailors answered.

"We haven't the range with these popguns, my lady. We'll fire as soon as our shot will reach them. Our best hope is to dismast her, and for that we must handle our guns as well as we're able—two of us to lay and haul back after the recoil, one to swab out and load, and one to carry powder."

"My lord and I can at least carry powder. It will be better than waiting. Show us."

As they reached the companionway, the first shot struck. They felt the small boat's timbers jar with the impact, somewhere aft, low down.

They followed their guide on into the dark.

Ailsa put Carn onto a lead rope and floated herself up to a little behind the crest of a wave, with only the top half of her head clear of the water. When that wave carried her astern, she dived and repositioned herself. Carn circled impatiently below her, but dutifully kept the lead rope just slack.

It took her a while to see, and then to understand, what the two ships were doing. Her eyes were lensed and shaped for underwater vision, and too dazzled by sunlight to pick out any detail. At first all she could be sure of was the two tall ships, the leading one bright, the other larger and more grim. They were making the thunder, and with it sent out white stuff like clouds, which rolled away on the wind. Then she heard a crash and a cry and the smaller ship seemed to stagger for a moment in its course. Squinting beneath half-closed lids, she saw airfolk at the front of the larger ship working some sort of dark pipe from which the thunder and the smoke emerged. And yes, the airfolk at the back of the small ship were doing the same, making a thinner boom, with less of the cloudy stuff. Ailsa realised that the airfolk were using the pipes to throw things at each other, not darts or spears, which were the merfolk's weapons, but dark balls which they crammed into the pipes between booms.

A heavier crash, and cries of many voices. The smaller ship staggered, swung sideways, wallowed. Part of the towering white fins that seemed to drive it were twisted away, falling, collapsing. The other ship came surging on with a mass of airfolk gathered at its front. Sunlight flashed off weapons. There was a louder crash, bellows, screams, fighting. She watched, amazed and distressed, until two figures appeared at the front of the stricken ship, one white and glittering like sunlit spray, the other dark and tall. The fight continued, with the attackers driving forward. Sharp whipping cracks rapped out amid the yells. The white figure—Ailsa, unthinking, had drifted herself near enough to see that it was a woman—turned her head, watched the fight for a moment, turned back and spoke.

"It is time to go," she said softly.

She had let her green cloak fall and stood at the rail in the dress that had been stitched for her marriage, though not to this man. Ten thousand seed pearls patterned its surface, and on it she had pinned every jewel she had brought, and they were many, for she was a king's daughter. The sun dazzled off her as if she had been white sea foam. On her cheek was a smoky burn, the back-flash from a pistol. The ship lurched and wallowed. The yells neared as the pirates started to force the companionway to the foredeck.

He flung his sword out to sea and with brisk fingers unbuckled his sword-belt. He grasped a stay, climbed, balanced on the heaving rail and helped her up to stand beside him. She laid her body against his, passed the belt around their waists and fastened it tight. The empty scabbard dangled by her side.

"I have brought you to this," she said, putting her arms around his neck. "It was all my doing. You had the whole world before you."

He bowed his head.

"My world is in your arms," he said.

The pirates erupted onto the foredeck and rushed towards them, but he clasped her to him and leapt clear. They hit the water with a glittering splash, and at once the weight of his armour carried them under. Her dark hair streamed above them as they sank, mixed with the pearl-like bubbles of their breath.

Ailsa saw the sword arc through the air, dived and was already swimming towards it as it splashed into the downslope of the next wave. She lashed with her tail and caught it not three lengths under. When she rose, the white figure and the black were poised on the rail at the very edge of the ship. A man and a woman. Lovers. Their pose and gestures signalled love. With one hand the man gripped the rope that rose beside him and with the other steadied the woman while she bound some kind of strap around their waists. She put her arms round his neck and spoke. He bowed his head to hers and answered. Time stopped.

The waves stood still, the spume hung brilliant in the air, the wisps of cloud-stuff remaining from the fight hovered motionless, and Ailsa's own heart paused between beat and beat. The lenses of her eyes seemed to adjust so that she could see every detail with diamond clarity.

And then they leapt, and the splash of their entry sparkled in the sunlight, while the pirates gathered with yells of anger to the rail and gazed down at the spreading circle of foam.

The moment held Ailsa in its trance. She had no need to try to understand what had happened. The moment was all that mattered, with its focussed brilliance and beauty, as if forces, whole lives, had been gathered into it from before-time and after-time, the way that light is gathered into a drop of spume or a jewel. They had made it so, in and for each other, choosing to leap, choosing to die. . . . Yes, die. Ailsa knew that airfolk could not live long in water, any more than she could in air.

The thought broke the trance. If she was quick, perhaps they did not have to die. She dived, twitching the lead rope as she lashed herself downward. Almost at once Carn was beside her, positioned so that she could grasp the hand-grip. Still swimming, she slid the sword under the centre-strap, laid her body against his and flicked him into full surge while she loose-rode him down.

But blue-fin, like merfolk, are creatures of the upper layers of ocean. The wild ones never enter the sunless underdeeps. The green-gold light changed through heavier green towards full dark in which they would see nothing at all. Carn tried to level out, and even with the leverage of the harness it was an effort to force him on down. She was fighting to hold course when she saw the lovers, right at the edge of her dwindling sphere of vision.

◆   ◆   ◆

Their lips were on each other's lips as the darkness took them.

"There!" she gasped. And Carn had seen them too, knew what he was here for, and drove on down. The water darkened. The woman's dress was a shadowy glimmer, almost in reach. A layer of deadly chill slid over Ailsa. Such layers exist in all deep oceans, and the Grand Gulf was deep beyond knowledge. The merfolk call these layers limits, and do not willingly go beyond them.

Now Ailsa could see the lovers no more. She loosed one hand from the grip, reached, groped, touched something narrow and hard, clutched it. The sudden weight loosed her other hand from the grip. She swirled and lashed upward, dragging the weight with her. Terror sluiced through her.

It had happened in the instant of turning. Before, still diving, she had been afraid, of the dark, of the cold, of going too deep to return, ordinary flesh-and-blood fears. This, filling her body as she forced her way upward, was terror. It was as if the cold and the dark had made themselves into a *thing*, alive, but huge as the immense underdeeps, dark beyond black, cold beyond ice, something that had been waiting there for the lovers to fall into its ice and dark, but now, now that she was dragging them back . . . She had not let go only because the nightmare had locked the muscles of her grip like iron.

She did not notice passing through the limit. Something broke into her nightmare, a soft touch against her cheek, Carn's querying snout. And it was no longer dark. Almost, but not quite. In wonder she looked up and saw that though she was still many lengths deep she could see far above her the ripple-pattern of the sunlit waves. She was exhausted, her heart thundering, her gills aching with the effort to sift the rush of water. There was a pain in her hand from the ferocity of her grip, and a fierce ache running up her arm from the wrenching weight she had dragged from below. She looked down and made out that she was holding the scabbard of a sword, still fastened to its belt, and the belt was buckled round the bodies of the two airfolk she had seen leap from the ship.

They wavered below her, a man and a woman, he in dark armour, she in a strange white covering which hid all but her head and her hands. (Merfolk wear armour if they need to but have no use for clothes.) This covering had glittered in the sun, and glinted now in the dimness, because it was sewn with innumerable seed pearls, among which were fastened many greater jewels. The faces were calm and pale, their eyes open but unseeing. The woman's dark hair floated all around them.

I am too late, thought Ailsa. They are dead. But still it did not cross her mind to leave them to drift down into the cold and dark below, and the things of cold and dark that waited for them there.

Carn was fidgety, but Ailsa murmured to steady him while she made her arrangements. She slid the sword into the scabbard to get it out of the way, unclipped the lead rope and ran it through the shoulder strap of the man's swordbelt, and then clipped it to the load hook so that Carn could take the weight. Now with both hands free she found the buckles on the man's armour and undid them. The thigh-pieces came loose and fell, but the body armour was held fast by the sword belt. She tied the loose end of the lead rope round the woman's chest, beneath the arms, and, supporting the man's weight in the crook of her elbow, managed to undo the buckle. The body armour was hinged at the shoulders, like a clam shell, with a hole for the man's neck. She eased the contraption over his head and let it fall. Below it she found that he too was wearing a covering, a soft brown stuff like cured sharkskin. She refastened his swordbelt round him, and retied the lead rope round his chest so that the two bodies, almost weightless now without the armour, floated side by side from the load hook. Finally she adjusted the harness as best she could to balance her own body against the trailing load, and clipped herself in. Before she flicked her tail to set Carn going, she cast a look down into the black deeps beneath her.

They were nearer than they had been. The limit itself was moving. She knew it, though she could feel no change in the water around her. The underdeeps—that whole immense mass of cold and dark—were rising towards her. Terror, nightmare, swept through her as before. Carn bolted.

He surged for the surface, for the warm and golden water beneath the wave roots. Once there, he levelled and surged on, still in a crazed panic beyond Ailsa's control. His madness had the effect of blocking her own, by giving her something urgent to do. At first she tried to master him, to force his head round, to pierce through his panic with shouted commands. She reached and gripped the bit-ring and heaved with all her strength. She had heard her father's huntmaster, Desmar, describe having done this with a bolting blue-fin, but Carn was too strong for her.

Then she realised that at least he was bolting for home.

Her best hope was to let him have his way. But swimming at full surge all that distance, with the inert load of the airfolk trailing behind, he could injure himself beyond recovery. Last year a group of young nobles racing for wagers on half-trained stock had brought them home in such a state that her father, furious, had banished the riders to remote reefs. Two of the fish had had to be put down. She would not let that happen to Carn.

It still did not cross Ailsa's mind to abandon the airfolk. She was sure that, having done what she had, she must now go through with it, and face whatever punishments she must. There was something about the woman, not only the covering and jewels that she wore, but the way that she had stood and moved, had held herself in the face of death, that spoke to Ailsa. She too was a king's daughter.

With one hand she clasped the grip and with the other unclipped her harness and free-rode. Now she had to transfer herself across Carn's body, round behind the big forefin. This was riding-school stuff, to be done at a steady pulse. She'd never tried it at full surge in the open sea. She shifted her left hand down to the centre-belt, which circled Carn's body just in front of the forefin, let go of the grip and trailed at arm's length. Now she changed hands on the belt and with her left arm reached round behind the fin and felt and found the belt again at the limit of her stretch. Arching her body so that the rush of water lifted her clear of Carn's, she let a twist of her tail flip her across the spiny ridge that ran from forefin to afterfin, and she was there. She rested a moment, transferred her right hand to grip the load hook, and then with a straining effort used her left to haul on the doubled lead rope until she had enough slack to thumb the loop off the hook and let go. As soon as he was free of the dragging load, Carn surged away, out of sight.

After that it was a matter of working out the easiest way for her to tow the two bodies. She finished with the rope running over the back of her neck and the airfolk trailing, one on each side, leaving her arms free to balance the load against the thrust of her tail. When the rope began to chafe her neck, she stopped and unfastened the top half of the man's covering. To her surprise he was wearing yet another layer of covering, a fine white stuff with delicate patterns at wrist and neck. She used the top covering to pad the rope where it chafed, and swam on.

As she toiled along, she brooded on the uncomfortable certainty that she must now face her father and explain not only that morning's delinquency—she had known what she would say about that before she set out—but her dealings with the airfolk. By custom so strong that it was almost law, merfolk had nothing to do with airfolk. All tales of such meetings ended in grief. Why should this be any different? It was some while before she became aware of a quite different kind of unease, coming not from inside her but from somewhere outside. Somewhere below.

At first she told herself that it was a sort of aftershock, a leftover bit of the panic that had gripped her in the cold and dark below the limit. She tried to drive it away by returning to the problem of what she could say to her father. She was still quite sure that she had been right to do what she'd done, but how could she put her reasons into words? They were all to do with the moment at which the man and the woman had stood on the rail of the ship and by the force of their love for each other had made that moment into a lifetime. How could she make anyone else see that? To do so, they would need to see the moment.

Something tapped at her mind. The unease—the certainty of it made it more than unease—flooded back. She stared downwards, but saw nothing, felt nothing. She did not need to. Here too, she could tell, the limit had risen.

Again on the edge of panic, she forced herself to swim steadily on, but as she did so, she began more and more to feel that an immense slow wave of cold and darkness was following her across the ocean floor. If she changed course, so would the wave. Indeed, she felt it was deliberately telling her so. Just as it had tapped at her mind while she was remembering the lovers' last moment of life, so now it was letting her know that it would follow her until she released them and let them sink through the dwindling light to where the cold and the dark waited for them.

She longed to rest but did not dare, knowing that the effort of swimming with the dragging load was all that was keeping panic at bay. By noon it was clear that she would not be home by nightfall. And then, well into the afternoon, she heard conch-calls, the thin, wavering wails that the huntsmen blew, keeping in touch along the line as they drove the game towards the waiting spear party. Like whalesong, the notes travelled far underwater. She heard one away to her left, and another nearer, another to her right, and a fourth yet further off, too widely spaced for a game drive. And no hunt was planned for today . . . but of course it was for her they were hunting. Carn had come home, spent and still in harness . . .

someone must have seen the direction. . . . She headed for the nearest conch.

It turned out to be Scyto, a dour-seeming but kindly old merman who had helped break and train Carn. The moment he saw her, he blew a short call and drove his blue-fin towards her.

"My lady!" he said. "Where have you . . . what are these?"

Before she could speak, he blew the call again.

"Did Carn come home?" she said. "Is he all right?"

"He came, and maybe he'll do. But these?"

"We must take them to my father," she said, refusing to explain.

"If you say so, my lady," he said, but clearly didn't like it.

A conch sounded nearby. Scyto answered, and Aspar came surging up, saying the same things and asking the same questions.

"We are taking them to my father," said Ailsa.

"Airfolk! Dead!" said Aspar.

"Do what you're told, lad," said Scyto. "Steady, there. Steady!"

This last to his blue-fin, which had shied as he was looping the lead rope onto the load hook. A moment later Aspar's blue-fin shied violently and might have bolted if Aspar hadn't forced its head round.

"What's into the blue-fin?" he muttered.

"Dunno," said Scyto. "You take the princess. Let's go."

Ailsa gripped the load hook and laid herself along the flank of the big blue-fin. Aspar flicked his tail and they pulsed away. Two more huntsmen curved in to join them, blowing their conches, and then others, so that they schooled along together, calling continuously that the hunt was over. It was a sound Ailsa could remember from her earliest years. She had always liked the huntsmen, and they had seemed to like her. Things seemed almost normal once more, so that for a while she lost the nightmare sense of being tracked from below by something huge and cold and dark, and began to worry again about how she could face her father. Then she noticed the huntsman to her left lean out and peer down, and another beyond him doing the same. The calls faltered and the Huntmaster, Desmar, riding lead, raised a hand to signal a halt.

"Anyone notice?" he said.

"Way down?" asked several voices.

"Blue-fin are twitchy as hell," said someone.

They hovered, craning to see what lay below, but there was only shapeless dark.

"Airfolk," grumbled someone. None of them would look towards the drowned lovers dangling at the rope's ends. Huntsmen were always superstitious. Their task depended so much on the luck of the ocean. Left to themselves they would have untied the rope and let the airfolk fall.

"We must take them to my father," said Ailsa.

"Right then," said Desmar. "Let's get on with it."

The king rode out to meet them above the slopes of the mountain. Relays of conch-calls had told him that his daughter was found. His green skin was flushed dark with anger, but he remained, as always, firmly calm. In silence he accepted Ailsa's formal salute, palms together, head bowed, tail curled under. In silence he glanced at the airfolk, turned his head and gestured. Master Nostocal, the court physician, bowed and drifted across to inspect them. Ailsa guessed that old Nosy must have come out with her father in case something had happened to her.

The king drifted aside with Desmar and spoke with him, staring down the mountain. He beckoned to two of the huntsmen. They saluted, listened to their orders and rode their blue-fin downward. At last he beckoned to Ailsa.

"You cut school," he said. "I had thought you were past that, but we will talk about it later. What then?"

She told her story as clearly as she could. He listened without interruption to her account of the fight and her dive to reach the airfolk. At that point he stopped her.

"You crossed the limit? You were not afraid?"

"There wasn't time. I had to reach them. But then, as soon as I turned back . . . It was worse than nightmares. . . ."

"Something specific had made you afraid?"

"Yes. I don't know what. When it happened, I just panicked, I didn't know why. But I got away, above the limit, and it was better there. But then whatever it was started to follow us up. That's why Carn bolted. I had to let him go. It wasn't his . . ."

"Yes. This thing. You didn't see it? Feel something in the water?"

"Not like that. I can't explain. But it's been following me . . . us . . . them . . . And the huntsmen felt it too. And all the blue-fin."

He floated silent, withdrawn. The dark green of his anger was gone, but that did not mean that her delinquency was forgotten. He would return to it in due time.

"You could have let them fall," he said.

"No. I mean, not once I'd followed them down and brought

them back up . . . it wouldn't have been right. You can see she's a king's daughter . . . I think . . ."

Even that certainty, so obvious while she had watched the lovers at the rail, was now blurred. What did she know of the kings of the airfolk?

Her father nodded and glanced enquiringly beyond her. Ailsa turned and saw Master Nostocal hovering there with an excited expression on his lined old face. He saluted and, barely waiting for permission to speak, blurted out, "The airfolk are still alive, my lord!"

"Alive? Airfolk die in water. Is this not known?"

"Hitherto, my lord, but these. . . . I have felt their pulses, firm, but slow beyond belief—eighteen of mine to one of theirs. They live, my lord."

"No doubt at all?"

"None, my lord."

"Then I cannot decide their fate alone. We must take them home and hold council. Ailsa, you will go straight to your rooms and stay there, not speaking to anyone of any of this, until I send for you."

Ailsa made the salutation and backed away. She could see Aspar waiting by his blue-fin, but chose a course that took her past the lovers. She slowed and gazed down at them. Even the unbelievable knowledge that they were still alive seemed vague to her as she saw once more in her mind the poised instant before they had leapt from the ship. The memory seemed still as vivid as the event itself, when she had watched it from the wave-top. But now it faded and something seemed to form where it had been, a cold, dark, numbing question.

"The king is mounted, my lady," said Aspar's voice. From

his tone Ailsa could hear that he had said it more than once. Dazedly she let him clip her into his harness and then he free-rode the blue-fin home.

They dreamed slow dreams of dark and cold.

Home was an immense undersea mountain, an extinct volcano riddled with tunnels and caves and underground chambers which the merfolk over many generations had shaped and enlarged to their uses. The palace was only a small part of the complex, running a hundred lengths or so along the southern slope of the mountain, above the solid, un-chambered spur along which Ailsa had slipped out that morning to find Carn. Now she waited at her window, look-ing out over this view, and thus it was that she saw the return of the two huntsmen who had ridden down the slope at her father's command. They rode a single blue-fin, which the one who held the reins struggled to control as it surged towards the main gate and out of sight.

Food was brought, not the punishment fare that used to follow her old escapades, but clam strips on a bed of sweet-weed, ripe sea-pears and manatee cheese. She ate and tried to read, but mostly she watched from the window as the Councillors gathered. Time passed. Twice more, unwilled, the scene she had witnessed that morning formed in her mind, and each time it was followed by the same chill question. The light on the wave-roof changed from gold to pink to purple, and when it was almost dark, a chamberlain came with a phosphor lamp and said it was the king's wish that the Princess Ailsa should attend him. This seemed strangely formal, and when she moved, expecting him to lead the way, he coughed and said, "His Majesty is in Council, my lady."

Startled, she fetched her diadem from its case and threaded its horns into her hair. Checking in the mirror, she decided that she looked silly wearing only the single large sapphire and an everyday necklace, so she added the white-gold carcanet with the rubies that had been her naming present from her grandmother, and the pearl and sapphire pendant and tail-bracelet that had been her mother's favourite jewels. The chamberlain nodded approval and led her first along the familiar passageways of the domestic quarters, and on down through grander windings to the Council Chamber.

Attendants waited. Doors were flung wide. Conches sounded. A voice cried, "Her Royal Highness the Princess Ailsa attends His Majesty in Council."

The chamber blazed with phosphor. Ailsa paused at the entrance to salute the king, finned herself gently down the aisle between the Councillors, and saluted again. Merfolk are weightless in water, so have no need for chairs. Instead of a throne, the king's office and authority were marked by a crystal pillar on which he rested the hand that held his sceptre. There was a smaller pillar to his left. At his feet lay the bodies of the airfolk. Somebody had combed the man's hair and beard and fastened his sword belt round him. The woman's white covering had been straightened and her marvellous long dark hair, which otherwise would have floated all around her, had been tidied into smooth waves and fastened with oyster-shell combs.

The king beckoned Ailsa forward and gestured to the smaller pillar. Nobody, she knew, had used it since her mother died. She turned, rested her right hand on it and waited while the Councillors murmured their greetings.

"My daughter will tell you what she did and saw," said the king.

Ailsa began with her ride out over the Grand Gulf, saying nothing about why she had chosen to go there. That was for her father alone. Otherwise she described all that had happened, including her own sensations, the detailed intensity of the moment when the lovers had made their choice to die, and the sudden mastering panic that had overwhelmed her when she had turned back from beyond the limit. She told the story collectedly, without any of the confusion and doubt she had felt when she had told it to her father. It did not take long.

"Thank you," said the king. "Are there further questions for the princess? No? Well, that is most of what we know. There was a fight between two ships of the airfolk. This pair leapt into the sea to escape their attackers. The princess dived, hoping to rescue them, and crossed the limit. She did that, she tells me, with no special fear in the urgency of action—no more, at least, than any of us might feel—but on turning back with the airfolk, she was overcome by inexplicable terror, a sense that something very large and cold and strange . . ."

He paused. Perhaps Ailsa alone in the Council Chamber knew why. She too had felt the crystal pillar tremble beneath her hand. Cushioned by the water in which they floated, the others might well not have sensed the shock. The pillars were based on solid rock, so it was the mountain itself that must have trembled.

"... large and cold and strange lay below her. This is not a young woman's fancy. She recovered herself and hitched the airfolk to her blue-fin to tow them home, but before long the blue-fin, a steady, reliable animal, bolted. The princess let him go and continued to tow the airfolk unaided. As she did so, she became convinced that whatever she had sensed beyond the limit was now following her. Again this is not mere fancy. The huntsmen who met her reported the same impression. Their own blue-fin, too, were barely controllable. When this was reported to me, I asked two of them to scout down the mountain but not to cross the limit. As they approached the limit, one of their blue-fin threw its rider and bolted, and but for good ridership the other would have done the same. As you are aware, the limit rises and falls a little with the seasons, but one of the men, who has often been down the mountain, reports that it is now many lengths higher than he has ever known it. Finally Master Nostocal, who has long had an interest in the anatomy of airfolk and has studied many bodies, found when he came to inspect these two that they still live, though in some kind of suspended animation. This is without precedent both in his own experience and in the books he has consulted since his return. Has anyone anything further to add? Councillor Hormos?"

Nobody knows how the merfolk came into being, though there are legends that say that at some point far in the past the strains of airfolk and fish came somehow to be mingled, and thus the first merfolk were born. Because of this hybrid inheritance they vary greatly in appearance, though most, like Ailsa, have a single tail, internal gills, and an upper body much like that of the airfolk. Ailsa's fingers were half-webbed, and she had a pair of silky waving fins running from her elbows to her shoulders, and another running almost the whole length of her spine. But double tails are not uncommon, especially in the northern oceans, and in one almost landlocked sea there is a race that has legs like airfolk and can breathe a long while in the air. There are even legends of merfolk who have been born on dry land, and have not for years realised their true nature.

At the other end of the range, and also rare, are merfolk who are almost wholly fish. It might be guessed that these would be despised, as being so near to an inferior sort of creature, but though merfolk hunt and eat and use the sea beasts, they also respect them, knowing that they themselves are in a sense interlopers. They therefore value members of their own race who most closely resemble fish, believing rightly that these have a truer understanding of the many mysteries of the sea.

Councillor Hormos was such a one, an undoubted merwoman, but with a large, solid, grouper-like shape, apart from human ears, in which she wore elaborate earrings. She floated vertically from her place, saluted the king with a movement of her tail, and spoke in a quick, breathy twitter that went oddly with her appearance.

"I believe," she said, "that Her Royal Highness has had the misfortune to disturb the Kraken."

The Council muttered surprise. The king nodded for her to continue.

"You will remember nursery stories about the Kraken," she said. "The unbelievably huge creature that will at the end of time arise from the sea floor and destroy the world. Your reasons have told you that there can be no such life form, and who knows the doom of the world? But there are fish that live far below the limit, fish whose ancestors in remote time made their way down into those lightless depths, and when they did so found that there was something already there, not of the same creation as sea-things and air-things, something whose nature is pure cold, pure dark, something utterly other. That is what fish know, in their small-brained way. They cannot put the knowledge into pictures or words, but it is still there, in their blood. It is in your blood too, and mine, and perhaps we can dimly sense it. Perhaps it is from this faint memory that we have constructed the nursery tale of the Kraken. And it is perhaps through that remnant of knowledge in her blood that the princess, and the huntsmen too, sensed the movement of something vast and strange in the deeps below them."

"Others, myself among them, have crossed the limit and returned," said the king. "We did not wake this creature. Why should the princess have done so?"

"She has told us she feels it was waiting for these airfolk to fall into its realm," said Hormos. "But she took them away, and now it is seeking for them. As I said, I would trust her feeling. It comes from the knowledge in her blood."

Another Councillor caught the king's eye, received his nod and rose.

"Could this thing actually destroy the world?" he asked.

The Royal Archivist sought permission and rose.

"Does anyone remember Yellowreef?" he wheezed. "It's a legend, of course, but some authorities believe there's history behind it. It was in West Ocean, a mountain city much like ours. The people there found a lode of emeralds, far down, near the limit, and mined them. They went down and down, making themselves a sort of armour to endure the pressure and the cold, until something came from even deeper and took the mountain in its grip and shook it so that it crumbled apart and the merfolk could live there no more."

Nobody spoke. In the silence Ailsa felt the crystal pillar shudder again beneath her palm. She caught her father's eye and knew that he had felt the same. She raised her hand for permission to speak. He nodded. She rose.

"Yes, we must take them back," she said. "Or it will shake the mountain to pieces like it did Yellowreef."

"But they still live," said the king. "They are very different from us, but they are people nonetheless, and under the protection of our laws. I could not send any of our own people to such a death without their consent."

"They've chosen already," said Ailsa. "I saw them do it. And it's the Kraken who's keeping them alive. It's got to be. It wants them alive. Perhaps it can't keep them alive for ever."

"Very well," said the king. "The Council must decide. Before we vote, I will tell you that while I have been here I have twice felt this pillar shake beneath my hand, and I think my daughter has felt the same. I have never known it do so before. Now it seems to me that we have only two choices. We cannot simply keep them here. If they wake, they will die. So either we can take them back to where my daughter saw them sink, or we can tow them to some shore and strand them in air, to live or die as their own fate falls. Will those in favour of the former course please rise?"

It was close. By only four votes the Council decided to

take the lovers back to where the Kraken, perhaps, waited for them.

Their dreams were darker, colder, slower yet. There was death at the edge of them.

They did the lovers full honour, schooling out as if for a royal funeral, the whole court, formally jewelled, to the sound of sad music. By now few of the merfolk had any doubt that they were doing what they must. Three times in the night the mountain had shaken so that all had felt it. Scouts reported that the limit had risen yet further up the slopes.

Ailsa rode near the front, knowing where she had gone yesterday. Carn was still too spent for work, so she had an elderly quiet blue-fin from the royal stables. The lovers lay on sleds weighted with boulders and buoyed with bladders so that they would not sink until they were needed to. Master Nostocal rode beside them, and took their pulses at intervals. He had reported that morning that their heartbeats were slower and weaker than before, and was afraid that whatever was keeping them alive was losing its ability to do so.

For a while, with so many people around her, Ailsa was not sure that she could sense the same immense mass of cold and dark that she had felt yesterday, tracking her across the sea bed. But even her stolid old animal was nervous, and the huntsmen riding scout on the flanks said they thought it was there. Slowly she began to feel more sure, and she knew for certain when the great tide below came to a halt.

"This is the place," she said.

They did not doubt her. They could tell, too.

The music changed. The merfolk gathered round the sleds and held them in position while the air was released from the bladders. Ailsa, full of grief at what she accepted must be done, was watching the stream of silvery bubbles shoot towards the wave-roof when a cold, dark thought slid into her mind. Not, this time, a question. A command.

"It wants me too," she said.

"No," said the king.

"I must go with them, or it will break the mountain."

"No, I will go," cried someone. Others joined, until the king raised his hand for silence.

"It's got to be me," said Ailsa.

He stared at her, and away, and bowed his head.

"Hold the sleds there," he said, and took her to one side.

"You are certain of this?" he said.

"Yes. It told me. As if it had spoken."

"Will you come back?"

"It didn't say."

Hard lines creased his face. This was how he had looked at her mother's funeral.

"Very well," he said.

She raised her hands to remove her diadem. To do the lovers honour, she had put on the same jewels as the night before, but there was no point in taking them with her. If she did not come back, her cousin Porphyry would become Prince. He should have them, for his wife when he married.

"No, wear them," said her father. "You must go as what you are, a king's daughter."

They went back to where the sleds were waiting. Ailsa took the middle of the rope that joined them, raised her forehead for her father's kiss, and nodded. The merfolk loosed their hold and the weight of the boulders carried her down. The light faded, more slowly than when Carn had dived at full surge. Ailsa was only vaguely afraid. The terror she should have felt was somehow numbed, like a pain being kept at bay by one of Master Nostocal's drugs. She could not guess what the Kraken wanted with her. Perhaps it would keep her in some strange half death, like that of the lovers, in its kingdom of dark and cold. The massive pressure of water closed around her. Light died. It became dark as night, dark as a starless midnight, darker than any night. With a plunge of cold she felt the limit pass.

Beyond it waited the Kraken.

Ailsa was aware of it in her mind, not through her bodily senses. In her mind she could feel the immeasurable length of it on either side of her, its immeasurable depth below, dark beyond black, cold beyond ice. It told her to let go of the rope. In her mind she saw the tendrils of dark that wreathed from it and took the lovers, playing over their bodies. But now there was light, light seen with her eyes, a dazzling spark as one of the tendrils lifted a jewel from the woman's dress. The light blazed from the jewel as the tendril turned it this way and that, and then vanished as the Kraken took it into itself.

Other jewels blazed or sparkled or glowed in turn, and were lost. The seed pearls on the woman's covering woke into an iridescent design which then flowed away, rippling like some luminous sea-thing, into the Kraken's inward blackness. When they were gone, Ailsa was once more in total dark.

Now in her mind she saw the Kraken moving its tendrils

to inspect the lovers. Despite the weight on the sled they had fallen no farther. Light glowed again, but this time she was unsure whether she was seeing it through her eyes or in her mind, faint streaking glimmers moving to and fro across and through the immense dark mass—dots of light, she thought, but moving so fast that they seemed to be glowing lines. She had no idea what this meant.

When the Kraken had done with the lovers, it briefly considered the sleds on which they lay, then turned its attention to Ailsa. Sensing the movement of the black tendrils towards her, she raised her hands, removed her diadem and offered it to them. As they touched it, the sapphire shone with a pure, pale light, more brilliant, more truly a jewel, than she had ever known it. Always before it had merely refracted the light that fell on it, tingeing that light with its colour. Now it was as if the Kraken was summoning out of it the sapphire's inner light, and drawing that light into its own blackness, just as cold calls heat into it but heat cannot call cold.

When the blue blaze of the sapphire was gone, she offered one by one her carcanet, pendant, earrings and tail bracelet and watched them sparkle or flame at the Kraken's touch. There was one small diamond in the carcanet that Ailsa had never particularly noticed as being different from any of the others which now shone out with the brilliance of Orion. When the Kraken had done with each piece, it took it into itself. Then it turned its attention to her.

The tendrils were soft, more feathery than the finest sea fern. She could scarcely feel their touch as they explored her shape, lingering a little at the waist where the smooth skin ended and the scales began. She saw again the strange darting lights, fewer than there had been with the lovers. When they had explored her tailfin, the tendrils moved up her body and gathered at the back of her head. Three times yesterday she had been asked the same dark question, but had not understood. Now she did.

The Kraken was not much interested in her. She was an oddity, with her airfolk torso and fish tail, but the ocean teems with oddities and the Kraken knew as much about them as it wished to. No, what absorbed it, what had caused it to move its vast mass across the ocean floor and shake the mountain in its anger, was the lovers. What could Ailsa tell it about them?

This time she did not need to put her story into words, which meant that she could tell it all, exactly as it had been. She felt that she could show, did in fact show the Kraken every sunlit droplet that had whipped from the wave-tops and every wisp of cloud-stuff that had puffed from the black tubes as the fight went on. She created again the arc of the sword through the air, created the precise poise, serene, passionate, unrepeatable, in which the lovers had balanced on the rail while the struggle had raged beyond them and the woman had buckled the sword belt round them so that they should go down unseparated into darkness. She created the final splash, and the attackers crowding to the rail.

At this point the Kraken seemed to lose interest. While Ailsa had been creating the moment, its whole mass had glimmered with a network of the streaking lines, but now these mostly died. At the same time her own mind went dull. If she had gone on to tell it, about her dive to reach the lovers, she would have had to do so with ordinary, fuzzy, gappy memory.

The brilliance of full recall was gone. That was something that the Kraken had summoned from her, much as it had summoned the inner light from her jewels. As the tendrils withdrew from the back of her head, she felt a vague sense of loss. It crossed her mind that the Kraken would now take her into itself too. She was too numb, too exhausted, to be frightened by the idea.

As she waited for whatever would happen next, she became aware of the cold, and the pressure. Even merfolk, used to the chill and weight of water, cannot survive long at such depths. Soon, she thought dully, I shall be dead. I'm sorry for father—first mother, now me.

A brief command came into her mind. She held out both hands and the Kraken placed something in each. She recognised the feel of the rope in her right palm, but not the hard, small, sharp-cornered thing around which her left hand closed.

Another command said Go, so she lashed with her tail and rose, hauling the sleds behind her. They came so easily that she supposed that the Kraken had loosed all the ropes and sent her back with the sleds empty, but when light began to glimmer round her and she could look back, she saw that the lovers' bodies were still there. The woman's hair was floating loose, so the Kraken had taken even the little mother-of-pearl combs that had held it in place.

Then the scouts, patrolling the edge of darkness, found her. Conches called, and the blue-fin came surging down, driven so hard that the cavity bubbles streamed in their wake. Hands took the rope from hers, her father grasped her in one arm and wheeled his blue-fin and surged with her up into the warm and golden waters where she belonged. From there the funeral party rode hallooing home, and the mountain emptied to greet them.

They dreamed of green shadowy light, of wave-lap, of half-heard voices. Their heartbeats quickened.

Ailsa gazed at the dark jewel, the Kraken's gift. It was more than black, beyond black. It was beyond cold—that is to say that it did not feel chill to the touch, but this wasn't because it was at the same temperature as the touching hand. Instead, contact made the hand aware of the soft warmth of living flesh, its own warmth. So with light. The jewel was faceted and polished like one of Ailsa's jewels, but no light shone back from any of its surfaces. Instead it sucked light into itself, calling it out of other things. If she took an emerald and placed it beside the black jewel, the emerald, which before had merely refracted the light from the phosphorescent corals that roofed the room, now blazed intensely green, blazed as a star does with its own generated light.

Looking at the black jewel, Ailsa knew that it was as close as she would ever come to understanding the Kraken's world, that world in which cold and darkness were life, and heat and light were what Councillor Hormos had called "utterly other."

"I'm sorry about Mother's jewels," she said.

"They're nothing. I thought I had given my daughter to try to save the mountain."

They were in one of his private rooms, where they had

supped together, something that she had never done alone with him before. The walls and floor were strewn with treasures. (Since merfolk do not walk, floors are as good a place as walls for pretty things.) All of them, jewels and coral and gold and mother-of-pearl and amber, seemed alive in the black jewel's presence, sending out their different lights in answer to its call.

And not only the jewels. Ailsa picked up the Kraken's gift and cradled it in her palm. Though it was no broader than the base of her middle finger, she could see that inside it the darkness went on for ever. Now she herself felt the same summoning call, and she answered. Answered willingly. Let something—the thing that made her Ailsa and no one else—be drawn into that darkness, let it close around her.

Yes, it went on for ever, before, behind, above, below. There was nothing else, anywhere. But it wasn't frightening. It had shape, structure, life, meaning, not in any ways she could understand—it was too other. But she was sure they were there.

A thread of understanding wound itself into her mind. Or perhaps it was in the Kraken's mind, and she was there too, because the thread seemed to glimmer in the darkness like the thoughts she had seen racing to and fro across the Kraken's huge mass in the darkness beyond the limit. Once again she heard the voiceless command, Go.

She withdrew, and the darkness released her.

She was floating in her father' private room, staring at the Kraken's gift, while that luminous thread found its place and meaning in her mind.

"I don't think it was me the Kraken wanted," she said

slowly. "It wasn't the airfolk either, really. Not for themselves, I mean. It was the moment. Just before they jumped. It was . . . I don't know. . . . They were going to die, so they took their whole lives, everything before and after, and pressed all of it into that one moment together. I saw it. I felt it. I shan't ever forget it. And the Kraken, all that way below . . . even right down there, the Kraken felt it too, and wanted it . . .

"I suppose it's a bit like the jewels. Jewels are about light, aren't they? It's what they do with light that makes them what they are. And that's why it wanted the moment—everything it could have of it—the airfolk—what I'd seen—to tell it about life. Our kind of life, merfolk and airfolk."

"Why should it want these things? And what gives it the right to destroy our mountain for a whim, because it has been prevented from adding some bright little object to its collection?"

"I don't think it's like that. Whims, I mean. I think it *needed* the moment. It had been waiting for something like that since . . . since . . .

"It's because we belong in the light, us and the airfolk. And that moment . . . it was so full of light—I'll never see anything like it again all my life. Not just sunlight and glitter . . . it was them, the way they loved each other . . . everything shone with it. . . . That's what the Kraken wanted . . . needed . . .

"The Kraken isn't going to die, you know. But when the sun goes cold and there's no light left, it will have the whole world, not just the bottom of the sea. But the moment will still be there, with all the other things it's collected ever since time began, waiting to be born again when light comes back.

That's why it needs them. . . . Yes, because it's our . . . our dark guardian . . .

"And I don't think it gave me this . . ."

She touched the black jewel.

". . . just to say thank you, just to be nice to me. It gave it to me because it thought we needed it. So that we can begin to understand its darkness. How other it is."

"You keep using that word. You don't just mean that it's very different from us?"

"No, that isn't the point. It's more than different. It's opposite."

"Well, I suppose you could say we need some inkling of our opposite in order to understand ourselves."

No, she thought. It was so much more than that, but he couldn't imagine it. How could he? Anyway, it didn't matter. She put the jewel down, and he nodded, closing the subject.

"Now," he said. "I want you to explain why you cut school yesterday."

"Because it was my last chance. From now on I'm not going to be able to do that sort of thing anymore. I'll have to do whatever I'm supposed to do because I'm your daughter. I won't be able to cut things. Nobody can make me do them, not even you. But I'll make myself."

"Dominie Paracan was hurt by your absence on your last day. It must have seemed like a deliberate slap in the face to him."

"Yes."

"You mean it was indeed deliberate."

"Dominie Paracan has never treated me fairly."

"He was instructed to deal with you rather more strictly than his other pupils."

"I guessed that. But it was never just strictly. I was always being punished for things I didn't deserve. He enjoyed setting traps for me in order to punish me. That's why I used to play truant. If I was going to be punished, I might as well deserve it."

He sighed. Ailsa had noticed that now, when he was alone with her, he didn't feel the need to keep his usual mask of calm in place.

"That is the trouble with power," he said. "It is the opposite of this jewel. It brings out the dark in you. Why didn't you tell me when he sent you to me for punishment?"

"How could I come whining to you? I don't want you to anything about it now, either. It's over, and he's a good teacher."

He nodded, approving. She caught his sidelong glance of amusement.

"Well, since you have not come whining to me now," he said, "I suppose I must deal this last time with your disobedience."

"A week confined to my rooms on punishment fare?"

He laughed.

"As last time?" he said. "That will start to-morrow morning, but you will have to leave your rooms to report on to-day's events to the Council. The Council will then declare a public holiday, as part of which I will remit a week's punishment for all offenders. This will happen to include you. To-morrow afternoon we will hunt, and I'm afraid that will be the extent of your holidays, because from now on you had better take your place at the Council, and sit in on as many committees as you can so that you can learn their work. I must warn you that most of our meetings are a lot more boring than the one you attended yesterday.

"Now you'd better get to bed. No. Leave the jewel with me. You'll be needing a new diadem."

"What will happen to the airfolk?"

"All we can do is somehow return them to their element."

They dreamed of sunlight and of leaves, and woke to the lap of wavelets on sand. They sat up and looked at each other, bewildered. She wore her marriage dress still, but every jewel upon it, down to the last tiny seed pearl, was gone. So was his armour, though his sword belt was across his shoulder and round his waist, with the sword in its scabbard. Their hair and garments were wet, and their flesh was pale and wrinkled, showing that they had been long in water. They felt sore around their chests, as if they had been bound around with ropes beneath the arms. Deep chill lingered in their bodies, that now seemed to drink hungrily at the morning sun.

They looked around. They were on a silvery beach, with blue sky overhead and a rippling blue sea before them. Behind rose heavy green woods, full of shadow. They had been lying upon two wooden sleds made from old sea-worn timbers and lashed at the joins with ropes twisted from an unfamiliar coarse fibre. The runners of the sleds touched the highest mark left by the receding tide, and the hummocked sand against the head timbers showed that they had been shoved rather than dragged up the beach. No footprints led inland, and the waves had washed out any marks that might have been left below high tide.

They helped each other to their feet and embraced. Dazed still, neither spoke. When they separated, the man eased his sword in its scabbard and

settled it home. The woman pointed at what might be a path into the
trees. They walked towards it, but when they were almost there, the
woman, as if on an impulse, put her hand on his arm and stopped him.
They turned.

"Our thanks," she called to the blank reaches of ocean.

They turned again and disappeared into the trees.

Ailsa watched them go.

A POOL IN THE DESERT

There were no deserts in the Homeland. Perhaps that was why she dreamed of deserts.

She had had her first desert dreams when she was quite young, and still had time to read storybooks and imagine herself in them; but deserts were only one of the things she dreamed about in those days. She dreamed about knights in armour and glorious quests, and sometimes in these dreams she was a knight and sometimes she was a lovely lady who watched a particular knight and hoped that, when he won the tournament, it would be she to whom he came, and stooped on bended knee, and ... and sometimes she dreamed that she was a lady who tied her hair up and pulled a helmet down over it and over her face, and won the tournament herself, and everyone watching said, Who is that strange knight? For I have never seen his like. After her mother fell ill and she no longer had time to read, she still dreamed, but the knights and quests and tournaments dropped out of her dreams, and only the deserts remained.

For years in these desert dreams she rode a slender, graceful horse with an arched neck, and it flew over the sand as if it had wings; but when she drew up on the crest of a dune and looked behind her, there would be the shallow half-circles of hoofprints following them, hummocking the wind-ridges and bending the coarse blades of the sand-grass. Her horse would dance under her, splashing sand, and blow through red nostrils, asking to gallop on, but she would wait for the rest of her party, less wonderfully mounted, toiling behind her. Then she would turn again in the direction they were all going, and shade her eyes with one hand, talking soothingly to her restless horse through the reins held lightly in the other; and there would be the dark shadow of mountains before her, mountains she knew to call the Hills.

As the years passed, however, the dreams changed again. She left school at sixteen because her parents said they could spare her no longer, with her mother ill and Ruth and Jeff still so little and her father and Dane (who had left school two years before) working extra hours in the shop because the specialists her mother needed were expensive. When Mrs Halford and Mr Jonah came to visit them at home (repeated efforts to persuade her parents to come into the school for a meeting having failed), and begged them to reconsider, and said that she was sure of a scholarship, that her education would be no burden to them, her mother only wept and said in her trembling invalid voice that she was a good girl and they needed her at home, and her father only stared, until at last they went away, the tea and biscuits she had made in honour of so rare an event as visitors in the parlour untouched. Her father finally told her: "See them out to their car, Hetta, and then come direct back. Supper's to be on time, mind."

The three of them were quiet as they went down the stairs

and through the hall that ran alongside the shop. The partition was made of cheap ply, for customers never saw it, which made the hall ugly and unfriendly, in spite of the old family photos Hetta had hung on the walls. The shop-door opened nearly on the kerb, for the shop had eaten up all of what had been the front garden. At the last minute Mrs Halford took Hetta's hand and said, "If there's anything I can do—this year, next year, any time. Ring me."

Hetta nodded, said good-bye politely, and then turned round to go back to the house and get supper and see what Ruth and Jeff were doing. Her father had already rejoined Dane in the shop; her mother had gone to bed, taking the plate of biscuits with her.

Ruth had been told by their father to stay out of the way, it was none of her concern, but she was waiting for Hetta in the kitchen. "What happened?" she said.

"Nothing," said Hetta. "Have you done your homework?"

"Yes," said Ruth. "All but the reading. D'you want to listen while you cook?"

"Yes," said Hetta. "That would be nice."

That night Hetta dreamed of a sandstorm. She was alone in darkness, the wind roaring all round her, the sand up to her ankles, her knees, her waist, filling her eyes, her nose, her mouth. Friendly sand. She snuggled down into it as if it were a blanket; as it filled her ears she could no longer hear the wind, nor anything else. When the alarm went off at dawn, she felt as stiff as if she had been buried in sand all night, and her eyes were so sticky, she had to wash her face before she could open them properly.

✦   ✦   ✦

It had been a relief to quit school, because she was tired all the time. There was more than she could get done even after there was no schoolwork to distract her; but without the school-work she found that her mind went to sleep while her body went on with her chores, and for a while that seemed easier. Sometimes months passed without her ever thinking about what she was doing, or not doing, or about Mrs Halford, or about how she might have used that scholarship if she had got it, if her parents had let her accept it, which they wouldn't have. Months passed while her days were bound round with cooking and housekeeping and keeping the shop accounts, looking through cookery books for recipes when her mother thought that this or that might tempt her appetite, sweeping the passage from the shop twice a day because of the sawdust, teaching Ruth and Jeff to play checkers and fold paper air-planes. When she had first started keeping the accounts, she had done it in the evening, after supper was cleared away and there were no other demands till morning, and the kitchen was peaceful while everyone watched TV in the parlour. But she found she was often too bone weary to pay the necessary attention, so she had taught herself to do it in the edgy time between breakfast and lunch, when the phone was liable to ring, and her mother to be contemplating having one of her bad days, and her father to call her down to the shop to wait on a customer. One afternoon a week she took the car to the mall and shopped for everything they had to have. After the narrow confines of the house, the car park seemed liberating, the neon-edged sky vast.

The months mounted up, and turned into years.

One year the autumn gales were so severe that ruining the

harvest and breaking fences for the stock to get through out in the countryside wasn't enough, and they swept into the towns to trouble folk there. Trees and TV aerials came down, and some chimney-pots; there was so much rain that everyone's cellars flooded. The wood stored in their cellar had to come up into the parlour, whereupon there was nowhere to sit except the kitchen. Everyone's tempers grew short with crowding, and when the TV was brought in too, there was nowhere to put it except on counter space Hetta couldn't spare. The only time there was armistice was during programmes interviewing farmers about how bad everything was. Her father watched these with relish and barked "Ha!" often.

That season in spite of the weather she spent more time than ever in the garden. The garden had still been tended by her great-grandfather when she was very small, but after he died, only her grandmother paid any attention to it. As her mother's illness took hold and her father's business took off, it grew derelict, for her grandmother had done the work Hetta did now, with a bad hip and hands nearly frozen with arthritis. Hetta began to clear and plant it about a year after she stopped school; gardening, she found, was interesting, and it got her out of the house. Her father grumbled about having to contain his heaps of wood chips and discarded bits too broken to be mended, but permitted it because she grew vegetables and fruit, which lowered the grocery bills, and she canned and froze what they didn't eat in season. No one else even seemed to notice that the view from the rear of the house looked any different than the front—although Ruth liked bugs, and would sometimes come out to look at the undersides of leaves and scrape things into jars—and so long as Hetta wasn't missing when someone wanted her, nothing was said about the hours she spent in the garden. Their house was the oldest on the street and had the largest garden. It had been a pretty house once, before the shop destroyed its front, but the shop at least made it look more in keeping with the rest of the row. There were proper walls around their garden, eight foot tall on three sides, and the house the fourth. It was her own little realm.

That autumn there was a heaviness to the air, and it smelled of rain and earth and wildness even on days when the sun shone. Hetta usually left as much as she could standing over the winter, to give shelter to Ruth's bugs and the birds and hedgehogs that ate them, but this year she brought the last tomatoes and squashes indoors early (where, denied the wet cellar, she balanced them on piles of timber in the parlour), and she cut back and tied in and staked everything that was left. Even with the walls protecting it, the wind curled in here, flinging other people's tiles at her runner-bean teepees and stripping and shredding the fleece that protected the brassicas. Sometimes she stopped and listened, as if the whistle of the wind was about to tell her something. Sometimes at sunset, when there was another storm coming, the sky reminded her of her desert. But she didn't dare stop long or often, even in the garden; her mother's bedroom window overlooked it, and the sight of Hetta standing still invariably made her hungry. She would open her window and call down to Hetta that she just felt she might eat a little something if Hetta would make it up nice the way she always did and bring it to her.

When the meteorologists began predicting the big storm on its way, the family gathered round the TV set as if the weather report had become a daily installment of a favourite soap opera. Her father snorted; he hated experts in clean business suits telling him things he didn't know. But he didn't protest when the TV was turned on early and he didn't declare the forecast rubbish, and he told Hetta to do her weekly shop early, "just in case."

Two days later the sky went green-yellow, grey-purple; *soon*, sighed the prickle of wind against her skin, and for a moment, leaning on her hoe, the sky was some other sky, and the smooth wooden handle in her hands felt gritty, as if sticky with sand. Her fingers, puzzled, rolled it against her palm, and she blinked, and the world seemed to blink with her, and she was again standing in the back garden of the house where three generations of her father's kin had lived, and there was a storm coming.

When the storm came in the deep night, Hetta was asleep. She knew she was asleep, and yet she knew when the storm wind picked her up . . . no, it did not pick her up, it plunged her down, forced her down, down into darkness and roaring and a great weight against her chest, like a huge hand pressing her into. . . .

She was drowning in sand. It wasn't at all as she'd imagined it, a peaceful ending, a giving up: she did not want to die, and what was happening *hurt*. She gasped and choked, nearly fainting, and the sand bit into her skin, sharp as teeth. She could feel the tiny innumerable grains hissing over her, offering no apparent resistance as she beat at them, pouring through her fingers, down her body, into her eyes and mouth, the unimaginable multitudes of them covering her till they weighed as heavy as boulders, a river, an avalanche....

Where were the others? Had they set out knowing a storm was on the way? Even in this area a storm this severe gave some warning....

In this area? Where was she? There was nothing to tell her—nothing but sand and wind roar and darkness. And ... who were *they?* She could not remember—she would not have set out alone—even a guided party had to take care—in the last few years the storms had grown more violent and less predictable—parties rarely went mounted any more—she—remembered—

Perhaps she slept; perhaps she fainted. But there were hands upon her—hands? Had her party found her again? She tried to struggle, or to cooperate. The hands helped her up, held her up, from her wind-battered, sand-imprisoned crouch. The wind still shouted, and she could see nothing; but the hands arranged the veil over her face and she could breathe a little more easily, and this gave her strength. When the hands lifted her so that one of her arms could be pulled around a set of invisible shoulders, and one of the hands gripped her round her waist, she could walk, staggering, led by her rescuer.

For some time she concentrated on breathing, on breathing and keeping her feet under her, tasks requiring her full attention. But her arm, held round the shoulders, began to ache; and the ache began to penetrate her brain, and her brain began to remember that it didn't usually have to occupy itself with negotiating breathing and walking....

It was still dark, and the wind still howled, and there was still sand in the heaving air, but it pattered against her now, it no longer dragged at and cut her. She thought, The storm is still going on all round us, but it is not reaching us somehow. She had an absurd image that they—her unknown rescuer and herself—were walking in a tiny rolling cup of sand that was always shallow to their feet just a footstep's distance before and behind them, with a close-fitting lid of almost quiet, almost sandless air tucked over them.

When the hand clutching her wrist let go, she grabbed the shoulder and missed, for her hand had gone numb; but the hand round her waist held her. She steadied herself, and the second hand let go, but only long enough to find her hand, and hold it firmly—As if I might run off into the sandstorm again, she thought, distantly amused. She looked toward the hand, the shoulders—and now she could see a human outline, but the face was turned away from her, the free hand groping for something in front of it.

She blinked, trying to understand where the light to see came from. She slowly worked out that the hand was more visible than the rest of the body it was attached to; and she had just realised that they seemed to be standing in front of a huge, rough, slightly glowing—wall? Cliff? For it seemed to loom over them; she guessed at something like a ledge or half-roof high above them—when the fingers stiffened and the hand shook itself up in what seemed like a gesture of command—and the wall before them became a door, and folded back into itself. Light fell out, and pooled in the sand at their feet, outlining tiny pits and hummocks in shadows.

"Quickly," said a voice. "I am almost as tired as you, and Geljdreth does not like to be cheated of his victims."

She just managed to comprehend that the words were for

her, and she stepped through the door unaided. The hand that was holding hers loosed her, the figure followed her, and this time she heard another word, half-shouted, and she turned in time to see the same stiff-fingered jerk of the hand that had appeared to open the door: it slammed shut on a gust of sand like a sword-stroke. The furious sand slashed into her legs and she stumbled and cried out: the hands saved her again, catching her above the elbows. She put her hands out unthinkingly, and felt collarbones under her hands, and warm breath on her wrists.

"Forgive me," she said, and the absurdity of it caught at her, but she was afraid to laugh, as if once she started, she might not be able to stop.

"Forgive?" said the figure. "It is I who must ask you to forgive me. I should have seen you before; I am a Watcher, and this is my place, and Kalarsham is evil-tempered lately and lets Geljdreth do as he likes. But it was as if you were suddenly there, from nowhere. Rather like this storm. A storm like this usually gives warning, even here."

She remembered her first thought when she woke up—if indeed any of this was waking—*Even in this area a storm this severe gave some warning.* "Where—where am I?" she said.

The figure had pulled the veiling down from its face, and pushed the hood back from its head. He was clean-shaven, dark-skinned, almost mahogany in the yellow light of the stony room where they stood, black-haired; she could not see if his eyes were brown or black. "Where did you come from?" he said, not as if he were ignoring her question but as if it had been rhetorical and required no answer. "You must have set out from Chinilar, what, three or four weeks ago? And then come on from Thaar? What I don't understand is what you were doing alone. You had lost whatever kit and company you came with before I found you—I am sorry—but there wasn't even a pack animal with you. I may have been careless"—his voice sounded strained, as if he were not used to finding himself careless—"but I would have noticed, even if it had been too late."

She shook her head. "Chinilar?" she said.

He looked at her as if playing over in his mind what she had last said. He spoke gently. "This is the station of the fourth Watcher, the Citadel of the Meeting of the Sands, and I am he."

"The fourth—Watcher?" she said.

"There are eleven of us," he said, still gently. "We watch over the eleven Sandpales where the blood of the head of Maur sank into the earth after Aerin and Tor threw the evil thing out of the City and it burnt the forests and rivers of the Old Damar to the Great Desert in the rage of its thwarting. Much of the desert is quiet—as much as any desert is quiet—but Tor, the Just and Powerful, set up our eleven stations where the desert is not quiet. The first is named the Citadel of the Raising of the Sands, and the second is the Citadel of the Parting of the Sands, and the third is the Citadel of the Breathing of the Sands. . . . The third, fourth, fifth, and sixth Watchers are often called upon, for our Pales lie near the fastest way through the Great Desert, from Rawalthifan in the West to the plain that lies before the Queen's City itself. But I—I have never Watched so badly before. Where did you come from?" he said again, and now she heard the frustration and distress in his voice. "Where do you come from, as if the storm itself had brought you?"

Faintly she replied: "I come from Roanshire, one of the

south counties of the Homeland; I live in a town called Farbellow about fifteen miles southwest of Mauncester. We live above my father's furniture shop. And I still do not know where I am."

He answered: "I have never heard of Roanshire, or the Homeland, or Mauncester. The storm brought you far indeed. This is the land called Damar, and you stand at the fourth Sandpale at the edge of the Great Desert we call Kalarsham."

And then there was a terrible light in her eyes like the sun bursting, and when she put her hands up to protect her face there was a hand on her shoulder, shaking her, and a voice, a familiar voice, saying, "Hetta, Hetta, wake up, are you ill?" But the voice sounded strange, despite its familiarity, as if speaking a language she used to know but had nearly forgotten. But she heard anxiety in the voice, and fear, and she swam towards that fear, from whatever far place she was in, for she knew the fear, it was hers, and her burden to protect those who shared it. Before she fully remembered the fear or the life that went with it, she heard another voice, an angry voice, and it growled: "Get the lazy lie-abed on her feet or it won't be a hand on her shoulder she next feels"—it was her father's voice.

She gasped as if surfacing from drowning (the howl of the wind, the beating against her body, her face, she had been drowning in sand), and opened her eyes. She tried to sit up, to stand up, but she had come back too far in too short a span of time, and she was dizzy, and her feet wouldn't hold her. She would have fallen, except Ruth caught her—it had been Ruth's hand on her shoulder, Ruth's the first voice she heard.

"Are you ill? Are you ill? I have tried to wake you before—

it is long past sun-up and the storm has blown out, but there is a tree down that has broken our paling, and the front window of the shop. There are glass splinters and wood shavings everywhere—you could drown in them. Dad says Jeff and I won't go to school today, there is too much to do here, although I think two more people with dust-pans will only get in each other's way, but Jeff will somehow manage to disappear and be found hours later at his computer, so it hardly matters."

Hetta's hands were fumbling for her clothes before Ruth finished speaking. She still felt dizzy and sick, and disoriented; but the fear was well known and it knew what to do, and she was dressed and in the kitchen in a few minutes, although her hair was uncombed and her eyes felt swollen and her mouth tasted of . . . sand. She went on with the preparations for breakfast as she had done many mornings, only half-registering the unusual noises below in the shop, habit held her, habit and fear, as Ruth's hands had held her—

—As the strange cinnamon-skinned man's hands had held her.

After she loaded the breakfast dishes into the dishwasher, she dared run upstairs and wash her face and brush her hair. . . . Her hair felt stiff, dusty. She looked down at the top of her chest of drawers and the bare, swept wooden floor she stood on and saw . . . sand. It might have been wood dust carried by yesterday's storm wind; but no tree produced those flat, glinting fragments. She stared a moment, her hairbrush in her hand, and then laid the brush down, turned, and threw the sheets of her bed back.

Sand. More pale, glittery sand. Not enough to sweep together in a hand, but enough to feel on a fingertip, to hold up in the light and look again and again at the flash as if of infinitesimal mirrors.

She fell asleep that night like diving into deep water, but if she dreamed, she remembered nothing of it, and when she woke the next morning, there were no shining, mirror-fragment grains in her bedding. I imagined it, she thought. I imagined it all—and it was the worst thought she had ever had in her life. She was dressed and ready to go downstairs and make breakfast, but for a moment she could not do it. Not even the knowledge of her father's certain wrath could make her leave her bedroom and face this day, any day, any day here, any other person, the people she knew best. She sat down on the edge of her bed and stared bleakly at nothing: into her life. But habit was stronger: it pulled her to her feet and took her downstairs, and, as it had done yesterday, led her hands and feet and body through their accustomed tasks. But yesterday had been—yesterday. Today there was nothing in her mind but darkness.

She struggled against sleep that night, against the further betrayal of the dream. It had been something to do with the storm, she thought, twisting where she lay, the sheets pulling at her like ropes. Something to do with the air a storm brought: it had more oxygen in it than usual, or less, it did funny things to your mind. . . . Some wind-roused ancient street debris that looked like sand had got somehow into her bed; some day, some day soon, but not too soon, she would ask Ruth if there had been grit in her bed too, the day after the big storm.

She took a deep breath: that smell, spicy, although no spice she knew; spice and rock and earth. She was lying on her back, and had apparently kicked free of the tangling sheets at last—no, there was still something wrapped around one ankle—but her limbs were strangely heavy, and she felt too weak even to open her eyes. But she *would* not sleep, she would not. A tiny breeze wandered over her face, bringing the strange smells to her; and yet her bedroom faced the street, and the street smelled of tarmac and car exhaust and dead leaves and Benny's Fish and Chips on the opposite corner.

She groaned, and with a great effort, managed to move one arm. Both arms lay across her stomach; she dragged at one till it flopped off to lie at her side, palm down. What was she lying on? Her fingertips told her it was not cotton sheet, thin and soft from many launderings. Her fingers scratched faintly; whatever this was, it was thick and yielding, and lay over a surface much firmer (her body was telling her) than her old mattress at home.

An arm slid under her shoulders and she was lifted a few inches, and a pillow slid down to support her head. Another smell, like brandy or whisky, although unlike either—her gardener's mind registered steeped herbs and acknowledged with frustration it did not know what herbs. She opened her eyes but saw only shadows.

"Can you drink?"

She opened her mouth obediently, and a rim pressed against her lips and tilted. She took a tiny sip; whatever it was burned and soothed simultaneously. She swallowed, and heat and serenity spread through her. Her body no longer felt leaden, and her eyes began to focus.

She was in a—a cave, with rocky sides and a sandy floor.

There were niches in the walls where oil lamps sat. She knew that smoky, golden light from power cuts at home. When she had been younger and her great-grandfather's little town had not yet been swallowed up by Mauncester's suburbs, there had been power cuts often. That was when her mother still got out of bed most days, and her grandmother used to read to Hetta during the evenings with no electricity, saying that stories were the best things to keep the night outside where it belonged. Cleaning the old oil lamps and laying out candles and matches as she had done the night before last still made her hear her grandmother saying *Once upon a time. . . .* The only complaint Hetta had ever had about her grandmother's stories was that they rarely had deserts in them. Hetta had to blink her eyes against sudden tears.

A cave, she thought, a cave with a sand floor. She looked down at glinting mirror-fragments, like those she had found in the folds of her sheets two nights ago.

I have never heard of Roanshire or the Homeland, or Mauncester. The storm brought you far indeed. This is the land called Damar, and you stand at the fourth Sandpale at the edge of the Great Desert we call Kalarsham.

Her scalp contracted as if someone had seized her hair and twisted it. She gasped, and the cup was taken away and the arm grasped her more firmly. "You have drunk too much, it is very strong," said the voice at her ear; but it was not the liquor that shook her. She sat up and swung her feet round to put them on the floor—there was a bandage tied around one ankle—the supporting arm allowed this reluctantly. She turned her head to look at its owner and saw the man who had rescued her from the sandstorm two nights ago, in her dream. "Where am I?" she said. "I cannot be here. I do not want to go home. I have dreamed this. Oh, I do not want this to be a dream!"

The man said gently, "You are safe here. This is no dream-place, although you may dream the journey. It is as real as you are. It has stood hundreds of years and through many sandstorms—although I admit this one is unusual even in the history of this sanctuary."

"You don't understand," she began, and then she laughed a little, miserably: she was arguing with her own dream-creature.

He smiled at her. "Tell me what I do not understand. What I understand is that you nearly died, outside, a little while ago, because your Watcher almost failed to see you. This is enough to confuse anyone's mind. Try not to distress yourself. Have another sip of the *tiarhk*. It is good for such confusions, and such distress."

She took the cup from him and tasted its contents again. Again warmth and tranquility slid through her, but she could feel her own nature fighting against them, as it had when the doctor had prescribed sleeping pills for her a few years ago. She had had to stop taking the pills. She laced her fingers round the cup and tried to let the *tiarhk* do its work. She took a deep breath. The air was spicy sweet, and again she felt the little stir of breeze; where was the vent that let the air in and kept the dangerous sand-tides out?

"Tell me a little about this place," she said.

He sat back, willing to allow her time to compose herself. "This is the fourth of the Eleven Sandpales that King Tor the Just and Powerful set round the Great Desert Kalarsham some years after the battle of the Hero's Crown and the second and final death of Maur, when it became evident that no easy cure for the desert would be found and that Damar's ancient forest was gone forever, and Geljdreth, the sand-god, would rule us if we let him. This Fourth Pale is called *Horontolopar* in the Old Tongue, and I am its Watcher, Zasharan, fifteenth of that line, for it was my father's mother's mother's father's"—his voice fell into a singsong and she did not count, but she guessed he named fourteen forebears exactly—"mother, who was first called Zasharanth, and installed by Tor himself, and kissed by Queen Aerin, who wished her luck forever. And we have had luck"—he took a deep sigh— "even tonight, for I did find you, though it was a narrow thing. Much too narrow. I would like you to tell me more about *Roanshire*, and *Mauncester*, where you are from, and how you came to be in such state, for no guide would have led or sent you so, and my eye tells me you were alone."

"Your eye?" she said.

"My Eye," he replied, and this time she heard. "I will show you, if you wish. The Eye may see more to this puzzle that you are: how it is that a sandstorm should have come from nowhere to bring you, and yet pursue you across my doorstep so viciously that the wound it laid open on your leg took eight stitches to close. My Eye lies in the place where I Watch, and it is much of how I do what I am here to do. It is only Aerin's Luck that I looked tonight, for this is an unsettled season, and no one has set out from Thaar in weeks. Perhaps you did not come from Thaar."

She laughed, although it hurt her. "No, I did not come from Thaar. And—and I have gone away—and come back. The storm—you brought me here two nights ago."

He looked at her calmly. "You have not been here above an

hour. You fainted, and I took the opportunity to dress your leg. Then you woke."

She was silent a moment. Her head swam, and she did not think another sip of *tiarhk* was advisable. "Are you alone here?"

He looked astonished. "Alone? Certainly not. Rarely does anyone else come to this end of the citadel, for I am the Watcher, and no other has reason to know of the desert door I brought you through. But there are some few of us, and the caves run far up into the Hills, and where they come out there is the filanon town Sunbarghon, although you would not find it unless they decided to allow you to, and Ynorkgindal, where they ring the Border, that the music of their bells may help keep us safe from the North, and the dlor Gzanforyar, which is mastered by my good friend Rohk. Perhaps you will meet him one day—" He blinked and gave a tiny shiver, and said, "Forgive me, lady, that was presumptuous."

She shook her head. "I should like to meet him," she said, but she heard in her voice that she believed there would be no such meeting. Zasharan heard it too, and turned his face a little away from her, and she saw how stiffly he sat. Her first thought was that she had offended him, but she remembered, *Forgive me, lady, that was presumptuous,* and before she could think, had reached to touch his arm. "But I *would* like to meet your friend, and see the caves, and your Eye, and—" She stopped. How long would the dream last this time?

He turned back to her. "There is something strange about you, I know that, and I see—I think I see—I—" He looked down at her hand on his arm, which she hastily removed. "You trouble me, lady. May I have your name?"

"Hetta," she said.

"Hetthar," he said. "Do you think you can stand, and walk? Do you wish food first? For I would like you to come to the place of my Eye, where I think you and I may both be able to see more plainly."

"I am not hungry," she said, and tried to stand; but as she did, her head swam, and Zasharan and the room began to fade, and she began to smell wood shavings and wet tarmac. "The sand!" she cried. "The sand!" And just before she lost consciousness, she flung herself on the floor of Zasharan's cave, and scrabbled at the sand with her hands.

She woke lying on her back again, her hands upon her stomach, but her hands were shut into fists, and the backs of them hurt up into her forearms, as if she had been squeezing them closed for a long time. With some difficulty she unbent the fingers, and two tiny palmfuls of sand poured out upon her nightdress. Slowly, slowly she sat up, pulling up folds of her nightdress to enclose the sand. She stood, clutching the front of her nightdress together, and went to her chest of drawers. She had been allowed to move into this room, which had been her grandmother's, when her grandmother died, but she had always been too busy—or too aware of herself as interloper—to disarrange any of her grandmother's things that weren't actively in her way. But they were friendly things, and once the first shock of grief was over, she liked having them there, reminding her of her gran, and no longer wondered if it might be disrespectful to keep them as they were. On the top of the chest there was an assortment of little lidded boxes and jars that had once held such things as bobby pins and cotton balls and powder, and were now empty. She chose one and carefully transferred the sand into it. She stood looking at its lid for a moment. She had chosen this one because it had a pretty curl of dianthus flower and leaf painted on its surface; her gran's dianthus still bloomed in the garden. She lifted the lid to reassure herself that the sand was still there—that it hadn't disappeared as soon as she closed the box—and for a moment, faint but unmistakable, she smelled the spicy smell of Zasharan's cave, and *tiarhk*.

When she dreamt of nothing again that night, she almost didn't care. When she woke up, she looked in the tiny box on her chest of drawers and the sand was still there on this second morning, and then she went downstairs to get breakfast. Today was her day to drive to the mall. Usually, if her list was not too long, she could spare an hour for herself. And today she wanted to go to the library.

It took more time to get to the mall than usual; she had had to go the long way round their block because of the fallen tree that still lay in the broken remains of their front paling, and there were other trees down elsewhere that the exhausted and overburdened county council had not yet cut up and hauled away. In one place the road had caved in where a flash flood had undermined it. There were detours and orange warning cones and temporary stoplights, and when she finally got there, some of the car park at the mall was blocked off. She'd have barely half an hour at the library, and only if she pelted through the rest first.

She didn't go to the library very often any more, since she had had to stop school. She didn't have much time for reading, and she couldn't think of any book she wanted to read: both fiction and nonfiction only reminded her of what she wasn't doing and might never do. She did read seed catalogues, intensely, from cover to cover, every winter, and the off-beat gardening books and even more bizarre popular science books Ruth bought her every birthday and Christmas, which, because Ruth had bought them, were friendly instead of accusing. The library felt like a familiar place from some other life. There were calluses on her hands that scraped against the pages that hadn't been there when she had been coming here several times a week.

None of the encyclopedias had any listings for Damar, nor the atlases, and she didn't have time to queue for a computer. They had added more computers since she had been here last, but it hadn't changed the length of the queue. She went reluctantly to the help desk. Geography had never been a strong suit, and by the time she was standing in front of the counter, she felt no more than ten and a good six inches shorter. "Er— have you ever heard of a place called Damar?" The librarian's eyes went first to the row of computers, all occupied, and she sighed. She looked up at Hetta. "Yes," said Hetta. "I've tried the encyclopedias and atlases."

The librarian smiled faintly, then frowned. "Damar. I don't recall—what do you know about it?"

It has eleven Sandpales and a Watcher named Zasharan at the fourth. "Um. It—it has a big desert in it, which used to be ancient forest." The librarian raised her eyebrows. "It's—it's a crossword puzzle clue," said Hetta, improvising hastily. "It's— it's a sort of bet."

The librarian looked amused. She tapped *Damar* into the computer in front of her. "Hmm. Try under *Daria.* Oh yes— Damar," she said, looking interested. "I remember . . . oh dear.

If you want anything recent, you will have to consult the newspaper archive." She looked suddenly hunted. "There's a bit of a, hmm, gap . . . up till five years ago, everything is on microfiche, and in theory everything since is available on the computer system but, well, it isn't, you know. . . . Let me know if I can find . . . if I can try to find anything for you." She looked at Hetta with an expression that said full body armour and possibly an oxygen tank and face-mask were necessary to anyone venturing into the newspaper archive.

"Thank you," said Hetta demurely, and nearly ran back to the reference room; her half hour was already up.

Daria. The Darian subcontinent in southwestern Asia comprises a large landmass including both inland plains, mostly desert with irregular pockets of fertile ground, between its tall and extensive mountain ranges, and a long curved peninsula of gentler and more arable country in the south. . . . Its government is a unique conception, being both the Republic of Damar under its own people and a Protectorate of the Homeland Empire and legislated by her appointed officers. See text articles. . . .

Damar. It existed.

She had been nearly an hour at the library. She ran out to the car park and banged the old car into gear in a way it was not at all used to. It gave a howl of protest but she barely heard it. Damar. *It existed!*

The ice cream had started to melt but her father never ate ice cream, and there were scones for tea with the eggs and sausages because scones were the fastest thing she could think of and her father wouldn't eat store bread. She ignored more easily than usual her mother's gently murmured litany of complaint when she took her her tray, and in blessed peace and quiet—Dane and his girlfriend, Lara, were having dinner with her parents, Jeff was doing homework in his room, their father was downstairs in the shop, and Hetta had firmly turned the still-resident TV *off*–began washing up the pots and pans that wouldn't fit in the dishwasher. She was trying to remember anything she could about Daria—they had been studying the Near East in history and current events the year her grandmother had died and her mother had first taken seriously ill, and the only thing she remembered clearly was *Great Expectations* in literature class, because she had been wishing that some convict out of a graveyard would rescue her. This had never struck her as funny before, but she was smiling over the sink when Ruth—whom she hadn't heard come into the kitchen—put her hand on her arm, and said, or rather whispered, "Hetta, what is *with* you? Are you okay?"

"What do you mean?"

"You haven't been yourself since the storm. I mean, good for you, I think you haven't been yourself in about eight years, except I was so young then I didn't know what was going on, and maybe you're becoming yourself again now. But you're different, and look, you know Mum and Dad, they don't like different. It'll turn out bad somehow if they notice. At the moment Dad's still totally preoccupied with the storm damage but he won't be forever. And even Mum—" Ruth shrugged. Their mother had her own ways of making things happen.

Hetta had stopped washing dishes in surprise but began again; Ruth picked up a dish-towel and began to dry. They both cast a wary look at the door; the hum of the dishwasher would disguise their voices as long as they spoke quietly, but their father didn't like conversations he couldn't hear, and the only topics he wished discussed all had to do with business and building furniture. "I—I'm embarrassed to tell you," said Hetta, concentrating on the bottom of a saucepan.

"Try me," said Ruth. "Hey, I study the sex lives of bugs. Nothing embarrasses me."

Hetta sucked in her breath on a suppressed laugh. "I—I've been having this dream—" She stopped and glanced at Ruth. Ruth was looking at her, waiting for her to go on. "It's . . . it's like something real."

"I've had dreams like that," said Ruth, "but they don't make me go around looking like I've got a huge important secret, at least I don't think they do."

Hetta grinned. Hetta had always been the dreamy daughter, as their father had often pointed out, and Ruth the practical one. Their grandmother had teased that she was grateful for the eight-year difference in their ages because telling stories to both of them at the same time would have been impossible. Hetta wanted fairy-tales. Ruth wanted natural history. (The two sons of the house had been expected to renounce the soft feminine pleasures of being tucked in and told stories.) The problem with Ruth's practicality was that it was turning out to have to do with science, not furniture; Ruth eventually wanted to go into medical research, and her biology teacher adored her. Ruth was fifteen, and in a year she would have to go up against their father about what she would do next, a confrontation Hetta had lost, and Dane had sidestepped by being—apparently genuinely—eager to stop wasting time in school and get down to building furniture ten hours a day. Hetta was betting on Ruth, but she wasn't looking forward to being around during the uproar.

"Do you know anything about Daria?"

Ruth frowned briefly. "It got its independence finally, a year or two ago, didn't it? And has gone back to calling itself Damar, which the Damarians had been calling it all along. There was something odd about the hand-over though." She paused. International politics was not something their father was interested in, and whatever the news coverage had been, they wouldn't have seen it at home. After a minute Ruth went on: "One of my friends—well, she's kind of a space case— Melanie, she says that it's full of witches and wizards or something and they do, well, real magic there, and all us Homelander bureaucrats either can't stand it and have really short terms and are sent home, or really get into it and go native and stay forever. She had a great-uncle who got into it and wanted to stay, but his wife hated it, so they came home, and you still only have to say 'Daria' to her and she bursts into tears, but he told Melanie a lot about it before he died, and according to her . . . well, I said she's a space case. It's not the sort of thing I would remember except that there *was* something weird about the hand-over when it finally happened and Melanie kept saying 'well of course' like she knew the real reason. Why?"

"I've been dreaming about it."

"About *Daria?*–Damar, I mean. How do you dream about a *country?*"

"Not about the whole country. About a—a person, who lives on the edge of the—the Great Desert. He says he is one of the Watchers—there are eleven of them. Um. They sort of keep an eye on the desert. For sandstorms and things."

"Is he cute?"

Hetta felt a blush launch itself across her face. "I—I hadn't thought about it." This was true.

Ruth laughed, and forgot to swallow it, and a moment later there was a heavy foot on the stair up from the shop and their father appeared at the kitchen door. "Hetta can finish the dishes without your help," he said. "Ruth, as you have nothing to do, you can have a look at these," and he thrust a handful of papers at her. "I've had an insulting estimate from the insurance agent today and I want something to answer him with. If Hetta kept the files in better order, I wouldn't have to waste time now."

She did not dream of Zasharan that night, but she dreamed of walking in a forest full of trees she did not know the names of, and hearing bird-voices, and knowing, somehow, that some of them were human beings calling to other human beings the news that there was a stranger in their forest. She seemed to walk through the trees for many hours, and once or twice it occurred to her that perhaps she was lost and should be frightened, but she looked round at the trees and smiled, for they were friendly, and she could not feel lost even if she did not know where she was, nor frightened, when she was surrounded by friends. At last she paused, and put her hand on the deeply rutted bark of a particular tree that seemed to call to her to touch it, and looked up into its branches; and there, as if her eyes were learning to see, the leaves and branches rearranged themselves into a new pattern that included a human face peering down at her. It held very still, but it saw at once when she saw it; and then it smiled, and a branch near it turned into an arm, and it waved. When she raised her own hand—the one not touching the tree—to wave back, she woke, with one hand still lifted in the air.

She did not dream of Zasharan the next night either, but she dreamed that she was walking past a series of stables and paddocks, where the horses watched her, ears pricked, as she went by, till she came to a sand-floored ring where several riders were performing a complicated pattern, weaving in and out of each other's track. The horses wore no bridles, and their saddles, whose shape was strange to her eyes, had no stirrups. She watched for a moment, for the pattern the horses were making (while their riders appeared to sit motionless astride them) was very lovely and graceful. When the horses had all halted, heads in a circle, and all dropped their noses as if in salute, one of the riders broke away and came towards her, and nodded to her, and said, "I am Rohk, master of this dlor, and I should know everyone who goes here, but I do not know you. Will you give me your name, and how came you past the guard at the gate?"

He spoke in a pleasant voice, and she answered with no fear, "My name is Hetta, and I do not remember coming in your gate. Zasharan has mentioned you to me, and perhaps that is how I came here."

Rohk touched his breast with his closed hand, and then opened it towards her, flicking the fingers in a gesture she did not know. "If you are a friend of Zasharan, then you are welcome here, however you came."

✦   ✦   ✦

On the third night she was again walking in a forest, and she looked up hopefully, searching for a human face looking down at her, but for what seemed to be a long time she saw no one. But as she walked and looked, she began to realise that she was hearing something besides birdsong and the rustle of leaves; it sounded like bells, something like the huge bronze bells of the church tower in her town, but there were too many bells, too many interlaced notes—perhaps more like the bells of the cathedral in Mauncester. She paused and listened more intently. The bells seemed to grow louder: their voices were wild, buoyant, superb; and suddenly she was among them, held in the air by the bright weave of their music. The biggest bell was turning just at her right elbow, she could look into it as it swung up towards her, she could see the clapper fall, BONG! The noise this close was unbearable—it should have been unbearable—it struck through her like daggers— no: like sunbeams through a prism, and she stood in air full of rainbows. But now she could hear voices, human voices, through the booming of the bells, and they said: *Come down, you must come down, for when the bells stand up and silent, you will fall.*

She looked down and saw the faces of the ringers, hands busy and easy on the ropes, but the faces looking up at her fearful and worried. *I do not know how,* she said, but she knew she made no sound, any more than a rainbow can speak. And then she heard the silence beyond the bells, and felt herself falling past the music and into the silence; but she woke before she had time to be afraid, and she was in her bed in her father's house, and it was time to get up and make breakfast.

✦　　✦　　✦

That afternoon when Ruth came home from school, she bent over Hetta's chair and dropped a kiss on the top of her head, as she often did, but before she straightened up again, she murmured, "I have something for you." But Lara, on the other side of the table, was peeling potatoes with a great show of being helpful, and Ruth said no more. It was a busy evening, for both the hired cabinetmakers from the shop, Ron and Tim, had been invited to stay late and come for supper, which was one of Hetta's father's ways of avoiding paying them overtime, and it was not until they had gone to bed that Ruth came creeping into Hetta's room with a big envelope. She grinned at Hetta, said, "Sweet dreams," and left again, closing the door silently behind her. Hetta listened till she was sure Ruth had missed the three squeaky stairs on her way back to her own room before she dumped the contents of the envelope out on her bed.

Come to Damar, land of orange groves, said the flier on top. She stared at the trees in the photo, but they were nothing like the trees she had seen in her dream two nights before. She shuffled through the small pile of brochures. As travel agents' propaganda went, this was all very low-key. There were no girls in bikinis and no smiling natives in traditional dress; just landscape, desert and mountains and forests—and orange plantations, and some odd-looking buildings. What people there were all seemed to be staring somewhat dubiously at the camera. Some of them were cinnamon-skinned and black-haired like Zasharan.

There were also a few sheets of plain stark print listing available flights and prices—these made her hiss between her teeth. Her father gave her something above the housekeeping money that he called her wages, which nearly covered replacing clothes that had worn out and disintegrated off their seams; she had nonetheless managed to save a little, by obstinacy; she could probably save more if she had to. Most of her grandmother's clothes still hung in the cupboard, for example; she had already altered one or two blouses to fit herself, and a skirt for Ruth. The difficulty with this however was that while her father would never notice the recycling of his mother's old clothes, Hetta's mother would, and would mention it in her vague-seeming way to her husband, who would then decide that Hetta needed less money till this windfall had been thoroughly used up. But over the years Hetta had discovered various ways and means to squeeze a penny till it screamed, her garden produced more now than it had when she began as she learnt more about gardening, and the butcher liked her. . . .

Perhaps. Just perhaps.

She did not dream of Zasharan that night either, but she smelled the desert wind, and for a moment she stood somewhere that was not Farbellow or her father's shop, and she held a cup in her hands, but when she raised it to taste its contents, it was only water.

She thought about the taste of desert water that afternoon as she raked the pond at the back of the vegetable garden. She wore tall green wellies on her feet and long rubber gloves, but it was still very hard not to get smudgy and bottom-of-pond-rot-smelling while hauling blanket-weed and storm-detritus out of a neglected pond. She didn't get back here as often as she wanted to because the pond didn't produce anything but newts and blanket-weed and she didn't have time for it, although even at its worst it was a magical spot for her, and the only place in the garden where her mother couldn't see her from her window.

She had wondered all her life how her great-grandmother had managed to convince her great-grandfather to dig her a useless ornamental pond. Her great-grandfather had died when she was four, but she remembered him clearly: in his extreme old age he was still a terrifying figure, and even at four she remembered how her grandmother, his daughter, had seemed suddenly to shed a burden after his death—and how Hetta's own father had seemed to expand to fill that empty space. Hetta's father, her grandmother had told her, sadly, quietly, not often, but now and again, was just like his grandfather. Hetta would have guessed this anyway; there were photographs of him, and while he had been taller than her father, she recognised the glare. She couldn't imagine what it must have been like to be his only child, as her grandmother had been.

But his wife had had her pond.

It was round, and there was crazy paving around the edge of it. There was a little thicket of coppiced dogwood at one end, which guarded it from her mother, which Hetta cut back religiously every year; but the young red stems were very pretty and worthwhile on their own account as well as for the screen they provided. She planted sunflowers at the backs of the vegetable beds, and then staked them, so they would stand through the winter: these sheltered it from view of the shop as if, were her father reminded of it, it would be filled in at once and used for potatoes. It was an odd location to choose for a pond; it was too well shaded by the apple tree and the wall to grow water lilies in, for example, but the paving made it look as though you might want to set chairs beside it and admire the newts and the blanket-weed on nice summer evenings; nearer the house you would have less far to carry your patio furniture and tea-tray. Maybe her great-grandmother had wanted to hide from view too. Hetta's grandmother had found it no solace; she called it "eerie" and stayed away. "She was probably just one of these smooth, dry humans with no amphibian blood," Ruth had said once, having joined Hetta poolside one evening and discovered, upon getting up, that she had been sitting in mud. Ruth had also told Hetta that her pond grew rather good newts: Turner's Greater Red-Backed Newt, to be precise, which was big (as newts go) and rare.

Hetta paused a moment, leaning on her rake. She would leave the blanket-weed heaped up on the edge of the pond overnight, so that anything that lived in it had time to slither, creep, or scurry back into the pond; and then she would barrow it to the compost heap behind the garage. She looked down at her feet. The blanket-weed was squirming. A newt crept out and paused as if considering; it had a jagged vermilion crest down its back like a miniature dragon, and eyes that seemed to flash gold in the late-afternoon sunlight—she fancied that it glanced up at her before it made its careful way down the blanket-weed slope and slid into the pond with the tiniest chuckle of broken water.

That night she woke again in Zasharan's rocky chamber. She lay again on the bed or pallet where she had woken before; and she turned her head on her pillow and saw Zasharan dozing in a chair drawn up beside her. As she looked into his face, he opened his eyes and looked back at her. "Good," he said. "I dreamed that you would wake again soon. Come—can you stand? I am sorry to press you when you are weary and confused, but there are many things I do not understand, and I want to take you to my Eye quickly, before you escape me again. If you cannot stand, and if you will permit it, I will carry you."

"Dream?" she said. "You *dreamed* I would return?" She was sitting up and putting her feet on the floor as she spoke—bare feet, sandy floor, her toes and heels wriggled themselves into their own little hollows without her conscious volition. For the first time she thought to look at what she was wearing: it was a long loose robe, dun-coloured in the lamplight, very like her nightdress at home—it could almost be her night-dress—but the material was heavier and fell more fluidly, and there seemed to be a pattern woven into it that she could not see in the dimness.

"Watchers often dream," he said. "It is one of the ways we Watch. No Watcher would be chosen who had not found his— or her—way through dreams many times." He offered her his hand. "But you—I am not accustomed to my visitors telling me they are dream-things when I am not dreaming."

She stood up and staggered a little, and he caught her under the elbows. "I will walk," she said. "I walked here before, did I not? The—the night I came here—nearly a fortnight ago now." He smiled faintly. "I would like to walk. Walking makes me feel—less of a dream-thing."

His smile jerked, as if he understood some meaning of her remark she had not meant, and they left the room, and walked for some time through rocky corridors hazily lit by some variable and unseen source. At first these were narrow and low, and the floor was often uneven although the slope was steadily upward; both walls and floor were yellowy-goldeny-grey, although the walls seemed darker for the shadows they held in their rough hollows. The narrow ways widened, and she could see other corridors opening off them on either side. She felt better for the walk—realler, as she had said, less like a dream-thing. She could feel her feet against the sand, a faint ache from the wound on her ankle, listen to her own breath, feel the air of this place against her skin. She knew she was walking slowly, tentatively, when at home she was quick and strong, and needed to be. Perhaps—perhaps they were very high here—had he not said something about hills?—perhaps it was the elevation that made her feel so faint and frail.

They had turned off the main way into one of the lesser corridors, and came at last to a spiral stair. The treads twinkled with trodden sand in the dim directionless light as far up as she could see till they rounded the first bend. "You first, lady," he said, and she took a deep breath and grasped the rope railing, and began to pull herself wearily up, step by step; but to her surprise the way became easier the higher they climbed, her legs grew less tired and her breath less laboured. They came out eventually on a little landing before a door, and Zasharan laid his hand softly on it and murmured a word Hetta could not hear, and it opened.

There were windows on the far side of the room, curtainless, with what she guessed was dawn sunlight streaming in; she flinched as the daylight touched her as if in this place she would prove a ghost or a vampire, but nothing happened but that its touch was gentle and warm. The view was of a steep slope rising above them; the room they were in seemed to grow out of the hillside.

There was a round pool in the middle of the floor and Zasharan knelt down beside it on the stone paving that surrounded it. "This is my Eye," he said softly. "Come and look with me."

She knelt near him, propping herself with her hands, for she was feeling weary again. Her gaze seemed to sink below the water's surface in a way she did not understand; perhaps the contents of the pool was not water. And as her sight plunged deeper, she had the odd sensation that something in the depths was rising towards her, and she wondered suddenly if she wanted to meet it, whatever it was.

A great, golden Eye, with a vertical pupil expanding as she saw it, as if it had only just noticed her . . .

She gave a small gasp, and she heard Zasharan murmuring beside her, but she could not hear what he said; and then the pupil of the Eye expanded till it filled the whole of her vision with darkness, and then the darkness cleared, and she saw—

She woke in her bed, her heart thundering, gasping for breath, having pulled the bed to bits, the blankets on the floor, the sheets knotted under her and her feet on bare ticking. It was just before dawn; there was grey light leaking through the gap at the bottom of the blind. She felt exhausted, as if she had had no sleep at all, and at the same time grimly, remorselessly awake. She knew she would not sleep again.

Her right ankle ached, and she put her fingers down to rub it; there was a ridge there, like an old scar.

She got through the day somehow, but she left a pot of soup on the back of the cooker turned up too high, so it had boiled over while she was scraping the seeds out of squashes over the compost heap, and her mother had called out, a high, thin shriek, that the house was burning down, although it was only burnt soup on the hob. Her mother had palpitations for the rest of the evening, was narrowly talked out of ringing the doctor to have something new prescribed for her nerves, and insisted that she might have burned in her bed. Her father complained about the thick burnt smell spoiling his tea, and that Hetta was far too old to make stupid mistakes like that. She went to bed with a headache, remembering that the blanket-weed was still waiting for her to haul it away, and found two aspirin on her pillow, and a glass of water on the floor beside it: Ruth. Their father believed that pharmacology was for cowards. The only drugs in the house were on her mother's bedside table, and Hetta would much rather have a headache than face her mother again that evening; she had forgotten Ruth's secret stash. She swallowed the pills gratefully and lay down.

When she opened her eyes she was again by the pool in Zasharan's tower, but she had moved, or been moved, a little distance from it, so she could no longer look into it (or perhaps it could no longer look out at her), and Zasharan sat beside her, head bowed, holding her hand. When she stirred, he looked up at once, and said, "I have looked, and asked my people to look, in our records, and I cannot find any tale to help us. I am frightened, for you sleep too long—it is longer each time you leave. You have been asleep nearly a day, and there are hollows under your eyes. This is not the way it should be. You live elsewhere—you have been born and have lived to adulthood in this elsewhere—where you should not be; you should be here; my Eye would not have troubled itself to look at any stranger, and my heart welcomes you whether I would or nay. There have been others who have come here by strange ways, but they come and they stay. If you wish to come here and we wish to have you, why do you not stay?"

She sat up and put her other hand on his and said, "No, wait, it is all right. I have found Damar in the atlas at home, and my sister has found out about air flights, and I will come here in the—in the—" She stumbled over how to express it. "In the usual way. And I will come here, and find you." She heard herself saying this as if she were listening to a television pro-gramme, as if she had nothing to do with it; and yet she knew she had something to do with it, because she was appalled. Who was this man she only met in dream to tell her where she belonged, and who was she to tell him that she was going to come to him—even to herself she did not know how to put it—that she was going to come to him in the real world?

"Air flights," he said thoughtfully.

"Yes," she said. "Where is the nearest airport? I could not find Thaar, or Chin—Chin—" As she said this, her voice wa-vered, because she remembered how hard it was to remember anything from a dream; and she was dreaming. *Remember the sand,* her dream-thought told her. *Remember the sand that lies in the little box on your chest of drawers.* "Oh—you will have to tell me how to find you. I assume there is a better way than . . ." Her voice trailed away again as she remembered being lost in the sandstorm, of being led blindly through the sand-wind, her arm pulled round Zasharan's shoulders till her own shoulder ached, remembered her curious sense that they were somehow kept safe in a little rolling bubble of air that let them make their way to the door in the cliff. *That is why he is a Watcher*, said the dream-thought. *There is little use in Watching if you cannot act upon what you see.*

"I do not know where the nearest airport is. What is an airport?" said Zasharan.

She knew, sometimes, that she spoke some language other than Homelander in her dreams; but then it was the sort of thing you felt you knew while you were dreaming and yet also knew that it was only a trick of the mind. The words she spoke to Zasharan—the words she had heard and spoken to the other Damarians she had met in other dreams—*felt* different. It was just a part of the dream, as was the different, more rolling, growlier, peaked-and-valleyed sound of the words Zasharan and the other Damarians said to her than what she spoke in Farbellow, when she was awake. (*I am awake now*, said the dream-thought.) It was only a part of the same mind-trick that when Zasharan said "airport," it sounded like a word that came from some other language than the one he was speaking.

She looked around, and saw a table in the corner, and books upon it (were these the records he had been searching for stories like hers?), and several loose sheets of paper, and a pen. She stood up—carefully, prepared to be dizzy—and gestured towards the table. Zasharan stood up with her. "May I?" she said. He nodded as anyone might nod, but he also made a gesture with his hand that was both obviously that of hospitality and equally not at all—she thought; her dream-thought thought—like the gesture she would have made if someone had asked her to borrow a sheet of paper.

She took a deep breath, and picked up the pen (which was enough like an old-fashioned fountain pen that she did not have to ask how to use it) and drew an airplane on the top sheet of paper. She was not an artist, but anyone in the world she knew would have recognised what she drew at once as an airplane.

Zasharan only looked at it, puzzled, worried, both slightly frowning and slightly smiling, and shook his head, and made another gesture, a gesture of unknowing, although not the shoulders raised and hands spread that she would have made (that she thought she would have made) in a similar situation.

Frustrated, she folded the sheet of paper, lengthwise in half, then folding the nose, the wings—she threw it across the room and it flew over the round pool where the Eye waited, bumped into the wall on the far side and fell to the ground. "Paper airplane," she said.

"Paper glider," he agreed. He walked round the pool, and picked her airplane up, and brought it back to the table. He unfolded it, carefully, pressing the folds straight with his fingers, smoothing and smoothing the wrinkles the bumped nose had made—as if paper were rare and precious, she thought, refusing to follow that thought any farther—and then, quickly, he folded it again, to a new pattern, a much more complex pattern, and when he tossed his glider in the air it spun up and then spiralled down in a lovely curve, and lit upon the floor as lightly as a butterfly.

She looked at him, and there was a sick, frightened feeling

in her throat. "When you travel—long distances," she said, "how—how do you go?" She could not bring herself to ask about cars and trucks and trains.

"We have horses and asses and ankaba," he said. "You may walk or ride or lead a beast loaded with your gear. We have guides to lead you. We have waggoners who will carry you and your possessions. There are coaches if you can afford them; they are faster—and, they say, more comfortable, but I would not count on this." He spoke mildly, as if this were an ordinary question, but his eyes were fixed on her face in such a way that made it plain he knew it was not.

Slowly she said, "What year is it, Zasharan?"

He said, "It is the year 3086, counting from the year Gasthamor came from the east and struck the Hills with the hilt of his sword, and the Well of the City of the Kings and Queens opened under the blow."

"Gasthamor," said Hetta, tasting the name.

"Gasthamor, who was the teacher of Oragh, who was the teacher of Semthara, who was the teacher of Frayadok, who was the teacher of Goriolo, who was the teacher of Luthe," said Zasharan.

Gasthamor, she repeated to herself. *Goriolo*. She doubted that the encyclopedia would tell the tale of the warrior-mage who struck the rock with the hilt of his sword and produced a flow of water that would last over three thousand years, but an encyclopedia of legends might. "You—you said the Queen's City, once before," she said. "What is the name of your queen?"

"Fortunatar," he said. "Fortunatar of the Clear Seeing."

She woke to the sound of her own voice, murmuring, *Gasthamor, Fortunatar of the Clear Seeing, the year 3086*. Her heart was heavy as she went about her chores that day, and she told herself that this was only because it was two more days before she could go to the library again, and look up the kings and queens of Damar.

She made time to finish cleaning the pool at the back of the garden, hauling the blanket-weed—now a disgusting sticky brown mat—two heaped barrowloads of the stuff—to the compost heap. When she was done, she knelt on the crazy paving that edged the pool, and dipped her dirty hands in the water. The sting of its coolness was friendly, energising; her head felt clearer and her heart lighter than it had in several days. She patted her face with one wet hand, letting the other continue to trail in the water, and she felt a tiny flicker against her palm. She looked down, and there was a newt, swimming back and forth in a tiny figure eight, the curl of one arc inside her slightly cupped fingers. She turned her hand so that it was palm up, and spread her fingers. It swam to the centre of her palm and stopped. She thought she could just feel the tickle of tiny feet against her skin.

She raised her hand very, very slowly; as the newt's crested back broke the surface of the water, it gave a frantic, miniature heave and scrabble, and she thought it would dive over the little rise made by the web between her forefinger and thumb, but it stilled instead, seeming to crouch and brace itself, as against some great peril. Now she definitely felt its feet: the forefeet at the pulse-point of her wrist, the rear on the pads at the roots of her fingers, the tail sliding off her middle finger between it and the ring finger. She found she was holding her breath.

She continued to raise her hand till it was eye level to herself; and the newt lifted its head and stared at her. Its eyes were so small, it was difficult to make out their colour: gold, she thought, with a vertical black pupil. The newt gave a tiny shudder and the startling red crest on its back lifted and stiffened.

They gazed at each other for a full minute. Then she lowered her hand again till it touched the pond surface, and this time the newt was gone so quickly that she stared at her empty palm, wondering if she had imagined the whole thing.

She heard bells ringing in her dreams that night, but they seemed sombre and sad. On the next night she thought she heard Zasharan's voice, but she was lost in the dark, and whichever way she turned, his voice came from behind her, and very far away.

She stormed around the supermarket the next day, and when she found herself at the check-out behind someone who had to think about which carefully designated bag each item went into, she nearly started throwing his own apples at him. She arrived at the library with less than half an hour left, but her luck had found her at last, for there was a computer free. *Queens of Damar*, she typed. There was a whirr, and a list of web sites which mentioned (among other things) internationally assorted queens apparently not including Damarian, paint varnishes, long underwear, and hair dressing salons, presented itself to her hopefully. She stared at the screen, avoiding asking something that would tell her what she feared. At last she typed: *Who is the ruler of Damar today?*

Instantly the screen replied: *King Doroman rules with the Council of Five and the Parliament of Montaratur.*

There was no help for it. *Queen Fortunatar of the Clear Seeing*, she typed.

There was a pause while the computer thought about it. She must have looked as frustrated and impatient as she felt, because a librarian paused beside her and asked in that well-practised ready-to-go-away-without-taking-offense voice if she could be of service.

"I am trying to find out some information about the queen of Damar," she said.

"Damar? Oh—Daria—oh—Damar. Someone else was just asking about Damar a few weeks ago. It's curious how much we *don't* hear about a country as big as it is. They have a king now, don't they? I seem to remember from the independence ceremonies. I can't remember if he had a wife or not."

The computer was still thinking. Hetta said, finding herself glad of the distraction, "The queen I want is Fortunatar of the Clear Seeing."

The librarian repeated this thoughtfully. "She sounds rather, hmm, poetical, though, doesn't she? Have you tried myths and legends?"

The computer had now hung itself on the impossible question of a poetical queen of Damar, and Hetta was happy to let the librarian lean over her and put her hands on the keyboard and wrestle it free. The librarian knew, too, how to ask the library's search engine questions it could handle, and this time when an answering screen came up, there was a block of text highlighted:

Shortly after this period of upheaval, Queen Fortunatar, later named of the Clear Seeing for the justice of her rulings in matters both legal and numinous, took her throne upon the death of her half-brother Linmath. Linmath had done much in his short life, and he left her a small but sound queendom which flourished under her hand. The remaining feuds were settled not by force of arms (nor by the trickery that had caught Linmath fatally unaware) but by weaponless confrontation before the queen and her counsellors; and fresh feuds took no hold and thus shed no blood. The one serious and insoluble menace of Fortunatar's time were the sandstorms in the Great Desert which were frequent and severe.

"Hmm," said the librarian, and scrolled quickly to the top of the document. *An Introduction to the Legendary History of Damar:*

All countries have their folk tales and traditions, but Damar is unusual in the wealth of these, and in the inextricable linkage between them and what western scholars call factual history. Even today. . . .

Hetta closed her eyes. Then she opened them again without looking at the computer screen, made a dramatic gesture of looking at her watch, and did not have to feign the start of horror when she saw what it was telling her. "Oh dear—I really must go—thank you so much—I will come back when I have more time." She was out the door before she heard what the librarian was asking her. Probably whether she wanted to print out any of what they had found.

No.

For three nights she did not dream at all, and waking was cruel. The one moment when her spirits lifted enough for her to feel a breeze on her face and pause to breathe the air with pleasure was one sunny afternoon when she went back to her pool and scrubbed the encircling paving. She scrubbed with water only, not knowing what any sort of soap run-off might do to the pond life, and she saw newts wrinkle the water with their passing several times. When she stopped to breathe deep, she thought she saw a newt with a red back hovering at the edge of the pond as if it were looking at her, and it amused her for another moment to imagine that all the newts she saw were just the one newt, swimming back and forth, keeping her company.

That night she dreamed again, but it was a brief and disturbing dream, when she sat at the edge of Zasharan's pool where the Watcher's Eye lay, and she strained to look into the water and see it looking out at her, but the water was dark and opaque, though she felt sure the Eye was there, and aware of her. She woke exhausted, and aching as if with physical effort.

She dreamed the same the next night, and the oppression and uselessness of it were almost too much to bear. Her head throbbed with the effort to peer through the surface of the water, and she fidgeted where she sat as if adjusting her body might help her to *see*, knowing this was not true, and yet unable to sit still nonetheless. There was a scratchy noise as she moved and resettled, and grit under her palms as she leaned on them. Sand. The ubiquitous Damarian desert sand; Zasharan had told her that usually there was no sand in the Watcher's chamber but that this year it had blown and drifted even there. She dragged her blind gaze from the water and refocussed on the sand at the edge of the pool: the same glittery, twinkly sand that had first given her her cruelly unfounded hope when she had woken at home with grains of it in her hands and nightdress.

She shifted her weight and freed one hand. *Help me*, she wrote in the sand at the edge of the pool, and as she raised her finger from the final *e*, the dream dissolved, and she heard the milk float in the street below, and knew she would be late with breakfast.

A fortnight passed, and she dreamed of Damar no more. She began to grow reaccustomed to her life above the furniture shop, housekeeper, cook, mender, minder, bookkeeper, dogs-body—nothing. Nobody. She would grow old like this. She might marry Ron or Tim; that would please her father, and tie one of them even more strongly to the shop. She supposed her father did not consider the possibility that she might not be tied to the shop herself; she supposed she did not consider the possibility either. She had raised no protest when her parents had sent Mrs Halford and Mr Jonah and the possibility of university and a career away; she could hardly protest now that she had a dream-world she liked better than this one and wished to go there. The paperback shelves at the grocery store testified to the popularity of dream-worlds readers could only escape to for a few hours in their imaginations. She wondered how many people dreamed of the worlds they read about in books. She tried to remember if there had been some book, some fairy-tale of her childhood, that had begun her secret love of deserts, of the sandstorm-torn time of Queen Fortunatar of the Clear Seeing, of a landscape she had never seen with her waking eyes; she could remember no book and no tale her grandmother told that was anything like what she had dreamed.

It took three weeks, but Ruth finally managed to corner her one Saturday afternoon, hoeing the vegetable garden. "No you don't," she said as Hetta picked her hoe up hastily and began to move back towards the garden shed. "I want to talk to you, and I mean to do it. Those dreams you were having about Damar lit you up, and the light's gone off again. It's not just the price of the ticket, is it? We'd get the money somehow."

Hetta dropped the hoe blade back behind the cabbages, but left it motionless. "No," she muttered. "It's not just the money." Her fingers tightened on the handle, and the blade made a few erratic scrapes at the soil.

"Then what is it?"

Hetta steadied the blade and began to hoe properly. Ruth showed no sign of going away, so at last she said: "It doesn't matter. It was a silly idea anyway. Doing something because you *dreamed* about it."

Ruth made a noise like someone trying not to yell when they've just cracked their head on a low door. She stepped round the edge of the bed and seized Hetta's wrist in both hands. Ruth was smaller than Hetta, and spent her spare time in a lab counting beetles, but Hetta was surprised at the strength of her grasp. *Talk to me,* said Ruth. "I have been worrying about you for *years*. Since Grandma died. You're not supposed to have to worry about your older sister when you're six. Don't you think I know you've saved *my* life? Father would have broken me like he breaks everyone he gets his hands on if I'd been the elder—like he broke Mum, like he's broken Dane, like he's broken Tim and Ron and they were even grown-ups—and Lara's going, for all that she thinks she just wants to marry Dane. You are the only one of us who has been clever enough, or stubborn enough, to save a little bit of your soul from him—maybe Grandma did, when she was still alive I wasn't paying so much attention, maybe you learned it from her—and I learned from you that it can be done. I know it, and Jeff does too—you know, with that pro-gramming stuff he can do, he's already got half his university paid for. When the time comes, nobody'll be able to say no to him. We're going to be all right—and that's thanks to *you*. It's time to save *yourself* now. That little bit of your soul seems to live in that desert of yours—if I were a shrink instead of a bi-ologist, I'm sure I could have a really good time with *that* metaphor—I've wondered where you kept it. But you're going to lose it, now, after all, if you're not careful. What are you *wait-ing* for? Lara can learn to do the books—I'll tell Dane to suggest it, they'll both think it's a great idea—I'll teach her. We'll eat like hell, maybe, but there's only a year left for me and two for Jeff, and the rest of 'em are on their own. Who knows? Maybe Mum will get out of bed. Hetta. My lovely sister. Go. I'll visit you, wherever you end up."

Hetta stood trembling. In her mind's eye she saw Zasharan, sand, trees, bells, horses, tree-framed faces, the Eye, the pool. For a moment they were more real to her than the garden she stood in or the bruising grip on her wrist. She realised this—realised it and lost it again as she recognised the landscape of her *real* life—with a pain so great, she could not bear it.

She burst into tears.

She was only vaguely aware of Ruth putting an arm round her shoulders and leading her back behind the storm-broken sunflower screen and sitting her down at the pool's edge, vaguely aware of Ruth rocking her as she had many times rocked Ruth, years ago, when their mother had first taken to her bed and their father shouted all the time. She came slowly to herself again with her head on Ruth's breast, and Ruth's free hand trailing drops of cold water from the pond against her face.

She sat up slowly. Ruth waited. She began to tell Ruth everything, from the first dream. She stumbled first over saying Fortunatar's name: *Queen Fortunatar of the Clear Seeing.* And she paused before she explained what had happened in the library the day before. "It's all *imaginary.* It's not only not real, it's not even history—it's just legends. I might as well be dreaming of King Arthur and Robin Hood and Puck of Pook's Hill and Middle Earth. If—if you're right that a little of my soul lives there, then—then it's an imaginary soul too." *Nothing,* whispered her mind. *Nothing but here, now, this.* She looked at the walls around the garden; even from this, the garden's farthest point, she could hear the electric buzz of woodworking tools, and the wind, from the wrong direction today, brought them the smell of hot oil from Benny's Fish and Chips.

Ruth was silent a long time, but she held on to one of her sister's hands, and Hetta, exhausted from the effort of weeping and explaining, made no attempt to draw away. She would have to go indoors soon, and start supper. First she had to pull the fleece back over her exposed cabbages; there was going to be a frost tonight. Soon she had to do it. Not just yet.

Ruth said at last: "Well, they thought for hundreds of years that bumblebees couldn't fly, and the bumblebees went on flying while they argued about it, and then they finally figured it out. It never made any difference to the bumblebees.

And I met Melanie's great-uncle once and he was no fool, and Melanie and I are friends because she's not really a space case, it's just that if she pretends to be one, she can tell her uncle's stories. Haven't you ever thought that legends have a lot of *truth* in them? History is just organised around facts. Facts aren't the whole story or the bumblebees would have had to stop flying till the scientists figured out how they could."

Hetta said wearily, "That's a little too poetical for me. Legends and poetry don't change the fact that I have to go get supper now."

Ruth said, "Wait. Wait. I'm still thinking. I'll help you with supper." Her head was bowed, and the hand that wasn't holding Hetta's was still trailing in the pool, and she flicked up water drops as if her thoughts were stinging her. "You know, I think there's a newt trying to get your attention. One of these big red fellows."

"Yes, I've met him before," said Hetta, trying to sound light-hearted, trying to go with Ruth's sudden change of subject, trying to accept that there was nothing to be done about Damarian dream-legends, and that this was her life.

"Not very newt-like behaviour," Ruth said. "Look." There was a newt swimming, back and forth, as it—he or she—had swum before. "Watch," said Ruth. She dabbled her fingers near the newt and it ducked round them and continued its tiny laps, back and forth, in front of the place where Hetta sat. Ruth dabbled again, and it ducked again, and came straight back to Hetta. "Put *your* hand in the water," said Ruth.

Hetta was still in that half-trance mood of having told her secret, and so she put her hand into the water without protest. The newt swam to her and crept up on the back of her hand.

She raised her hand out of the pond, slowly, as she had done once before; the newt clung on. She stared into the small golden eyes, and watched the vertical pupil dilate as it looked back at her.

"Maybe Queen Fortunatar of the Clear Seeing is trying to send you a message," said Ruth.

Hetta dreamed again that night. She came through the door she had first entered by, when Zasharan had saved her from the storm. She came in alone, the sand swirling around her, and closed the door against the wind with her own strength. She felt well and alert and clear-headed. She dropped the scarf she had wrapped around her face, and set off, as if she knew the way, striding briskly down the corridors, the sand sliding away under her soft-booted feet, and then up a series of low stairs, where the sand grated between her soles and the stair-stone. The same dim light shone as it had shone the night that Zasharan had guided her, but she often put her hand against the wall for reassurance, for the shadows seemed to fall more thickly than they had done when she was with him. She was not aware of why she chose one way rather than another, but she made every choice at every turning without hesitation.

She came to the spiral stair, and climbed it. When she put her hand to the door of the Eye's chamber, it opened.

Zasharan was standing on the far side of the pool. Hetta raised her hands and pushed her hair back from her face, suddenly needing to do something homely and familiar, suddenly feeling that nothing but her own body *was* familiar. She let her palms rest against her cheekbones briefly. The sleeves of the strange, pale, loose garment she was wearing fell back from her forearms; there was a shift beneath it, and loose trousers beneath that, and the soft boots with their long laces wrapped the trousers around her calves. Her right ankle throbbed.

Zasharan made no move to approach her. From the far side of the pool of the Eye, he said, "I thought you would not return. It has been a sennight since you disappeared. If there had not been the hollow in the sand beside the pool where you had lain, I might have believed I had dreamed you. I went back to the little room by the lowest door where I first brought you, and the dressings cabinet still lay open, and the needle lay beside it with the end of the thread I had used on your ankle, and one bandage was missing; and I could see where your blood had fallen in the sand, for no one goes there but me, and I had not swept nor put things to rights. I—when you first came, I—I thought I knew why you were here. I thought—I thought I had read the signs—not only in the sand, but in your face. I was glad. But you do not wish to come here, do you? That is what I missed, when I searched the records. That is why your story is different. Sandstorms are treacherous; I knew that; I just did not see what it meant here. It is only the blood you shed here that brings you back, the blood you shed by the treachery of the sand. That is all. I must let you go. I am glad you have come back once more, to let me say good-bye, and to apologise for trying to hold you against your will."

There were tears under Hetta's palms. She smeared them away and dropped her hands. "I—I *dream* you." She meant to say *I only dream you, you are just a dream.*

Zasharan smiled; it was a painful smile. "Of course. How

else could we meet? You have told me of *Roanshire*, in a land I do not know. I should have realised . . . when you never invited me to come to you in your dreams . . ."

"*I only dream you! You are just a dream!*" Hetta put her hands to her face again, and clawed at her hair. "I looked up Queen Fortunatar in the library! She is a *legend!* She is not real! Even if she were real, she would have been real hundreds of years ago! We have airports now, and cars, and electric lights and television and computers!"

Zasharan stepped forward abruptly, to the very edge of the pool. "Queen Fortunatar is in your library?" he said. "You have read about her—you sought to read about her in your waking Roanshire?"

"Yes, yes," said Hetta impatiently. "But—"

"Why?"

"Why? Why did I?—because I *wanted* her to be real, of course! Because I want you to be real! You do not want to waste your dreaming on my life—you do not want to visit me there!—although I wish Ruth could meet you—oh, this is *absurd!* I am *dreaming*, and Queen Fortunatar is a *myth*, a fairy-tale—she is not real."

"Everything that is, is real," murmured Zasharan, as if his mind were on something else. Then he walked round the pool and held his hand out towards her. "Am I real? Take my hand."

Hetta stared at him and his outstretched hand. This was only a dream; she had touched him, dreaming, many times on her visits here; he had half-carried her out of the sandstorm, he had dressed her ankle, he had held a cup for her to drink from, he had led her to this room.

She raised her hand, but curled it up against her own body.

What if, when she reached out to him, her hand went through his, as if he were a ghost? As if he were only imaginary, like a legend in a book?

Like a dream upon waking?

She held out her hand, but at the last moment she closed her eyes. Her fingers, groping, felt nothing, where his hand should be. She felt dizzy, and sick, and there was a lumpy mattress against her back, and sheets twisted uncomfortably round her body, and a fish-and-chips-and-wood-shavings smell in her nostrils.

And then it was as if his hand *bloomed* inside of hers; as if she had held a tiny, imperceptible kernel which the heat of her hand had brought suddenly to blossoming; and her feet in their boots were standing on sand-scattered stone, and she opened her eyes with a gasp, and Zasharan drew her to him and he let go her hand only to put both arms round her.

He said gently, "You must find your own way to come. The way is there. I do not know where; I do not know your world, your time, with the cars and the electricithar. If you wish to come, you must find the way. I will wait for you here."

She turned her head as it lay against his shoulder, and stared at the water of the pool at their feet. Somewhere deep within it, she thought a golden eye glittered up at her.

She woke feeling strangely calm. It was just before dawn. The first birds were trying out the occasional chirp, and the chimneys across the street were black against the greying sky. She climbed out of bed and put her dressing gown on and crept down the first flight of stairs, careful of the creaking boards, to Ruth's room. Ruth woke easily; a hand on her shoulder was enough. She put her lips to Ruth's ear. "Will you come with me?"

They made their way noiselessly downstairs, past the shop, into the back room and the garden door. There they paused briefly, baffled, for that door could not be opened silently. Hetta stood with her hand on the bolt, and for a moment she thought she saw Zasharan standing beside her, his hand over her hand. He was looking at her, but then looked up, over her shoulder, at Ruth; then he looked back at Hetta, and smiled. *I thank you,* he said: she did not hear him, but she saw his lips move. *My honour is yours,* she said, formally. Then she pulled the bolt and opened the door, and it made no sound. "Whew!" Ruth sighed.

When they reached the pool at the end of the garden, Hetta pulled Ruth into a fierce hug and said softly, "I wanted to say good-bye. I wanted someone here when I—left. I wanted to thank you. I—I don't think I will see you again."

"You are going to go live in a legend," said Ruth. "I—I'll re-member the bumblebees. I—make up a legend about me, will you?"

Hetta nodded. She knelt by the pool. Its surface was still opaque in the grey dawn light, but when she put her hand to the surface of the water, the newt crept up immediately into her cupped palm. As she knelt, an edge of her dressing gown slipped forward—"You're bleeding!" said Ruth.

Hetta looked down. The scar on her ankle had opened, and a little fresh blood ran down her leg. The first drop was poised to fall. . . .

She jerked upright to her knees and thrust her foot out

over the pool. The blood fell into the water: one drop, two, three. The newt was still clinging to her hand. "Ruth—"

"Go," said Ruth harshly. "Go *now*."

Hetta slipped forward, into the water, and it closed over her head.

It was a long journey, through water, through sand, through storms and darkness. She often lost track of where she was, who she was, where she was going and why; and then she felt a small skipping sensation against the palm of one hand, or the weight of a small clawed thing hanging to the hair behind her ear, or saw a goldy-black glint of eye with her own eye, and she remembered. She swam through oceans, and through deserts. She was swallowed and vomited up by a green dragon in a great stinking belch of wet black smoke. She eluded sea serpents by drifting, for, like sharks, they respond to movement; and water goblins by hiding in mud, because water goblins, being ugly themselves, are determined to notice only beautiful things, even if this means missing dinner. She was guided on her way by mer-folk, who have a strong liking for romance and adventure, and in whose company she sang her first songs, although they laughed at her for only being able to breathe air, and said that her little gold-eyed friend should teach her better. She spoke to sand-sprites, who have small hissing voices like draughts under doors, and she listened to the desert feys, who rarely speak to humans but often talk to the desert. She was almost trampled by the sand-god's great armoured horses till her little friend showed her how to hide in the hollow behind their ears and cling to their manes; but Geljdreth stood between her and what she sought and longed for, and at last she had to face him with nothing but her own determination and wit and the strength of her two hands, and a little friend hanging over one ear like an ear-ring. And, perhaps because she was from Roanshire in the Homeland where there were no deserts, and she had not lived her life in fear of him, she won out against him, and loosed his horses, and crippled his power.

At last her head broke the surface in a small calm pool; and there was Zasharan, waiting to pull her out, and wrap her in a cloak, and give her *tiarhk* to drink, as he had done once before, though he had wiped her face free of grit then, not of water. She turned to look back into the pool, and she saw a gold eye looking back at her, and she could not tell if it were a very large eye or a very small one. "Thank you," she said. "I thank you."

Somewhere—not in her ear; in her heart or her belly or the bottoms of her feet—she heard *My honour is yours.*

"Welcome home," said Zasharan.

Ruth had grown up, married, had two children, and written three best-selling books of popular science concerning the apparent impossibilities the natural world presents that scientists struggle for generations to find explanations for, before she found herself one day tapping *the legends of Damar* on her computer. Her search engine produced few relevant hits; after a brief flurry of interest for a few years following independence, Damar had again drifted into the backwaters of international attention.

It only took her a few minutes to find a reference to Queen Fortunatar of the Clear Seeing. It described her half-brother,

her success as an adjudicator, and the sandstorms that particularly plagued her reign. After a few compact paragraphs the article ended:

One of the most famous Damarian bards also began telling stories during Fortunatar's reign. Hetthar is an interesting figure, for part of her personal legend is that she came out of time and place to marry Fortunatar's Fourth Sandpale Watcher, Zasharan, and it was said that after she came, no one was ever again lost to the storms of the Kalarsham, and that the sand-god hated her for this. But her main fame rests on the cycle of stories she called The Journeying, and whose central character has the strangely un-Damarian name of Ruth.